There's Always Chocolate!

Abby Irish

Order this book online at www.trafford.com
or email orders@trafford.com

Most Trafford titles are also available at major online book retailers.

Note for Librarians: A cataloguing record for this book is available from Library and Archives Canada at www.collectionscanada.ca/amicus/index-e.html

Printed in Victoria, BC, Canada.

ISBN: 978-1-4269-1805-6

Our mission is to efficiently provide the world's finest, most comprehensive book publishing service, enabling every author to experience success. To find out how to publish your book, your way, and have it available worldwide, visit us online at www.trafford.com

Trafford rev. 10/22/2009

Trafford PUBLISHING www.trafford.com

North America & international
toll-free: 1 888 232 4444 (USA & Canada)
phone: 250 383 6864 • fax: 812 355 4082

Chapter 1

A new chapter

Where there's a funeral, there's rain. It's just a fact of life. Or death, rather. Today's funeral was no different. Today, there was enough rain to choke a duck.

An early summer shower has drowned the cemetery throughout the early hours of the morning, soaking the fresh cut grass. The bright green sleeves of the trees cried onto the fresh mounds below them. Only in the past hour or so had the downpour settled into the gray drizzle that now sprinkled the brown coffin before us. Small streams of water trickled from the standing wreath of deep pink roses near the coffin. The rabbi was speaking quickly, as to not get too wet. Others surrounding him, including myself, had umbrellas to wash away the wetness of the day.

Standing next to my children, and leaning on my eldest, Michael, I looked away from the clean wooden box. Mud caked the edges of my navy leather pumps. Cameron bought shoes for me Valentine's Day this year. Well, not exactly *bought.* He gave me a gift certificate. I finally used it, just yesterday. Otherwise, this certificate would still be in my nightstand drawer waiting with all the other thousand gift certificates he has given me. The Macy's certificate was closer this time – footwear is far more interesting to me than tire rotations. At least I used this one in a timely fashion, so to speak.

I fought the urge to wipe the mud away. Several seconds went by.

I couldn't stand it any longer. I bent down and wiped away the mud with my bare hand. *Shoot.* Now my hand was muddy. I shook it behind me, hoping the mud would fall to the wet ground below and then the intermittent drizzles would cleanse my fingers. It didn't work. I bent down, for the second time in two minutes, and wiped my hand on the soaked grass. My hand slipped out from under me, and I pitched forward onto my knees.

"Oof." I stifled my surprised grunt. Then I stifled my urge to swear like a sailor. My dark nylons are soaking at the knees. *Stupid rain…*

"God damn it," I whispered to myself hoping no one else heard me, especially the Rabbi.

I stood back up as best as I could without making a scene. It was a little late. Several people turned their eyes away quickly, as if they didn't want me to know they caught my grace. A secretary from Cam's office shook her head quite dramatically before returning her attention to the Rabbi.

What? Like they've never seen anyone keel over at a funeral? That's within the rules, isn't it?

Whatever. I am not going to worry about it now. Not everyone worried about appropriateness, certainly not the three women standing across from me, on the far side of the coffin. Clearly, they don't give a hoot about appropriateness today. Why else would they be wearing candy apple red attire, high spiky heels, long showy fingernails, and carrying umbrellas that match? What were they thinking this morning when they were dressing? Did they get their invitations wrong today? Would they show up at a bar mitzvah party tonight in black nylons and headveils? I don't even know who these women are. I didn't invite them. I actually didn't do any of the inviting today.

I wiped the mist from my cheeks.

At least the painted hussies kept my mind off the rain and mud, off the dozen or so friends and family sinking sullenly in the mud, off my own clamminess.

Off Cameron's coffin.

I peeked at the coffin, and then turned away, focusing on the Rabbi at the edge of the enormous mud hole. The simple ceremony is supposed to be short. He was saying all the right 'Rabbi' words, which just meant he makes bad jokes about everything under the sun,

(Today there was no sun). I know I am not supposed to laugh. Well, I did, just once, when he joked about Cameron's tendency to talk loudly during a Yom Kippur service a few years back. I had tried to tell Cam that vocalizing the loudest wouldn't bump him to the head of the line into Heaven. There was no telling anything to that man. His eyes were pointed forward and stormed ahead at his own pace, my opinion be damned.

Now look where he is. Did he get his way and go to the head of the class? I certainly hope I won't find out for quite some time. I am not ready to join him in the near future, or ever for that matter.

Damn him.

A loud crack vibrated the ground as a giant bolt of lightening struck a huge tree branch nearby. I think it was on the first tee...oh excuse me, the fir tree. *No more golfing for Cam.* Everyone jumped except for me. I am in another world. I need to figure out who these three women are and what they are doing here; invading my space, my privacy, and my husband.

The droplets swelled to golf balls and are assaulting the ground with such intense force that some of the guests are leaving before the Rabbi could finish his act. Their next destination is my home, for the food festivities, Stage Two of a Proper Funeral. After all, this is a party of sorts. Instead of Cameron's death, we celebrate his life. In turn this means we probably should be throwing this 'party' at his old office, instead of our home. He did spend a lot more time working than being a Dad and husband. The rules say we go to my home.

Finally, the Rabbi wrapped up his one-man act. We all darted to the shelter of our cars, with most of the ladies heels plunging into the mud for at least fifty yards. I struggled to the 'complimentary' black limo, in the drizzle, when one of my pumps stuck deep and hard. For the second time in half an hour, I pitched forward into the mud.

"Mom!" my oldest daughter called out, too far away to move to me quickly.

The Rabbi made a half-assed move as if to help, but really, what help can a Rabbi offer with a damsel in distress, rather in the mud, if she isn't holding a signed check in the air.

I raised my head to the sky and just stared for a moment or two. I was thinking about crying and started to, but then I just rolled it into laughter.

I glanced up toward the sky, "What more can you put on my plate today?"

I'd already lost my husband, the rain is pouring down, and everyone is soaking wet. I have to laugh. Everyone can hear me, and I don't want to stop. My children are stunned. The Rabbi's eyes popped out. I think because I got more laughs than he did, because my laughter caught on and now everyone is either giggling or laughing, not at me, but with me, *I think.* The whole world laughs with you, right? Laughter is the best medicine, right? A smile a day makes the pain go away, right?

Even when you want to hide in a small, unencumbered hole in the ground, the hole can keep getting deeper and deeper. Eventually, you will have to climb out and be free.

෴

The limo dropped us off in the front of my home where the flagstone walkway begins by the curb, curves around, and ends up at the entry to my home. Michael, my eldest, is 24 years old. He helped me out of the car and helped brush off what he could of the caked-on mud from my navy blue dress. When he was a little boy, I gave him a nickname just between the two of us … 'Bud.' Michael is a handsome young man. He is tall, dark-haired and has hazel-green eyes, just like his father's. Michael plans to be the youngest Sports Anchor on ESPN with his newly earned degree in Journalism. Currently he is working at an unknown TV station in the middle of a small town doing it all to please the boss.

Cameron always said, "You have to start as a peon and work your way up the ladder. If you work hard, it will pay off for the future for you and your family."

Those were words to live and die by. However, Cam died before he could reap the rewards of his hard work. He always believed in working hard and pretty much 24/7. No time for family vacations or second honeymoons, just work, work, work, a little golf game with clients, and back to work some more. Making his clients happy and making money was his business and he did it well, too well.

Melanie came out of the limo next. Melanie just turned 21. Bar scene here she comes! Her life is just beginning, as she puts it, then Dad had to go and do this to HER. Melanie is a beautiful young woman, the spitting image of her mother, of course. Cameron wouldn't have had it any other way. I gave her the nickname, "Pumpkin," when she was born. She was large, round, and peach-colored. We found out we were pregnant the Halloween before she was born. Melanie has her senior year in college left and is looking, rather will be looking, for a job in the fashion industry. Anything will do as long as it has to do with clothes design and New York or Paris, or both! That does not leave many options.

My twin girls came out at the same time. I am not talking about giving birth right now. I mean they climbed out of the limo simultaneously. They are identical eighteen-year old young girls. I say 'girls' because they haven't grown up yet. They will in the near future, God help them, and God *please* help me get through it all.

The twins were our surprise babies. When and how they were conceived is beyond my recollection. I rarely ever saw Cam, even in those days --- especially in those days. He had his two children already, his boy and his girl, the 'Perfect Family.' Then the twins went and ruined His Plan. Gave him another reason to work long hours away from home.

Julie and Jenna just finished their frosh year in college and studied sorority life and fraternity men, not necessarily in that order. They haven't decided on a major yet, and have no idea what they would like to study, or if they would like to study. Julie and Jenna have always followed a beat to their own drum(s).

Cameron always said, "It's not a question of '*If* you are going to college,' it is a question of '*Where* are you going to college?"

Therefore, they had one year under their belts, no questions asked. They were inseparable. They have the same personality: very outgoing, curious and a little mischievous. It has always been difficult for people to tell them apart. Even I still have trouble every now and then. However, Michael and Melanie can always tell them apart. Siblings always do.

ꙮ

At a snail's pace, I crept in through my front door. I see Carol running amuck from the kitchen to the dining room carrying food, back and forth, trying to place everything just so. Carol, my six-foot svelte friend, was in charge of setting an attractive table with salads and desserts. To be honest, I couldn't have cared less what we served today, if anything. Carol had to take control, and I let her. Carol and I have known each other for a bazillion years. We met at a summer sleep-away camp, back in the 60's, in upstate New York where all the rich Jewish kids went for the entire summer, (This way parents could travel around the world without their children). We stayed friends ever since.

"Amy," Carol said on one of her laps around me, "one of the chocolate cheesecakes fell off the table as I was trying to shove, uh, fit more desserts. I'm sorry dear." My mom had brought out a few cheesecakes the day before when she flew in from New York. Thankfully, there were two more.

As Carol ran past me, I patted her on the arm. "That's okay."

"I let Tom and Jerry clean it up from the floor." Tom and Jerry are the family dogs. They are colossal chocolate brown bloodhounds, named after the cartoon characters from the 60's. , any flavor cheesecake, was their favorite food to clean up. I spilled often, so I knew.

"That's okay." I smiled and tried patting her arm again but missed in the gush of wind, and almost lost my balance. So instead, I vaguely followed her trail, ending up just walking around in limbo.

ꙮ

My home sits on the bottom of a cul-de-sac in an upscale lived-in neighborhood. It is a large, ranch style older remodeled home, just big enough for **Cam's** family and the dogs. It has four good-sized bedrooms, four baths, with a small rectangular pool and spa in the backyard, and plenty of grass for the dogs to run around on. It has a white picket fence that I'd made Cam put up as soon as we moved in. Back then, I could actually assign him house tasks and expect *some* to actually get done.

Cam liked subdued colors in and around our home. It's tastefully decorated in several shades of cool blues and beiges. The lit candles are mine. I just love scented candles.

I stopped at the window and stared at my roses. We have a dozen or so different shades of rose bushes out front to bring color up against the walls of our castle.

"My, my, what lovely roses you have Amy," one of the secretaries commented as she snuck up behind me, and barely touched my right shoulder, as if she had to touch me.

"Yeah, I know," I replied without even looking, and then walked away.

Today, the Kayden home is full of guests and food. Never have there been so many people gathered in our home for any event, **EVER**. Cameron didn't like parties, get-togethers, or anything that involved numerous people, meaning more than the immediate family. However, today, it was not up to him. How would he feel about this? He is probably grumbling and turning over in his grave.

I walked a few more laps around the house, with the guests giving me space. They seemed to know I needed to be alone, even in their midst.

One of the law firm partners, Ken, approached me. He touched my arm, ever so, lightly, "Amy, if there is anything you need, let me know. You can always leave a message at the office for me."

What in the hell is that supposed to mean? You are on call only with the office phone. What happened to home phones, cell phones and such? That was real sincere.

"I think I have had enough of office phone calls, don't you?" I jerked to the opposite side of Ken and briskly walked down the hallway. I was steaming and needed to let it out, somehow.

When I found myself back at the twins' bedroom where Tom and Jerry were captive, I stopped my roaming. The howling and tail wagging began as soon as I opened the door. Now this is my release to all tension. My babies and I have unconditional love for each other, always and forever.

"Hey boys, Mommy's here. I missed you this morning." I crawled onto the bed and let them jump on me and slobber me with kisses.

"I love you boys. You are my babies."

Tom jumped on top of me until I fell backwards on one of the beds. Both, Tom and Jerry licked my salty tears off my face and then lay down next to me, as close as they could get. There was no room for **anyone** else. When we, Cam and I, normally went to bed, Tom and Jerry joined us of course, right in the middle. That is where they think they belong. For a long time, Cameron would grit his teeth and pace around the bed before getting in it every night.

"The bed has gone to the dogs," he would grumble powerlessly. Eventually he got used to it.

I was lying on one of the beds with my 'puppies' for what seemed like an eternity. It was nice and quiet in Julie and Jenna's room, also known as Sugar Plum and Babe, my little nicknames for the girls since they were toddlers. They were so sweet and innocent then. They both have beautiful auburn shoulder-length wavy hair. They stand 5'5" with hourglass figures. I don't ever recall looking like that in high school, in college, or ever for that matter. I was still waiting in line to reach 5'3".

∾

I slowly and quietly entered the main part of the house again. Everyone is eating, drinking, making small talk, and laughing. In fact, it seemed as though everyone was in a cheery mood and having a great time, all at Cam's expense. I mean, in his honor.

I stood in the entry hallway holding up the wall. God forbid it fall on me today. I didn't want people touching me, feeling sorry for me, pitying me or anything. I just wanted the day to end. The women in red strolled through my front door. I got the chills.

"Sorry dear," the petite one said to a surprised woman near the door. "We are so late. We needed to go refresh ourselves before arriving. All that rain!"

Carol rushed over. "I don't think we met. I'm Carol, Amy's friend. And you are..." The women started to 'chit-chat' and totally ignored Carol. "Well, I guess I need to see what is happening in the kitchen." Off and running back to the kitchen Carol went, while keeping her right eye on all three hussies.

One of the ladies in red, did manage to sign the guest book, for all of them, somewhat. Her penmanship was that of a ten year old, from where I was observing. When the ladies moved toward the food, Carol ran over to check out the names.

"What in the heck does this say?" She tried from every angle to make out the writing but still was perplexed. I'm not sure if she saw me or not as I stood there, still holding up the wall. I too was trying to read their writing from a distance.

Carol tried to sound the names aloud when Melanie snuck up behind her.

"Who are those ladies?" Melanie asked.

"Oh!" Carol startled in surprise bobbling the guest book in the air. It landed right next to the Rabbi, who was helping himself to another clean plate.

He put the plate down, not too far, and picked up the guest book. "Oh, my," the Rabbi said, equally startled. "Well, let me see." He peered at the guest book. After a moment he looked up and announced, "Sorry, can't read it. It isn't written in Hebrew." He gave a modest chuckle.

"Real funny," Melanie said flatly, as she turned away from him, shaking her head, and popping a mini-éclair in her mouth.

Carol seized the guest book back from the Rabbi and placed it back by the entrance to my abode. "Oh Melanie dear, come in the kitchen and help me set out a few more desserts honey."

"But Carol, I don't really want to." Melanie protested as Carol pushed her in the direction of the kitchen. "Carol, you know I can't do anything in there. I can't …"

Melanie was not one for being in the kitchen very long. She rarely entered the kitchen or knew which direction it was in the house, even by the wondrous odors. She does not like to cook, bake, BBQ or clean up after a meal. So what was the purpose of her being there, ever?

I stood with my back leaning on the wall in the dining room watching people gaze at the food. One of 'ladies in red' started drooling when she saw the table. I just wanted to take one of the cheesecake knives and stick it where the sun doesn't shine. I imagined myself killing her with a dessert knife. It felt rewarding in my head, and I felt a little relief, and smiled to myself.

"These look so yummy girls. Get yourselves a big plate and dig in."

She and the other two didn't hesitate and piled it on. They proceeded to walk around the house huddling together. I could barely hear the women whispering amongst each other and walking ever so slowly around my home to see my precious belongings. They picked up, touched, and gawked.

I hugged my sweater tightly. This was worse than feeling everyone's eyes on me at the funeral, and definitely worse than a gynecological check-up. At least there I know who the doctor is, what he is doing, and when it would end.

Michael was standing while my parents, two small old Jewish people from New York, sat on one of the living room couches. "Grandpa, don't eat so much. You'll get sick."

"Yeah, yeah. I know. It's okay. I am not going to live forever."

"I'm not going to let you live past tomorrow if you don't slow down and stop eating so much Morty. You are going to make yourself sick." My Mom slapped him on the hand to no avail. "You are embarrassing me dear. Slow down. If you throw up, I won't clean it up, or feel sorry for you. Do you hear me Morty?" Nearby guests looked over at them.

Dad shook his head in agreement to keep Mom happy. "Yeah, yeah, I know," as he waved off his young bride of 55 years.

Actually, there aren't many relatives at all. Cameron grew up in a foster home. He never felt comfortable there and knew he had to do something with his life. He was a very bright man, and received multiple academic scholarships for college and law school. I know that is why he was so hard on the children growing up and becoming a 'somebody.' Cam wanted our children to know that people had to study and work hard for the good things in life. Nothing comes easy to those who wait. Or die.

On my side of the coin, my parents and only brother came for the funeral. My parents flew in from New York, and Michael was in charge of taking care of them, for the entire trip. Thank goodness, they love Michael. Old Jewish people can be a real pain in the … neck. However, Michael knew he was in the 'Will' and did whatever they asked him to do.

My brother, Rich, a somewhat handsome, not so tall, divorce attorney practicing in New Jersey, flew in with my parents. He came without his wife. He stepped up next to me in the hallway.

"Sara isn't feeling well lately, Amy. I'm sorry she didn't come with me. Please accept my apologies for her."

"I really didn't expect her to show up anyway, Rich. I never do," I walked away towards the bedrooms. I wasn't angry, just disappointed. Rich didn't need to apologize for his so-called wife.

Lying down again, just for a moment, so I thought, I must have fallen asleep with Tom and Jerry, because the sound of low voices on the other side of the door startled me to consciousness. *How long have I been out?* Focusing on the voice, I sat up and peered under the doorway. There were shadows of high-heeled shoes. Not just one pair either, but several pair of shoes.

"Whose room do you think this is Jeanette?"

"I'm sure it's one of the kids. Let's take a peek."

The doorknob turned slowly until the door opened a crack. I shuffled back quickly and Tom and Jerry jumped up off the bed, into the air, and landed face to face with all three women. They howled loud enough to wake the dead. Well, maybe not *that* loud.

The one closest to the door, holding the door knob, threw her plate on the woman next to her, who in turn, threw her iced tea and plate on the third woman, who then slipped and fell backwards with her food all over her red luminous outfit. There was chocolate cheesecake, chocolate cake, pasta salad, bread pudding and more all over my newly cleaned travertine floor, and on all three women. Tom and Jerry weren't done. In unison, they pounced on the mess, intent on cleaning it, with their tongues. I could hear people's footsteps racing down the hallway to see what had stirred up the dogs. What were these women thinking? They probably weren't.

On any other given day, I would be in their faces asking a million questions. I would want to know their business. I would probably be giving them the evil eye. But not today. Today was my day to be numb. Tomorrow is another day!

I stood in the doorway just to peek at all the commotion going on in the hallway. I could see and hear Tom and Jerry munching away at everything edible in sight. Tom and Jerry were slobbering all over the women while Carol giggled, just a little. I was trying to keep my laughter under my breath. Tom was actually on top of one of the women in red licking her face. He was hovering over her body as if he were protecting his young. Her neck and chest covered in chocolate cream pie. She was stunned to see a giant tongue coming right for her. It was like being in the movie, 'Honey, I shrunk the kids!'

Nathan and Chase, the best neighbors in the world, came down the hallway. They each tried to help one of the other two women up from the floor. Well, needless to say, they too ended up on the slippery floor on top of the women.

Chase declared, "This isn't what I had in mind at all." Then slowly and carefully, he stood up, brushed himself off and left. Nathan followed suit.

All three women were in a daze on the floor while the dogs were having the feast of their lives. Finally, the women helped each other up and decided that they had enough, and left abruptly through the front door.

Back in the core part of the 'party,' Julie and Jenna are scoping out Michael's friends from high school that came to the house after the funeral. Cameron used to coach baseball for Michael's teams from the time he could play tee ball, at age four, through the eighth grade. Many of Michael's friends showed up to pay their last respects to one of their old coaches from way back when.

Once Cameron made 'Partner,' he had to focus more on his work, therefore working more and coaching less was in store for Cameron's future, his son, and all of the women in his life as well. He made sure he made it to all of Michael's games throughout high school. Cameron really wanted to be around Michael much more than he was able to the last few years. Michael was usually stuck with a bunch of girls watching the Lifetime Channel, eating chocolates, drinking diet sodas, and talking about their time of the month. It was always someone's time of the month in the Kayden household. I always thought we should have bought stock in Tampax.

Now that the twins are "legal," they feel so grown up and are ready to date real men. Not just the 18 or 19-year-old freshmen in college, but real men, older men, like 22 or 23. Jenna and Julie huddled together trying to decide whom to talk to first. Now that Michael's old friends were all out of college and wearing suits, they were very appealing to the girls. *I just love a man in a nice pin-stripped suit.* I guess that is one of the reasons I married Cam. He looked so handsome all dressed up in his pin-stripped suit ready to go to court or the office each morning of our marriage. Little did I know that the court and office would see him more than me after the suits arrived.

There were my girls, surrounded by "older" men. *I guess Christmas came early this year.* The 'older' men joined in and were trying to guess which one is Julie and which is Jenna. This is how they had all the men's attention. Julie and Jenna giggled, smiled 'big,' and flirted with the boys, rather men.

Michael noticed his youngest sisters with his friends, shook his head from side to side, rolled his eyes, and tried not to look. His little siblings were trying to pick up his friends in his home. They are old enough to do what they please, so they think. Michael continued to listen to his grandmother complain about his grandfather's eating habits. The Klein's are the only grandparents the Kayden children have ever had. All the kids love them both dearly, and not because they are all in the 'Will.'

The next few hours seemed like days. The smorgasbord seemed never-ending. The food kept on coming out of the kitchen, on its own, at a steady pace. People kept on eating as if there was no tomorrow. The only person who hasn't eaten anything this afternoon was me. I did not seem to have much of an appetite these past few days. I am sure it will come back, but losing a few pounds couldn't hurt much. I always think I could stand to lose a few pounds here and there, mostly here, and maybe a little there too. Cameron thought so too, but never said anything aloud to me. I don't think he would have ever dared anyway. I certainly could always tell by the look on his face when I would wear clothes he thought weren't 'fitting.' The look was as bad as drinking sour milk.

Carol was still running the show. My Dad was still eating, and the kids were all in good spirits. I just observed everyone around me, as if I were invisible, until my Mom grabbed me from behind.

"Come here darling and sit down with your Mother." She grabbed my right hand with her left, and led me to the couch in the living room and said, "Here, eat. You will feel better, I promise." She is a very sympathetic person and always knows the right thing to say in any situation. HA!

I started to nibble at the cheesecake. It was the best, New York Cheesecake. Why shouldn't it be? My mother brought it all the way from New York just for the occasion.

"There, there now, don't you feel a little bit better honey?"

"Yes Mother. This is just what I needed." I took a deep breath and another nibble of the delectable dessert. My mom smiled and patted me on the back of my hand that held the fork. The cheesecake was normally good, but not today.

"Amy, Darling, everything is going to be alright dear, I promise. I know how you feel honey. Really I do."

How could she? Dad was still alive and well, and eating non-stop. She will know how I feel when her refrigerator stays full for at least a full day!

"I remember when I went to visit your Aunt Sophie for a few days awhile back. I left your father by himself, God forgive me. I thought he would die without me, but he didn't, *sigh*." My Mom shifted closer to me and patted my arm while I was trying to take a bite of cheesecake. She continued …

"I came home in the middle of the afternoon a few days later, quickly looked in the refrigerator to see what was left, if anything. I screamed when I looked and saw all the food still there. I slowly turned towards the bedroom to see your father lying on the bed not making a sound in the least." She grabbed my hand, the one with the fork in it, and held it to her heart and took a deep breath. "I thought he was dead. I thought he had left me forever and no one called me to let me know. I screamed and held my heart, then jumped about 10 feet in the air when I heard your father snoring as he turned over onto his back. Now, that was scary. So, honey, I do know how you feel. And the food in the frig, well, apparently your father was invited to the neighbors to eat every meal. Every meal, can you believe?" She finally let go of my hand. It is so numb from her squeezing so damn hard that I may never be able to eat cheesecake again (At least not with my right hand).

Mom thought she was being sympathetic, supportive, and a loving Mother. However, she didn't really understand. I know she thinks she does, but then all Jewish Moms think they know everything about everything. I guess I am included in that group as well, except I really do know everything!

Chapter 2

Home Alone

Summers usually go by so slowly, like a snail inching across a wide sidewalk in the middle of the day in the intense heat. The kids are usually bugging me about what to do, where to go, and how much money they will need. It didn't happen this summer. The last couple of months seemed to fly by without looking twice, thrice, or four times for that matter. I really don't know what happened to the summer months. Maybe I fell asleep like 'Rip Van Winkle' and woke up at the end of summer. I didn't grieve at all for Cameron. Maybe I just don't know how to grieve. Maybe it still hasn't hit me yet or maybe I was waiting for Cameron to come home from the longest golf game of his life. I just don't know how to feel yet. I am sure it will be a downpour when the time is right.

Michael was back at work. Mel was finishing her internship, while Julie and Jenna were finishing a summer school class. This way the girls will be officially sophomores in the fall. At least that is what they told me. I know they are all growing up. It is too bad Cameron won't see his offspring venture out into the world as adults, just liked we planned. They all seemed to take on more responsibilities amongst themselves instead of asking me for help or advice. That was a good sign, wasn't it? I must have done something right in their upbringing.

With a new season approaching, I decided to start anew, with my housecleaning for the fall, by taking each room by storm, one at a time. I feel it is always good to start something new with a clean slate. I cleaned out the closets and drawers, one by one. When it came to our closet, Cameron's and mine, I stopped. I slowed down, as if I was stuck in a time warp. I was alone in my closet, and time was standing still, at least for me it was. I touched Cameron's pin-stripped suits. I smelled his button-down white shirts, and eyed his ties on the rack. I sighed with heavy droplets waiting to fall from my deep brown eyes. I sat down in the middle of the closet and closed my eyes. The droplets let go, but I can't. I just can't. The closet must be left alone, at least for the time being. I wanted to keep my past a part of my future. I was not ready to let go of everything just yet. One day at a time.

Dealing with Cameron's folders, law books and files from the office was much easier. In fact, I relished it. You see, everyday, and I mean everyday, Cameron would bring home at least one box of work to do each evening, and usually would leave it at home.

"Amy, I'm home. I brought some work so you can help me tonight. You know, some filing. I know how good you are with organizing." One would have thought we were moving with all the boxes lined up against the wall in our bedroom, and in the family room as well.

I walked into the family room. I was having a stare-down with all of Cam's boxes lined up against the wall. They always seemed to outnumber me, and win. Not today. I quickly ran for the phone and called Cathy, Cameron's secretary, from the law firm.

"Cathy, have I got some presents for you. Bring your husband's truck." The house looked immaculate after the mass papers, folders, books, and file cleanout. It is time for me to move on! I can't change the past, and I need to keep moving on into the future. My future, and mine alone. It was past seven and I went into the kitchen to pour myself a glass of red wine. Victory was mine today. The boxes are gone, and I won this round fair, and square, (Oh, like the boxes.).

Fall is always so peaceful, colorful, and cool around our home. For one reason, all the kids are back at school. That alone is enough to celebrate with a glass of red wine. Secondly, the leaves start changing colors as they start disappearing from the trees. Cameron used to go out in the yard, with Tom and Jerry, to rake up the leaves in the late Fall.

This was one chore Cameron actually enjoyed doing. It was his thinking time. I am sure he was thinking about the next step in his trials and other cases.

Tom and Jerry mainly watched their Dad do the raking, piling and cleaning up the leaves. They lazily sat besides one of the humongous tree trunks in the middle of the yard and watched with one eye open. Nevertheless, they were with him all the way. Thirdly and last, the coolness in the air was back, especially in the evenings, as well as taking tranquil lengthy walks with Tom and Jerry, wearing my jeans and sweaters. It is my favorite time of the year. How I wish we could have fall all year round.

While walking one evening with my boys I smell wood burning. There are always logs stacked in everyone's yard. Puffs of silent grayish-white smoke arise from the chimneys sporadically. That is enough to keep me going forever. I love to cuddle on evenings like this when the air is chilled, have some hot cocoa, and maybe a s'more or two. I would have preferred to cuddle with Cameron, but he always brought work and cuddled with his files instead of me. I got used to it.

October 1st is the day I start decorating for Halloween by bringing out all the candles of the season. Pumpkin, Spice, Vanilla, and Cinnamon scents are set in each room. When the kids were still in high school, the nights were cool and quiet. They were all busy doing their homework, going to school dances or watching school sports. Now the evenings were exceptionally quiet. It was just the boys and me sitting out in the backyard gazing at the twinkling stars. They are great company, the dogs, I mean. They never ask for money or complain about anything. They don't talk back, or throw laundry on the floor in the utility room. They don't leave glasses half full by the computer. They do follow me from room to room, including the bathroom though. You never know if I might need some assistance in there.

I wasn't lonely, yet. I am used to being alone even when I wasn't. Unbelievably, I wasn't depressed either. I guess it just hasn't hit me yet. I knew one day Cameron would pass away at an early age, because he worked so intensely and didn't take care of himself, by eating healthy or exercising. God forbid he would go for a walk with me when I took the boys.

I didn't expect anything to happen this soon, or rather I wasn't rightfully prepared for this to happen so soon. Nevertheless, I have to move on and deal with what my present and future hold for me. Right now, I have a beautiful home, my four wonderful healthy children, and my two boys by my side, figuratively and literally speaking.

The silence is thick in the air. Just sitting in my rocker in the cool air out back makes me feel like time is standing still. I slowly stood up from my white wicker rocker in the backyard. I unhurriedly walked into the kitchen and locked the French door, after Tom and Jerry picked their heads up and decided to follow me now. Great watchdogs, huh.

"Boys, did you hear anything?" Like I would get an answer from dogs. "Come with Mommy. I want to check the locks." I waved my hand for Tom and Jerry to follow me. I don't know why. They will follow me anyway.

I started with the kids' rooms. I turned all the lights on, checked the closets, under the beds, and in the bathrooms. Paranoid, I know. But still.

"Nothing in here. No chainsaw murderers, no rapists, no boogie man…" I tiptoed slowly down the hallway into the living room, dining room, and family room. The dogs followed me. "Aren't you guys supposed to be in front of me? How are you going to defend me from behind, huh? Great guard dogs you turned out to be."

Still nothing. "Paranoid whacko," I said as I stood tall, as tall as I can be at 5'2", and started walking back to my room. Suddenly I stopped in my tracks. "The lights!" The dogs bumped into my rear, which to me is a big target. "I forgot to put the outside lights on. That's it!" I sighed and turned around. I really need to get a timer for those.

Briskly, I went over to the front door, which is a French door with many little rectangular windows, to turn on the outside lights. Just as I reached to flip the light switch, a shadow moved outside.

"AHH!" I screamed.

The shadow moved again and something crashed as Tom and Jerry howled and jumped around. I bolted to the kitchen. *A butcher knife, a butcher knife…!*

"Amy!" a voice called out. "It's me. Amy!"

I stopped with my hand on a knife handle at the butcher block. "Carol?" I croaked

"Amy? Is everything okay? Let me in." The person tapped the glass on the door. "Honey, I brought you some Carvel with chocolate jimmies."

Carvel with chocolate jimmies. Yes, it has to be Carol.

I went to the door, flipped the outside lights on, and let in my oldest friend. The dogs were still going nuts and running back and forth from the kitchen to the front door. They bolted out as soon as I opened the door. The ground covered in jimmies, which they love better than chocolate cheesecake.

"Sorry," Carol said, squeezing by the furry vacuum cleaners. "I know how much you love chocolate jimmies. When you screamed, you scared me and I jumped and then…" she gestured to the mess under the dogs. "I think I broke your planter too. Sorry hon."

"Just come in," I said, laughing.

Carol followed me into the kitchen, which I'd repainted a pale tone of peach. I always hated the sky blue that Cameron loved so much. It was so, so blue.

"So this is what you've been up to," she said, looking around at my freshly painted walls. "It's been forever since I've seen you. Do you know how to return calls?"

"Oh stop. It hasn't been that long. I waved to you yesterday in the front yard while I was cutting some roses for the kitchen table."

"Was that you? I thought it was the mailman." Carol smiled lightly. "What's going on, Amy? Everything okay with you?"

"Just enjoying the silence, that's all." I sighed.

"That's all… Well, Larry and I just drove over to Carvel, without the kids for a change. It was our date night, and we had ice cream, and I thought I would bring some back for you. But it looks like Tom and Jerry are getting it all."

"Thanks anyway." I took a deep breath, and Carol did too. Then we stood there, just looking at each other. But it wasn't the awkward kind of silence. It was the good kind. I'd forgotten how good that could be.

"Sit down. I'll get coffee." I started the Mr. Coffee, decaffeinated of course, without waiting for a response from Carol. Let me tell you, no one makes a better cup of coffee then Mr. Coffee, at least not in this house. Meanwhile I grabbed bottled water for Carol while we waited for the coffee. Carol and I sat down, face to face at the kitchen table. We just looked at each other and sighed.

"SO.....how's everything, the kids, dogs, you, since yesterday?" Carol eyed me.

"Oh, you know."

"No, I don't. So, tell me," Carol looked right into my eyes.

I just sat there staring at her, and then the coffee pot made a noise and gave off a last steam, so I think it is ready.

"Want a cup?" Maybe coffee would help me avoid Carol's line of questioning.

"Sit," she ordered. "I'll get it."

I shook my head. My house was Carol's house, and Carol's house was my house. We both flew in and out as if both of us were Tasmanian devils. We always left both kitchen doors unlocked. At least I used to.

"Thanks," as she put my mug in front of me on the kitchen table. We both just sat for a while. The coffee mug warmed my palms. I put my head down on the table and sighed.

Carol took a sip of the steaming hot coffee and placed it back down on the table quietly. "What can I do for you Amy? How can I help you? Tell me please." She touched my hand with hers.

"Well," I met her eyes, "my floors need washing."

She smacked my hand. "Seriously, anything you need from me, you know you have it."

"I am serious. You can mop the floors tomorrow morning, along with cleaning the windows. How about deodorizing the bathrooms too? They aren't really dirty, just a little dusty."

She sipped her coffee, her eyes peering over the mug at me. "Okay, I catch your drift. I will leave you alone, for now." She stood up and straightened her blouse. "You know where to find me. Anytime you want, you can run down to my house and listen to me yell at the kids and Larry. My house is your house."

"It is quiet around here," I admitted. "You know me Carol. I just need some thinking time, alone. I'll come around." I stood and walked her to the front door.

She gave me a big hug. "Come over anytime. I mean it."

"I know."

I locked the door for the second time tonight, and put the alarm on. When I turned around, Tom and Jerry were sitting and waiting for me to tell them what to do next.

"Well boys, it's just me and you. Let's go to bed. Off with you." I waved them on and they shot ahead of me. "Oh, sure, now you take the lead."

Chapter 3

Pajama Weekend

Butterball turkey, stuffing, gravy and potatoes all sound so good. The smells, tastes, colors, of all the delectable fall foods make my mouth water, especially if it isn't burnt. This is the one holiday meal my grandmother taught me well. Grandma Klein would sit me up on a chrome stool with the red shimmering plastic cover cushion. She would show me everything she put into the foods as she was cooking. They were never sure measurements, just what she thought would taste the best. She would also tell me jokes (in Yiddish and I would have to pretend I know what she meant), taste the foods as we went along, and we always had the best time of our lives in her kitchen. I can still smell Grandma. She always smelled like whatever she was cooking. Oh, the good ole days. I knew I would miss her.

This Turkey Day my kids and I are spending some quality time together. Let's not forget Tom and Jerry. They have all their girls home to give their undivided attention to them, and only them.

"Hey girls," I said, whisking into the family room. The twins had fashion mags on their laps and Melanie was lying sprawled out on the couch eating oatmeal raisin cookies. I made them every year for Thanksgiving because they were Cameron's favorite. Some habits never die. "Why don't we each pick out a DVD we just can't live without. Let's make this the greatest Thanksgiving." I crouched in front of the entertainment center to pick out my all-time favorite.

"How is that Mom?" Melanie asked.

"We all agree to watch the movies together, no matter what. I'll make a contract for us all to sign," I learned some things from being married to a lawyer. "and if any of us break the contract, she has to do everyone's laundry on Sunday morning, before leaving for school again. Plus cook and serve Sunday morning's breakfast." I waited for a response, or two, or possibly three. No one uttered a sound. "It'll be fun. Feet up, cookies in our laps, dogs to snuggle… Don't everyone talk at once."

"Okay, sounds great to me," the twins chimed in at the same time. (It's scary sometimes when they say the exact thing at the exact same time). They looked at each other and giggled.

"Oh, okay." Mel took another cookie from the bowl. She held it up to the light. "Hey, Mom, this one isn't burnt. Good job."

I threw a sofa pillow at her. I thought about throwing a cookie, but didn't want it used against me in a court of law, as a weapon.

We all sat comfortably waiting to watch one of my favorite movies, which happened to be Cameron's favorite of all time, *Field of Dreams.* When Cam and I saw it for the first time, actually in a theatre, he had tears in his eyes at the end and turned the other cheek as we were leaving the theatre. He wouldn't admit it touched him, but I knew it did, and left it at that.

"Great. Let's all get cozy in our pajamas and meet back here in five, girls. I'll make a couple of bags of popcorn, in the microwave of course. Let's move it."

We all raced around the house and met back in the family room on the couch. I brought the popcorn out in a few bowls, along with a few cans of Fresca that were ice cold, ready for consumption. It was the girl's favorite soft drink since it has zero calories. Every daughter of mine has been on every diet at one time or another, and me too for that matter. The Fresca balances out the popcorn and cookies for the evening.

When my movie was over, it was still early in the evening, so Melanie grabbed her favorite, *Scream.* The rest of us really didn't appreciate scary movies like Mel, even with a little comedy in them, but Melanie had no fear whatsoever. The twins started to go to their room.

"Night Mom," they whispered in unison.

"Come on now," Melanie said. "We all agreed and signed at the dotted line didn't we?" Melanie just loved to rub things in especially when it came to teasing her little sisters. Mel could be in the house alone, in the dark, in the middle of the night, with the windows wide open, doors unlocked and partially open, wind blowing and leaves rustling around, and a huge storm brewing in the dark of the night, and I don't think a slasher movie would bother her in the least. She was right, though, we all did agree to watch together, and we all signed at the dotted line.

"Let's go girls. Back in here. We made an agreement." I gave Melanie a '*why-do-you-do-this-to-me*' stare. She smiled innocently. "Before we start Melanie's 'choice' of movie, we need to check the house." They all knew exactly what I meant.

Melanie sighed. "You are all such a bunch of babies." The rest of us fanned out to lock up the house. "I can't believe you are all so scared," she called out.

None of us answered her. We finished our little chore, and we all ended up back in the family room together again for round two and started Mel's movie.

We were all just getting comfy, including the boys on the floor, when we saw a light flash through the front French door.

Jenna jumped up. "What was that?"

"Oh Jenna, breathe again, will you?" teased Mel. "It was something in the movie. Now sit down. They're about to kill off the blonde chick with the humongous boobs."

The rest of us looked at each other warily. Tom and Jerry didn't budge, so why should we? Then again, why would they? They were happy as clams on the floor being close to Julie, who was using them as cushions. After a few seconds, we all settled down and tried to focus on the movie. The murderer drew his sword and held it high up in the air ...

Once again, there was a flash of light. It was much brighter now, and we all flinched. Tom and Jerry gave out a few howls as they jumped up, to defend our lives, or theirs' who knows.

"Okay," I pointed to the dogs, "that was real this time. The dogs even saw it."

"Ouch," Julie groaned while she rubbed the spot on the back of her head, which had hit the floor when Jerry jumped up.

"What was it Mom?" Jenna grabbed my arm.

"I'm not sure. But let's stay calm." I sat there, frozen, just like the rest of the girls. One of us has to do something.

We all turned to look at each other, like who is going to go to the front door and look.

"OH, MY, GOD," Melanie said, standing up and brushing the popcorn off her pants. "I will see what is going on out there. I'm sure it's the boggie man come to chop us all to bits."

"Mel!" Jenna whispered.

Melanie pushed pause on the recorder, and walked around the corner, disappearing, into the darkness. The rest of us sat still, not even blinking, while we waited, to hear something from Melanie.

The front door slowly creaked open. Then silence. Ten seconds, thirty, forty …

"What happened to her?" Jenna whispered.

"Maybe she's dead," Julie whispered back, as she covered her mouth.

Dead? I jumped up and flew down the hallway. Around the corner, I flew as fast as I could in my pj's and slippers. One of my slippers slipped in one direction and I went in the other. A spill on the floor for me, and I landed right at Melanie's feet.

"God damn it." I laid there on the travertine.

Melanie looked down at me. "Mom, what IS your problem?"

"You're alive."

"Of course I'm alive!" She bent down and put her hands under my armpits. "You can get up now. Everything is fine. There's just a basket out here."

"Well, I hope there isn't a baby in it," I replied out of recourse.

"Oh mother. You are so weird."

I brushed myself off. "I think I pulled a muscle, or at least split my pj's in the back."

Mel looked at me as if I was an idiot running around the looney bin with my pants down.

I moved to the door. "There's a basket out there?" Melanie joined me. There was a brown, round, wicker basket, but it was too dark to see if anyone was standing with it. "Mel, go take a look out there by the rose bushes, okay Pumpkin?"

"Me? Why are you throwing me to the wolves?"

"Because I have two spare daughters on the couch, and there's only one Mom. GO." I gave her a nudge.

No one was around.

When she came back inside the house, she and I brought in this huge wicker basket. It had green cellophane wrapped around it and a huge green and gold bow. It was almost too pretty to open.

"I'll carry it Mom. I know what a weakling you claim to be." Melanie carried it into the kitchen for me, as I stared at her.

I locked the front door, twice to be sure, and joined the girls in the kitchen. Julie and Jenna crowded around it. "Wow. How exciting. Look at all that stuff in there." They had already unpacked the half of it to see *What Lies Beneath* (one of Mel's other favorite movies).

"Candy, chocolates, pretzels, mustards, jellies and jams, a card from Blockbuster so we can rent some movies, and a huge bag of hot cocoa mix." Julie clapped. "Someone knows what I like."

Jenna's eyes were as big as candy apples. "Who do you think it's from? Why are we so lucky to get a goody basket?"

Jenna pranced around the kitchen island with the chocolates and candies in her hands.

"No card?" I asked.

"I don't see one." Melanie ran her fingers throughout the basket and then scanned the floor.

We all looked in and out of the basket again, (except Jenna who is still prancing around the kitchen as if she found a pile of gold bricks), but nothing. "OK, let's backtrack to the front door and look there girls." Funny, having a mission got rid of the scary movie 'heebee jeebees'. We happily tromped back to the mysterious, dark front door.

Melanie even went into the bushes. "Nothing, but a rawhide bone." She held up a gnawed, dirty, beige thing between her thumb and forefinger. Instantly Jerry flew out of the house, grabbed the rawhide bone from Melanie, and darted back, into the house. Tommy boy didn't even know what happened. I'd always wondered if that dog was 'mentally challenged.'

"Well, at least Jerry found what he was looking for. Come on in girls. There is no sense in standing outside in the dark." The girls continued to search anyway. "Girls, it's too dark to keep looking now. I'll get up early tomorrow morning and look again. There isn't anything more we can do right now. Hello? I am locking up now!" They all marched on in and I locked the door again, for the third or fourth time this evening. *Who is counting?*

Back in the kitchen, staring at the basket of goodies, Julie started to foam at the mouth seeing all the delectable snacks. "Let's dig in."

They tore into the chocolates and candy bags.

"Girls, girls? What are you doing? We don't know who sent us this package. I am not going to make any trips to the emergency room tonight. We need to find out who this is from before you dig in." They moaned and made faces. "C'mon now, you should all know better than that. Let's get back to Mel's movie. I did make oatmeal raisin cookies!" Yeah, the girls faces really lit up now.

I marched them back into the family room. With all their groaning and moaning, you'd think it was a forced prisoner march and not a happy family night of killer knives and serial murders. What's a mother to do?

∾

Early the next morning I showered for the day and was dressed in a flash. It was a beautiful clear brisk morning. I sat in the backyard in my white wicker rocking chair listening to the birds sing, enjoying the sunshine, and Mr. Coffee was doing his job in the kitchen. What more can a woman want on a day like today?

"The Note!" I suddenly thought. "We never found a note that should have been with the basket last night." I was looking right at Tom and Jerry beneath my feet. "I better get going."

All the girls were still fast asleep; after all, it was only eight in the morning. Who else would be up so early besides the boys and me? I carefully opened the front door. I don't want the girls to hear. Digging in the bushes was a lot less spooky in the daytime. Aside from sticking my arm on some rose thorns, it couldn't have been a happier stroll through the garden. No note, though. I even looked in the gutter by the street. Nothing turned up.

Walking into the kitchen, I packed up the basket of goodies and put it in the laundry room. "I know the girls won't look there, will they?" Tom and Jerry just tilted their heads as usual when I ask them questions. "They won't think about doing their laundry until Sunday morning, right before it is time to go back to school. I think they would all rather cook than do laundry. I would rather do laundry. I can't burn the laundry", *could I?* I left the basket on top of the washing machine for the time being, (talking to Tom and Jerry makes me feel sane, better than as if I was talking to a wall).

I waited for the girls on the backyard patio, enjoying the coolness of the early morn once again. I had the biggest smile on my face, sitting there thinking and looking at my tranquil backyard. It felt so good to be home with all my girls, knowing they were safe in their own beds fast asleep. I wish Michael were here too, but the real world called! Tom and Jerry stretched out on the wet grass. It was going to be a magnificent day.

I sat quietly for about fifteen minutes before I realized it was Thanksgiving! "OH MY GOD! I forgot to take the turkey out of the freezer yesterday. Or the day before yesterday. Or whenever the hell I was supposed to take it out." Who remembers these things? This called for extreme measures.

I darted into the house, and into my bathroom, where I turned the tub faucet to steaming hot. The boys ran with me. Tom actually slammed into the wall; he was running too quickly on the travertine floor. His loud yelp echoed throughout the house.

"Mom? What was that?"

"Great. Tom. You woke up Jenna." I raised my voice at least an octave: "It's nothing honey. I just dropped Grandma Klein's favorite rooster pitcher. I'll fix it, again. Go back to sleep." I rushed into the pantry, where we have our extra frig and freezer, to get the turkey. I wanted to get it into the tub before the girls spotted me. They swore I would do this. I swore I wouldn't. *I channel Grandma Klein on Thanksgiving, for goodness sake.*

I paused in the doorway. Grandma Klein suffered from Alzheimer's, didn't she? *Damn it.*

My rushing was for naught. Julie came out into the hallway half-asleep before I'd even reached the frozen bird.

"What are you doing Mom?" She yawned. "What happened to Tommy boy?" He was whimpering in the corner. She bent down to pat his head and gave him a couple of kisses. I would've sworn the dog grinned mischievously at me.

I turned my number three daughter around and pushed her back into her room. "Nothing sugar plum. Go back to bed. It's vacation for you. It's too early for you to be up yet." She stumbled down the hallway and back into her room.

I ran back into the pantry for the turkey one more time. "It shouldn't take that long to defrost, right Jerry?" He wagged his tail. "Oh, my. Who made turkeys so big? It's all those preservatives and crap." I muttered, practically dragging the frozen carcass down the hallway, and flipping it up over the edge into the tub. I turned off the water, and closed the door. "Whew! Saved by the tub." Jerry wagged his tail at me. Tommy boy grinned again. I just knew it. "Now, for the rest of the meal."

∞

This year I had wised up and assigned a dish to each daughter, (one of us should know how to cook). They were required to put something colorful on the table that was edible and considered a vegetable and healthy, not something hazardous to the stomach. I asked them all about a week ago what they would make. Melanie decided that she would make the yams with marshmallows. Julie offered to make corn and peas with butter, and Jenna said she would make the cranberry sauce. I nixed that one. Opening a can of cranberry sauce and putting the contents on an appealing and colorful plate isn't enough work. Try and try again.

"Jenna, please put a little more effort into your dish. It is Thanksgiving. It only happens once a year, you know."

"How about the stuffing, Mom?"

"From scratch?"

"Of course not. From the box. Get real Mom."

I agreed, of course. It was better than canned cranberry sauce. Martha Stewart, Jenna was not. Neither was I, for that matter. I definitely look a lot better anyway. No offense Martha.

I was in charge of the turkey, mashed potatoes, green bean casserole, and rolls, (Yes, store-bought rolls. I don't like taking chances on those. I could tell stories about my homemade rolls, but don't get me started today). The turkey was my extravaganza for the day. Thank goodness Thanksgiving is only once a year.

I thought I would at least get the mashed potatoes made, and not from scratch, (Julia Child I am not). That takes too much work for one person. We usually have a late lunch for Thanksgiving and then munch again in the evening on the leftovers. I paused with my hand on the cupboard. Cameron loved the late lunch too, since he usually didn't have time to eat lunch at work and pretty much would forget about eating until dinner every day.

I opened the cupboard and set a box of cereal on the counter. It was hard enough to think of preparing one humongous meal a day, the Kayden girls were 'on their own' for breakfast today. So let them eat Cocoa Krispies! (That is my favorite cereal. Why not, it has chocolate in it!).

While the green bean casserole was cooking/baking in the oven, and the potatoes are in the microwave doing whatever they do, I ran back to the bathroom to see how the turkey was doing in the hot tub. *Shoot.* The water was too cool. I pulled the plug. Out with the cool, and in with the hot. A few drops got on my socks.

In my dash to get back to the kitchen to check on the food, I slipped, again "***God damn it***," I whispered under my breath. At least Melanie didn't see this maneuver. I picked myself up, and walked briskly, to my bedroom closet to put on my sneakers. This was going to be a sneakers kind of day. I can feel it.

Back in the kitchen I flew. How long was a casserole supposed to stay in the oven? Are the potatoes done? I turned the oven light on and checked the casserole through the window. The edges were dark brown. "Looking good so far boys." Tom and Jerry tilted their heads and wagged their tails in a tick-tock motion. I checked the potatoes, then ran back to turn the water off in the tub. Tom and Jerry are right there with me every step of the way, and a few extra steps because I tripped over Jerry at least twice in the hallway.

Still no one else was up. Whew!

Setting the table in the dining room was special. We normally don't eat in there. I want it to be a special Thanksgiving for us all. It is our first Thanksgiving without their dad. I placed our Thanksgiving placemats on the table. Each child had made a placemat for Thanksgiving in kindergarten. This way they had set places to sit each year. Cameron and I always used paper placemats the twins made one year ---their handprints, drawn and colored into turkeys. I'd covered them with clear plastic so we would be able to use them from year to year on Thanksgiving.

"Oh." I pulled back in surprise. I'd placed all six out on the table, out of habit. Instead of pulling off Michael's and Cameron's, I just left them. They will be here in spirit, I thought to myself.

Back into the kitchen I ran, to check the casserole. This time I turned off the oven, then left the casserole in there.

Back to the bathroom I ran, to check 'big bird.' The water had cooled down quickly again. Out with the cool, and in with the hot. I am beginning to feel like I am a yo-yo.

"I hope this is working," I said to Jerry. "You know what? If it isn't, I'll cook it anyway. At least most of it will cook, right?" Jerry wagged his tail again. "Good. Then we're in agreement."

When I returned to the kitchen for the umpteenth time, Melanie was up and helping herself to a cup of coffee.

"Morning Pumpkin," I said with a big smile huffing and puffing as I walked over and gave her a big hug, and to rest on her shoulders for a minute.

"Why do you look like you just came back from a smelly gym? What have you been doing all morning?

"Just cooking, just cooking."

"Lord help us." She grabbed the cereal box and a bowl. "Where is the milk?" Looking on the counter wasn't the right place, anyone knows that, even a Kayden girl.

"Where I normally keep it. Under the living room rug. Where do you think it is Mel?" Can you tell I was a little annoyed?

One by one, the girls arose from their slumber into the kitchen for a cup of coffee. I guess going away to college they all learned to drink coffee. It must be all those late night study sessions, huh.

Once all my girls were awake, at least in the physical sense, I reminded them of their 'dish' for today. "Girls, remember what I said just last week about everyone helping out with the Thanksgiving dinner today?" They all tossed their heads about, sighed, and gave me looks of despair. "What did you think? That I'd do it for you? Chop, chop. Let's get to it."

One by one, the girls prepared their part of the great Thanksgiving feast. When the delicacies were finished an hour later, I placed them all in the fridge in the pantry. "Girls, this is going to be the best Turkey Day ever."

"*Turkey!*" I forgot about the turkey. Running down the hallway I shouted, "Girls, we're going to have Thanksgiving dinner instead of lunch this year." I didn't tell them the reason. "So fill up on cereal and coffee."

I heard Melanie grumble something, but the exact words escaped me, (Probably for the better).

Something seemed odd this Turkey Day, but it wasn't until later in the morning that I realized the reason: We didn't have to watch football this year. The testosterone kings weren't yelling at us to move away from the TV. The silence was nice, deafening, but still nice.

ᔓᔕ

The turkey had been in the oven, hmmm, a long time now. Cameron and lately, Michael, had always carved the turkey for everyone on our special holidays together. But, with no men, the honor went to the Estrogen Queens.

"Mel, Jenna, Julie, who would like the honor of carving the turkey today?" I announced it like it was the honor of the century. They all turned and looked at each other and then at the walls. "I am not getting an answer, girls." I guess I didn't expect one either. Hacking into the bird for half an hour, getting all juicy and hearing all the "I want white... I want dark..." was definitely no day at the spa. I waited a few seconds while the girls looked at each other in despair.

"Okay then, we will all take turns carving the dead beast. Girls, lets go. Everyone needs to be in the kitchen now. This is going to be a family effort. Come on, it'll be fun."

Tom and Jerry were the first to arrive. They sat right in front of the turkey with their tongues hanging out, and saliva started to drool and hang out on the sides of their mouths, like shoelaces from a sneaker. What a sight that is. One by one, the girls came into the kitchen. I held the carving knife and asked who would like to go first. Jenna offered and carved off a leg.

"OK, now that was pretty easy. I am done," Jenna smiled. "Who's next?"

"Me, I guess," Julie moaned. She decided to cut the other leg. What would one expect from a twin? "Mel, now it's your turn."

"Huh," Melanie huffed in a low muffled sound. "OK, now." Melanie started to carve some slices from the side. She placed them on the serving platter I had set out on the counter. It was pretty messy and getting worse as she went on. Pieces crumbled and chunks flicked in all directions. Thank goodness she doesn't plan on being a surgeon, of any kind.

"Think you could massacre it any more, Mel? This isn't one of your favorite movies, you know." Julie yelled.

"It looks like my high school science experiment, gone wrong," Jenna added.

I stepped in as Mel pulled the knife from the bird and pointed it at her sisters.

"OK, enough Mel. I got it from here." I think she screwed up so she wouldn't have to do anymore. "You can all go do what you were doing until I have it all done," Like I knew what I was doing. I took the carving knife from Melanie and placed it down for a minute to figure out the rest of this tedious operation. The girls left, without delay I may add, but Tom and Jerry are troopers and stayed by my side. They are such good boys. I know what they ***really*** want and what they ***were not*** getting. OH, who am I kidding, of course they are going to get some.

How could I deny my babies on Thanksgiving, or any other day for that matter?

A half hour later, at least it seemed like an hour later, I finally finished carving the turkey. It did not look like a turkey anymore, or anything else I could possibly describe. Calling it a science experiment would be kind. I wasn't even sure it was edible now. But, then Tom and Jerry didn't drop dead from the scraps, so I guess it would be safe for my daughters to consume. At least most of it cooked through, I think. The hot water immersion technique came through, again.

It was about five in the afternoon. I had the table set and reheated all the vegetables. I placed everything on the table. I lit some cinnamon and pumpkin scented candles. I called the girls in for supper.

"Food!" They all came running into the dining room. Tom and Jerry were the first ones there, again. Actually, I don't think they ever left the turkey's sight. We all sat down. Melanie looked at the empty seats and then back at me. "Mom?" Her eyebrows lifted from their normal frowning position on her face.

"I know Pumpkin. I just thought, you know, just in spirit. I am sure your dad is watching over us now, and probably laughing about this whole day so far," I looked around at the girls, hoping they wouldn't know what I was talking about. I didn't bother to explain. "I also wish Michael could be here with us all."

"Yeah," Mel said. "Then he could have carved the stupid bird."

All the girls laughed, and then we began to eat our Thanksgiving feast. Tom and Jerry sat patiently waiting for leftovers. They would walk around the table to each one of us with those sad eyes and moan, just to make sure we know they are here. As we were all trying to finish what was on our plates, we realized our eyes were bigger than our stomachs. None of us could move. We all just sat there in silence.

It was actually a sad few moments. I don't think any of us looked up at each other, probably because we each had a few tears in our eyes and were too proud to show each other at the table how we really felt. Cameron didn't like it when the kids' cried. He always told them to cut it out, suck it up and knock it off. He didn't do well with emotions for himself or anyone around him. I guess that is why I didn't cry much when he died. He would have been proud.

"Usually Dad yells at us for putting too much food on our plates, and not eating it all," Jenna said quietly.

"Yeah, he is – was -- always making jokes at the table by asking us silly questions about boys too," Melanie chimed in.

"Yeah, that's your Dad girls. Always trying to make **you** look silly."

We lapsed into silence again. We really hadn't talked about Cameron much.

A few seconds went by and then Jenna shouted out, "What's for dessert?"

"Dessert!" My shoulders sagged. "I totally forgot about dessert, babe. Oh my God. I don't have any Sarah Lee in the freezer or anything else. I am so sorry, girls…Oh, I know! Let's get some chocolate bars, marshmallows and graham crackers and make s'mores out back. What do you say?"

"I don't know," Jenna said. "Seems like a lot of effort." She unbuttoned her top pants button. I guess a few helpings of yams, potatoes, casserole, and a little cooked turkey did the job. She grinned.

"Hey, how about we open up the some of the candy from the basket we found yesterday Mom?" Julie asked. I sat there with no expression whatsoever, hoping the basket would magically disappear into thin air. "C'mon, Mom. Why not? That's what it's for, to eat, right?" Julie added with a huge smile on her face and her eyes sparkling wide open.

Now all of them were ganging up on me, yelling "please," and "c'mon Mom."

"Fine, fine, fine. Enough already. I'll go get the basket."

I didn't even get a chance to stand, though, because they all immediately shot out of their chairs. What happened to "too much effort?" I shouted.

Later that evening, after another round of dessert, we were all in our pajamas and this time we watched Jenna's movie. She picked out *Home Alone.* I think she wishes she was, 'Home Alone,' sometimes. I don't think the twins ever were home alone at any point in their lives. They are always together. We all watched until we all started to fall asleep. Melanie was the only one who made it all the way through without dozing off for a few minutes.

We all said good night to each other with hugs and kisses. Real hugs and kisses. Then I said, "Group hug girls, come on." Just as I'd predicted, it was the perfect Turkey Day.

~

Friday morning came early, as usual. I was the first one up and ready for the day ahead. The girls will sleep until almost noon and I will let them. It was nice and quiet all morning long. It was just the boys and me, out back, with a cup of coffee, and the birds singing above the treetops.

It was just about eleven in the morning when I heard the doorbell ring. Tom and Jerry raced through the house, as if they were trying to "catch the bunny." They obviously reached the front door before me. It was the Mailman. He had a package. It was big. He had a hard time balancing it on his chest and trying to look through the glass door. Such nerve.

I said thank you, and practically dropped it on the way in. The dogs were still yelping and howling even after I closed the door. They sniffed the box and wagged their tails.

I looked for a return address. It said it was from Cameron's office building. It wasn't from his firm or even the same floors.

"That's strange," I said to the boys. They tilted their heads to one side. I carried the box into the kitchen and opened the top island drawer to get my big scissors. I tried to keep it quiet, so I wouldn't wake the girls.

There were masses of bubble plastic inside. I had to dig to see what was there. I found a white business envelope. Quietly I looked around to see if any of my offspring has risen for the day. Nope, the coast is clear. Inside the white envelope were two tickets to see one of Cameron's favorite singers, John Fogerty. I dug around for a note and found some scented candles and Godiva chocolates. "Cameron didn't eat chocolate." Thank goodness I do. I smelled the candles. They were vanilla scented. At the bottom, I found a beautiful white linen handkerchief with the initial "C" in the middle. It smelled like a rose, a pink one maybe, clearly a woman's perfume. What was Cameron hiding?

My signature scent isn't rosey.

"What the hell?" I kept on digging around for a card of some sort. It wasn't until I rechecked the bubble wrap that I found one. It's addressed to me.

I looked around the kitchen and down the hallway to see if any of the girls were up yet. I threw the items back in the box and quietly took it to my room. The boys followed ever so quietly too. I locked the door behind me and sat on the bed with the box. The rose scent drifted through the room.

Do I want to know who sent this? My hands were shaking. I wasn't sure what to think or do right now. I took a deep breath and picked up the envelope. My name is on the front. I carefully opened the back and took out a piece of paper:

Dear Amy,

We are so sorry for your loss. For your loss is our loss too. We knew Cameron and were very impressed with his work as an attorney. He was a good friend. He helped us out in so many ways, not just legal. We had bought these tickets sometime ago for you to enjoy for the holiday season. We weren't sure if we should send them to you now, but thought it would be best, and Cameron would want you to go. Enjoy the concert.

Cameron told us how you love scented candles and Godiva chocolates too. Hope you and the children enjoyed the basket for Thanksgiving. Once again, we are so sorry for your family's loss and wish you and your family a happy and healthy holiday season.

The Big MAC Corporation.

The Big MAC Corporation? Just then, I heard a knock on the door. "Mom, its me, are you okay?" Melanie asked.

"I'm fine Pumpkin." I wiped my moist eyes. "I am just changing. I will be out in a minute hon." I hid the box under my bed. I then decided to put a clean pair of pajamas on and lay back for the day.

The rest of the weekend went smoothly. We watched Julie's favorite movie, *Multiplicity,* on Saturday afternoon, (figures it was one of the 'twins' movie choice). It was a lazy day with billowing clouds in the sky and a slight chill in the air. It was the perfect day to stay indoors and watch a movie or two. We ate popcorn and drank hot cocoa. We all stayed in our pajamas on Saturday. The phone didn't ring once. Even the girls' cell phones didn't ring. It was so relaxing and comfortable. I wished it would never end.

Sunday morning and the girls were making ugly faces as they were racing for the washing machine. I always say, "First come, first served." They all argued and decided, together, to put all the whites in a load, then the colors, then the darks, then the linens. They actually agreed and did their laundry together. It's amazing what happens when they go away to college. On the other hand, do you think I had something to do with their upbringing? I think I will take all the credit on this one.

The day flew by while the girls packed to go back to school. The twins always share the car and the driving. There was a discussion, or was it a fight, about who was driving. It didn't matter to me as long as they were there safely and in the light of day. They didn't have far to drive, thank goodness. They were only an hour or so away from their Mom. Or is it the other way around?

Melanie had her own car. She was driving back alone and needed to be on the road fairly soon. I don't like any of them driving in the dark anywhere. *I really don't like them driving.* I said goodbye to Mel in the driveway. We held each other and hugged. I held onto my pumpkin for a long time. I had tears forming in my eyes and I didn't want her to see, so I kept on hugging her.

"You've got your father's smile pumpkin," I whispered in her ear. "You know that?"

"Yeah," she whispered back. "And I got my mother's cooking skills. Damn it all."

I laughed and squeezed her. Finally, when I caught my breath and was able to hold back the tears, I let go.

I let go.

Chapter 4

Sunday, Sunday

Slowly I moseyed back into the old homestead. My head, bent to the side, and so was my smile. What smile? I had tears in my eyes. I hated to see my girls go. I know they need to fly on their own. I need to keep pushing them out of the nest. My lonely empty nest, the place I call home.

Tom and Jerry waited at the front door. Their tails were motionless. They too, were sad to see our girls leave. I patted their heads, "Well boys, it's just you and me, again." Slowly I walked inside, locked the door, took a deep breath and sighed. The backyard invited me to sit back in my white wicker rocker, close my eyes, and relax.

I thought I was dreaming. I could hear the phone ringing. I shook all over and opened my eyes. I clumsily ran to pick up the phone, but the message machine had already started. I pushed a million buttons trying to turn the machine off, without success.

"God damn this phone." I just picked up the phone.

"Hello, hello."

Michael called. "Just called to see how Thanksgiving was, Big A. I just got off work and -----."

"I'm here Bud. Just ran in," trying to catch my breath, being startled, and pushing a zillion buttons. "So, what's new?" I clicked a few more buttons to stop recording our conversation, but to no avail. *Stupid phone.*

"Just called to talk to you, Big A."

"Big A is a fat man who played football back in the day, and drinks too much beer. I am your mother, not Big A."

Laughter was on the other end of the conversation. "Touchy, touchy, **Mother dearest."**

"That's better. Thank you for calling. I would have rather you been here. The weekend was lonely without you."

"I find that hard to believe. You had all those crazy girls home. I'm glad I wasn't there to witness PMS every day." Michael loves to tease me, any chance he gets.

"Knock it off. They're your sisters and I know you love them. You don't have to like them, but you do have to love them. I am the Mom and my word is final!"

"Whatever. I just wanted to let you know that I am coming home for Christmas, for just a couple of days. I will have to work New Year's Eve. They just set out the schedule for December." He was strangely silent for a few seconds. I was beginning to think something was wrong.

"I also wanted to let you know that I am bringing someone." There was a pause, "Maybe."

There was dead silence. I took the phone away from my ear and stared at it for a second. I thought it was out of order, or maybe my hearing was out of order. I bit my lip and then waited. Finally, I shouted, "Well who are you bringing home? A girl, I hope. What is her name? Where did you meet her?" I questioned him all at once. I knew I flew off the cukoo's nest now, but it was too late to retract.

"Oh, boy. I knew you were going to ask a million questions as soon as I mentioned the words, 'Bringing someone home with me.' I met her at a baseball game. I have been dating her for the last few months. I just didn't want to say anything, for several reasons. I know how you are Mom. You want to know everything there is to know about her, right now!"

"Well, I'm just excited for you Bud. That's all. I want you to have someone in your life besides all your sporting events. So, what's her name?"

I paced the kitchen floor, going in circles and probably making Tom and Jerry dizzy, as well as myself. I didn't care. My son has a girlfriend!

"Liz. That's her name. I am bringing her home on Christmas Eve, maybe, if you behave between now and then. I have the evening broadcast to finish. It will be very late when we get there, Mom. I know, to drive very carefully because I have to watch out for everyone else on the road."

I was smiling when he said that. I taught my children well, at least about driving carefully.

I could hear the sarcasm in his voice.

The phone was quiet. I was waiting for more information, and instructions. However, Michael, being just like his father, didn't venture any further with more incidentals. "Okay." I slowed my pace down now. "What else can you tell me about Liz? How old is she? What else WILL you tell me?"

"Mom, calm down. She's tall compared to you. Everyone is. You are a midget, Big A."

"You mean 'petite,' and stop calling me that name."

"Of course you are. She has brown hair, I guess. She does have a last name, and that's all I'm going to tell you," Michael demanded.

I took a deep breath and smiled underneath it all.

"Well, okay then, Bud. I just want to be prepared, for when she comes to stay with us. She is going to stay with us, right? You aren't planning to stay in a hotel or something." I wasn't sure how that sounded but I thought I was being very calm for a Mom.

I waited anxiously for an answer or two. I bit my lip, again and raised my eyebrows till I heard his voice.

"Mom. Here we go…questions and more questions." He sighed. "She will stay with us. You figure that out. Anyway, I need to run now. We are going out for an early dinner. Later, Big A." Michael hung up the phone.

I wanted to scream at him again for calling me 'Big A' again. I couldn't, not because he hung up so quickly, but because I had a huge smile on my face and I couldn't yell at him when I am smiling. You know what I mean. All Moms do.

I am so happy for him. I hope she knows what she is getting into. *Did I think that?*

"Tom, Jerry, your brother has a girlfriend!" The dogs howled and jumped around the kitchen. They probably thought I was giving them the rest of the turkey for their dinner tonight. I know, I know, it's the tone of my voice that makes them so excited.

I was so thrilled for Michael. I didn't know what to do. Do I call the girls and let them know that their brother is bringing home a girl. Pacing the kitchen in circles around the island, "Maybe I should start cleaning the rooms. What do you think boys?" They gazed at me waiting for something yummy, or anything, to fall off the counter. My head started spinning and my heart is skipping some beats. All I can do right now is smile from ear to ear. I need to do something. I need to use some of this energy.

"Boys, how would you like to go for a walk?"

The tails were a 'waggin.' We, including myself, all ran over to the garage door for the leashes.

I beat the dogs. Wow, I must have a lot of energy right now.

I practically ran all the way to Carol's house with Tom and Jerry following me for a change. I knocked on the kitchen door, and just walked in with the boys. I could see Carol's kids running amuck all over the house.

"Hey Carol, where are you? Adam, go get your mom please."

Adam screamed, "MOM."

"Adam, dear, sweetie, I could have done it that way too." Adam was busy stuffing his face with a big slice of pumpkin pie.

"Want some pie Mrs. Kayden? It's really good, so I know you didn't make it." He grinned and stuffed away.

Carol walked in the kitchen casually, "What's up Amy?" wiping her hands on a dishtowel. Carol always has a dishtowel in her hands or in her pocket. I think it is calming to her, sort of like a security blanket. "Adam, could you go in the other room. I'm beginning to have a 'children's headache.'" Carol placed her arm over her forehead as if she was in pain, or will be soon if he doesn't leave NOW.

"Yeah, right," as he shuffled his feet into the family room, but not without another slice of pumpkin.

"That kid will eat the tin if that is all that is left," Carol joked.

"The girls left, and Michael called."

"Oh, are you sad, hon?" She held her arms out to me and hugged me. She stopped and gazed at me for a second. "You certainly don't look sad. What's going on?" She looked bewildered. She placed her hands on her hips, tilting her head.

"I am not sad at all! Michael called ……how about you come walk the boys with me and I'll let you in on the gossip."

"Larry, the kids are yours forever. I'm going with Amy." She announced it to the whole house, but only the walls were paying attention.

Once outside, and walking towards the park with Tom and Jerry, Carol inquired, "What's up hon? Everything okay? Did Michael do something stupid, again?" sounding disappointed.

"Everything is good. Michael called……" I left Carol hanging in mid sentence.

"Yeah, yeah and what? Tell me already, what's with Michael?"

"Well, it seems as though he has a girl, or rather a young lady he is seeing." I kept on walking faster and faster. "He called to say that he is bringing her home for Christmas."

Being Jewish, we aren't supposed to celebrate Christmas, but we have always celebrated the family being together, the opening of gifts, the glitter, and glamour of the festive time of year. We don't go to temple, but we do light the Chanukah candles. It's just a tradition my family has had since I was a little girl. Cameron was okay with it since he never had a real family. Besides why can't we have the best of both worlds?

"Well, well, well now. Hmmm. Isn't that something. Finally!" Carol laughed and her hands went airborne, thanking god. She could practically touch him with her height, or at least a lot closer than I will ever be. She smiled from ear to ear. I think she happier for him than his own mother. How can that be? Carol watched my children grow up, as if she was their second mother. When she put her hands up in the air, the leash dropped and Tommy boy took off towards the park. We both ran after him, or rather, Jerry ran first, and was dragging me behind him.

Jerry was pulling so hard on his leash that I had to release it, as I fell into the sandbox. All that dirty sand, broken toys, probably some cat poop, sand ticks, and more, is now all over me.

"God damn it. Yuck!" Who knows how many kids have been in here peeing, or picking their noses, or something else they were picking.

"Gross, gross, gross." I jumped out of there as fast as I could, as if there was a skunk coming after me ready to spray. I shook myself as if spiders were crawling all over me. "I hate this." There might have been one in there, who knows. I don't want to think about it.

Carol's hands were in the air and her long legs were taking giant strides across the soccer field, in the middle of a game I might add. It was Sunday, in the late afternoon, and that was soccer time. Here comes Carol!

After shaking the' *hee-bee gee-bees'* off me, I started to run after all of them onto the soccer field as well. My left sneaker fell off during my 'trip.' It is probably at the bottom of the sandpit. It was going to stay there now, for all I care. The sand trap can have it. I took off the other sneaker and threw it in the sandbox as well. Now they will have a matching pair to play or pee on in there.

Here we are, two crazy women running after two rambunctious hound dogs. A whistle blew on the field and all the girls know they have to sit down in their spots. The referees were running after Tom and Jerry with their whistles in their mouths, changing their footings every few steps trying to keep up with the dogs. They looked like the three stooges. Tom and Jerry were having the time of their lives leaping around and playing soccer. They got a hold of the ball and booted it. They were both prancing around on the soccer field, with their leashes in toe, and having a "ball," no pun intended, NOT.

The girls sat on the field giggling and laughing, but I didn't see the parents or the referees doing the same. They all had a time schedule to keep. Two of the dads started to run after the dogs and fell on top of one another in a muddy area. A few of the other parents were shouting obscenities at Carol and me. I dare not mention what they were saying, but you catch my drift. Now we had a few more people chasing my boys, on and off the field. What a sight to see. It looked like a comedy show or *America's Funniest Videos.*

I was watching Tom, as I continued to chase him, as he stopped in front of a baby stroller and took some licks of the little boy's ice cream. The Mother cringed at the site. Jerry saw a blanket on the sidelines with what else, FOOD. It was a smorgasbord. He grabbed a few bites before running back onto the field with Tommy boy to play some more soccer.

Enough is enough. I placed two of my fingers in my mouth and whistled loudly for the entire park to hear. You would have thought the fire department was on their way. The dogs stood dead in their tracks. Their tongues were hanging a mile out of their mouths as they were breathing heavily and saliva was thrown everywhere, including one of the 'chasing' dad's faces. The soccer ball rolled slowly into the goal.

"Tom, Jerry, come here." I pointed to my feet. They turned around and came trotting back to me with their leashes, and tails behind them. Carol followed, as well as a couple of parents who wanted to give me a piece of their minds.

"Carol, let's go. NOW!"

We briskly walked back into our safe zone.

"There's no place like home." I smiled at Carol.

"I'll see you tomorrow hon." I could see Carol sneak back into her kitchen, without making a sound. The walls will never tell.

I scolded the boys all the way to the front door. I sat there with them on the front step of the porch, looking out to the west side of the early evening skyline.

"Sigh."

The sun looked so pretty this time of day. The reds, oranges, and yellows were all fading away and turning into greens, blues and purples. What a beautiful sunset. The three of us just sat there, resting mainly.

I couldn't be angry with Tom and Jerry. They just wanted to have some fun, and they did. I kissed them on their heads and gave them some hugs. I just love these guys.

"Now don't run away from me again boys. You hear me?"

I know they hear me, but do they comprehend? Who knows. Dogs can pretty much understand our tones, but the words? I don't know, (It would be great to know exactly what they are thinking. But that could be saved for another book, another time, or maybe I should ask the dog whisperer?).

Cleaning the girls' rooms would take up the rest of the century. Since I had so much energy to use up after Michael's phone call, let the sterilization begin! The girls weren't going to be home until Christmas break, so this was a good opportunity to see their rooms looking clean, uncontaminated and smelling fresh. Lighting scented candles at the end of the onslaught is always a sign of cleanliness and a job well done.

The doorbell rang as I lit a candle in Mel's room. The dogs raced to the front door barking away. They were just doing their job.

"Good boys," I replied to their efforts. The grandfather clock in the living room just struck seven. Where had the time gone? I raced through the hallway to the front door, remembering now that I forgot to turn the outside lights on, again, and it was already dark. I stood back a few feet from the door and yelled, "Who is it?"

"My name is Joe and I was at the game this afternoon. I watched you walk home," he proudly told me.

My heart rate just sped past 30 mph, the speed limit in our neighborhood. I almost jumped out of my skin. My legs were getting weak. He followed me home. How creepy. Why would he do that? What should I do now?

"What do you want?" While waiting for a response, I flew into the kitchen, probably going 60 mph, picked up the phone, and dialed 911. Joe started talking to me, but I really wasn't listening. My hands were shaking, my mouth became dry and I could hardly speak.

"There is a stranger at my front door. It's dark outside and I'm alone. Can you please send someone, NOW? He told me that he had followed me home and is now waiting for me to open the door." I could barely speak. I felt my mouth was as dry as the Sahara desert.

"Are you okay right now?"

"Yes, no, I don't know. I am shaking like crazy. My legs are about to give out. I feel like I may fall on the floor at any moment. I may pass out. I can't catch my breath. I am really thirsty."

"First of all, stay calm."

"That's easy for you to say. You are nice and cozy at the police department, with a billion officers to protect your life."

Give me your address, and keep him in a conversation. Is that possible?"

I shook my head, and tried to breath slowly … in the nose, out the mouth.

"Mam, are you there? What is your address and I will send a squad car right over."

I was still shaking all over, but said okay, and gave her my address. I caught my breath and decided to take 'Joe' on my own terms.

"I'm sorry Joe, I didn't hear you just now, and my two ferocious bloodhounds are barking and foaming at the mouth. Let me try and put them in the laundry room with two huge bones to chew on."

He was laughing on the other side of the door. Two seconds later, I heard a siren. *Who's laughing now Joe*, I thought to myself. I could see the red and blue lights blinking through the glass part of my french door. I turned the outside lights on and waited until one of the two police officers approached the front door. He didn't.

One of the two policemen had a megaphone and yelled at Joe to put his hands in the air and turn around, slowly. I saw through the French door that Joe's eyes widened, as well as his mouth. Now all the neighbors were turning their outside lights on and peering out their living room windows. What chickens. Tom and Jerry were still barking away and now were attacking the door. They wanted in on this adventure too.

Joe did as they said. He put his hands in the air, leaned up against the door. The young good-looking, police officer walked over to him while the elder officer had aim on him with his gun standing by the squad car, and conversing with someone on his radio to home base, I assume. The young hunk, rather police officer, who was frisking Joe asked him his name, where he lives, and to state his business. He didn't wait for an answer, and just took his handcuffs out, and started to read Joe his rights as he pushed Joe's face down to the ground and handcuffed him. The police officer was strong and young (Did I already mentioned that?). It looked as though he was having just a little too much fun.

Joe was shoved into the squad car. The elder policeman walked to the door just as the young hunk disappeared down the road. He jotted down my story, what little there was.

"Mam, we need you to come down to the station. You need to identify this man in a lineup and press charges, if necessary."

I didn't even have time to give him an answer. My mouth was hanging open. I think I was in shock. I had never witnessed a scene like this before, well, I have but it was on TV, and not on the porch of my home. It happened all too quickly. I closed the door behind me, locked it, and took a deep breath. Tom and Jerry were still yelping away. Since I still had the phone in my hand, I called Carol and Larry. "Which one of you would like to escort me to the police station right now?"

Larry yelled away from the receiver, "Carol, it's for you."

Before I had time to take a few deep breaths, and try to control my heart from jumping out of my chest, Carol came crashing to the front door with her apron on, mobile phone in one of her pockets, and a dishtowel in her right hand.

I gladly opened the door for Carol.

She was huffing and puffing, "You need me hon?" She had a big smile and gave me an even bigger hug. I think she enjoys my stress.

Carol drove down to the station with me, in total silence. I was still shaken up a bit. Carol understood as she patted my hand. Neither Carol nor I have ever been to the local police station before. We looked around not knowing where to go or who to talk to once we were on 'the inside.' We strolled to the front desk. A chubby, bald, elderly man was sitting on a stool reading the paper through his bifocals, while a cigar was hanging out of his mouth. "Can you help me Sir?"

The bald man looked up from his sports page, with one hand holding up his brain (I suppose), "Well, let's see. Can I help you? Hmm. This is a police station. I am a police officer. The hair coloring is on aisle 10, next to the stress balls. It will depend on the problem Mam, but I think I most possibly can!"

Ignoring his witty comments, "I was asked to come down to the station. I don't want to press any charges." I paused for a moment not knowing what to do next. I reached into my purse to find my drivers license for an ID. There were good-looking police officers all around us, doing whatever police officers do at the station, mainly flexing their muscles. Carol's eyes popped open, as well as her mouth. I had to close it for her in fear of her drooling all over her apron.

Baldy said, "Have a seat. Someone will be with you shortly … Ms. Kayden." As he stared at my driver's license.

"Mrs. Kayden, if you don't mind."

"Whatever." He didn't even look at me when he spoke.

A few minutes, feeling like hours, had gone by and we were still sitting in the waiting area, along with a bunch of hookers, some druggies, and a very diverse group of people I would never want to have lunch with on a Wednesday, ever. Carol and I were the only normal people here, at least what I considered normal. *Does that make us the minority?* One officer came out from a back room, "Ms. Kayden, please follow me." He didn't bother to wait for us. He turned around, and was gone, in a flash.

"My name is Mrs. Kayden," as I ran to follow him. "My friend, Carol, is out there, can she please join us?" I pointed out to the waiting area behind me now.

"Are we having a tea party that I don't know about?" He didn't wait for an answer from me. He left the room to retrieve her.

"Thank you very much."

"Yeah, yeah. Two lumps please," and laughed all the way back to his 'office.'

Suddenly a curtain opened up and lights were upon several men in a lineup. "Well Ms. Kayden, can you pick out the man that was harassing you? Please indicate, by number, which one is the perpetrator Ms. Kayden."

"The name is Mrs. Kayden for the third time." Don't they listen? "I don't want to press any charges. Just question him please. He didn't do anything but scare me (to death). I freaked out and just did what was natural, and called the police. I was alone in the house. Please can we just forget this whole thing, and everyone can go home?" I asked sympathetically.

The police officer sighed, and shook his head and looked up as if God was going to give him the answer. Apparently, this happens all too frequently. Everyone in the room sighed a few times and then the officer signaled to let everyone in the lineup go free.

"Thank you so much. I feel terrible about this. I am so embarrassed." I sighed with relief.

"That's ok Mam. We go through this everyday. Just go home, lock your doors, and don't call us – we'll call you," an elder Policeman said as he shook his head and took the pencil from behind his ear and walked out of the room.

As Carol and I were leaving, one of them shouted, "Hey lady!" Carol turned around and looked at the elderly police officer in surprise. "Not you, the other one, the short one."

I was so humiliated. I slowly turned around with my head tilted downward so no one would recognize me (not that anyone would here), and as I did, there were probably a hundred eyes checking me out. "You forgot your purse lady," he said laughing, and lifted my purse in the air for everyone to see. I slowly walked back and grabbed it. It was my black "coach" purse, (fake of course).

"Thank you very much. My name is Mrs. Kayden, not Hey Lady. Please remember that next time," I said quietly and softly as I walked away, blushing a deep red.

"You mean we have to go through this again soon?" he laughed even harder. A few of the other men also were laughing now. I just wanted to get out of there.

I was almost in tears in the car. It was the longest ride home ever. "Thanks Carol." She knew exactly what I meant, and nodded.

"Anytime you need me, you know I am here for you. Even if I am there, (pointing to her house) I am here," she said with a smile on her face. We hugged and said good night.

I locked up the house, again, turned on the outside lights, the alarm, and the TV as well. I fed the dogs and gave them clean, fresh water.

After my accident in the sandbox this afternoon, doing some major disinfecting in the girls' rooms, and a surprise visit to the local police station, I decided to take a bubble bath. I lit the vanilla scented candles and just relaxed. Tom and Jerry were lying on the bathroom floor waiting just for me.

A half hour went by and I was still sitting in the tub. The water was only lukewarm and time to get out and hop into bed with the boys. I put on my teal satin pajamas and felt so clean and refreshed. I forgot to eat dinner! Now you wonder why everyone thinks I'm not such a good cook. I was a little hungry. I waltzed into the kitchen and made myself a turkey and cranberry sauce sandwich. Of course, Tom and Jerry were right there waiting for something to drop off the counter. The sandwich was delish. So who says I can't cook? I had a Fresca with it, of course.

Ten o'clock in the evening and all is well in the Kayden household. The boys and I were cozy in bed watching reruns of *Seinfeld.* I put the timer on so the TV won't be on all night long. We all just relaxed and slowly dozed off one by one. I heard Jerry snoring loudly. He must have had a great time at the park this afternoon. It probably bothered his allergies a little too. I fell asleep not too long after the boys. Two in the morning and I jumped up and remembered 'the box!'

Chapter 5

'Tis the Season

Waking up on a beautiful, crisp, early Monday morning is my favorite time, and day of the week. Sitting outside in my wicker rocker, a mug of coffee in one hand, listening to the birds chirp, the boys at my side, and the smell of the crisp morning air, what more can a girl ask for? AHH.

The leaves have fallen from the trees, breathing in cool crisp whiffs of fresh air, and the usual holiday music is playing in all the stores. Gift shopping for the kids usually starts, well, let's put it this way, it never ends. I shop all year round for my children's gifts. Somehow, the last couple of months, Santa's closet isn't near as full as it used to be. Time to catch up!

Twinkling lights, music, and the scents of the season, are heaven to me. Well heck, no one wants to smell my cooking or baking this time of year, or any time of year for that matter. Those smells could be strong enough to wake the dead. Do I dare?

I wish Christmas was all year long. Really, I do. Even though I am Jewish, I still decorate my home for the season, inside and out. Why shouldn't my family enjoy the festivities and glitter of the season like everyone else?

Remembering back when Cam and I celebrated our first Christmas together, we had one string of lights on our third floor apartment balcony. It looked so perfect to me. However, it was sparse compared to everyone else, but it was just right for us. I couldn't wait until we could afford a big house, have oodles of lights, a huge decorated tree, and a wreath welcoming family and friends into our home for the holidays. The wreath never appeared. Take a guess.

∾

I don't know how this Christmas will be without Cam. I imagine pretty much the same, since it was always just the six of us. Closing my eyes, knowing Cam won't be joining us for Christmas, I decided this is going to be the best Christmas ever. I am going to make damn sure of it, whether the kids like it or not.

Sauntering back into the kitchen for a refill, I can hear the ticking of the second hand on the grandfather clock in the living room, I can smell the aroma of the perked coffee all around me. I can even hear the birds chirping in the backyard. No kids to yell that they are going to be late for school, no husband to kiss good-bye at the garage door, no deciding what I should attempt to make for dinner, just the dogs lying beside me. It was quiet, too quiet.

"Well boys, what do you say?" as I sat down ever so slowly at my kitchen table, all alone.

They looked up at me, groaned, and decided to change positions at least 10 times to find a comfy spot on top of my feet.

"Sigh. Some help you guys are."

I always did the shopping for everyone's gifts. Cameron never had the time nor desire to shop unless it involved golf clubs. Attempting to bake was a tradition, at least with me. I don't know why. I do remember being in Grandma's kitchen and watching her bake up a storm. Me, I just create the storm and everyone else has to pick up the pieces. Baking is just one of those homemaker chores that you have to do, sometimes, I guess. No one in my house really appreciates the art of baking. The only time they notice is when they smell something burnt and then yell, "Mom, what did you forget about in the oven?"

Sitting straight up in my chair, "An early food shopping it shall be."

The dogs looked up at me, wondering what was that about, and slowly bowed down to the kitchen tile.

Looking great by wearing nice, clean jeans, a holiday sweater, makeup, hair done, a little jewelry, not too much, (You know the old saying, 'less is more.' What **little** I have on is **more** than in the drawer), always makes me feel like I am ready to take on the world, or my small part of it, or something like that.

Looking ahead, into the parking lot, noticing hardly any cars, I know I outsmarted them all and had beaten them all to the punch. I am so smart. The carts are all over the parking lot, and the front of the store. I went to reach for one, and someone pulled it away.

"Hey lady. You need to shop somewhere else. The employees here are on strike. Can't you see the signs they are holding?"

"Oh. You scared me. I wasn't paying attention to the signs. Sorry."

Apparently, there has been some kind of feud going on the last month. I am in my own world, and have been for some time now. I need to start crawling out of the manhole I made.

"Well, I can still shop here, right? I mean, you can't *forbid* me to go in?" I brushed my hair back with a swift quick hand movement, while standing tall in my 5'2" stature in my sneakers.

"You can, but we are asking everyone to go somewhere else until this strike ends, Mam."

I hate when people call me 'Mam.' Now I plan on going on.

"Do I look like a Mam to you? I don't want to have to go somewhere else. I live here, and I am going in there." I flipped my hair back with my hand, again.

"I really don't need to explain anything to you." Huffing and puffing I grabbed the cart back from the man and made my way through the entrance of the store.

The shelves looked almost bare on each aisle. Apparently, since the employees were all outside, there wasn't anyone left to unload the trucks in the back or stock the shelves. Not wanting to look foolish, I was trying to find something, anything, I could buy. Strolling up and down each aisle looking for anything that looked vaguely familiar to me, I finally found something. Soup! I found some mushroom soup.

It may not be for the holidays, but I am determined to walk out of this store with a bag of something, and soup is it. The cans made a lot of noise as I tossed them into the empty cart. No one was around. I waited patiently at the checkout stand.

"Is there anyone here to help me?" I felt like I was in a "Twilight Zone" episode.

The manager of the store came running and apologized. He rang up my few cans of mushroom soup. The charge was less then five dollars and I gave him my debit card to use.

"Don't you have a five dollar bill lady?"

"I want to use my debit card if you don't mind," looking around again to see if there was anyone, and I mean anyone else besides me in the store. Nope.

"C'mon lady, it is less than five bucks. Don't you have a five dollar bill?" He rolled his eyes and huffed and puffed, just like I did before.

"No I DO NOT. I don't carry cash with me. I need these cans. So if you don't mind, I am in a hurry as well," motioning him to continue.

He charged my debit card. "Paper, or plastic Mam?"

"Plastic will be just fine, thank you. And don't call me Mam." I put my plastic bag back in the cart and marched back to my car.

As I was strolling along with my cart of cans, one of the wheels of the cart found a pothole. Losing my balance, I stumbled and almost fell into a huge puddle. Lucky for me, I was holding onto the cart handle, which helped me break my fall, and then the cart went flying on two wheels instead of me, thank goodness. The cart sailed through the parking lot, and stopped right at the trunk of my car.

"I meant to do that," I said to myself loud enough for anyone in earshot to hear. I brushed off some dirt, and continued to towards my car, holding my head up with dignity.

Once I put my bag of soup cans in the car, put my seatbelt on, I just hung over the wheel. How humiliating was that? The whole scene was utterly ridiculous. Not only that, but now I have to go to another store and do this all over again, but hopefully they will have other groceries beside mushroom soup, and no potholes!

Back into the holiday mode, I drove to another grocery store, which is just outside my five mile radius. Going inside, it looked perfectly normal. Looks can be deceiving you know. . . . .

People were milling around, carts available, and food on all the shelves with a festive "jingle bells" playing in the background. It was actually a bit crowded now that I think about it. Reaching for a cart, I was minding my own business when Chase and Nathan saw me down the vegetable aisle.

"Hey Amy," Nathan had a huge 'Santa' smile on his face. He came darting over and gave me a big hug. Chase quickly pushed their cart right next to mine and gave me a hug too.

"How are you dear?" Nathan always is so sincere and truly cares about people.

"Are you doing ok sweetheart? Anything we can do for you?" as he patted my back and stroked my long brown hair.

"I'm fine, really I am," (My smile probably looked as fake as trying to enjoy eating one of my own pancakes). "You guys should come over for coffee and just chat with me. Bring some of your snicker doodle cookies. I just love them. Definitely better than mine," (that made both of them smile). Just as I was talking to Nathan and Chase, a rather tall angry-looking man with a noisy cart, swiftly went by and almost knocked us off our feet.

"Hey you, that wasn't very gentlemen-like." I huffed and puffed under my breath. My eyebrows turned down and I could feel hot air coming out of my ears.

"We'll see you later Hon. We'll come over soon," Nathan whispered. Before I knew it, Nathan and Chase disappeared to the fruit aisle, (no pun intended).

The man with the speedy cart went around to the next aisle. The aisles were crowded, and there were some roadblocks down each aisle. I turned my cart around and tried to chase him down.

"I'm going to give him a piece of my mind," dashing down the next aisle as quickly as possible.

He quickly turned down the next aisle after I entered it. This went on for two more aisles. Finally, I got smart! I skipped an aisle and waited about thirty seconds. We both went crashing down the same aisle where all the mushroom soup cans were stacked to the ceiling, (well, it looked high to me). The man with the quick cart and I crashed at the soup display at the end of the aisle. Mushroom soup cans went flying everywhere, literally. They were in both our carts, on the floor, even one in my purse!

"What in hell's name do you think you are doing flying up and down every aisle at eighty miles an hour?" I could feel the heat in my face starting to make me turn red.

When he turned around to answer me, I realized whom it was. He was the dad from the soccer game that showed up at my front door. Now what do I say or do? My face turned a bright red now, and I felt like I was having a hot flash, even though I haven't had any of those yet. Placing my hands on my hips, then waist and back again was all I could do, seeing the embarrassment in both of us. We looked away, hoping the other one would just disappear. I waited a few seconds. *Damn.* He didn't disappear. Neither did I.

"I am so sorry for yelling like that just now. I also want to apologize for the other day, you know what I'm talking about. Don't make me say it." Joe just stood there with one eye squinting and one side of his lip higher than the other, as if he was having a stroke or something, (we can only hope).

I didn't want to look at him straight in the eyes, so I started stacking all the mushroom soup cans from the floor and put them all in my cart. He stacked the soup cans in *my* cart as well. Once we made eye contact while we were stacking, I realized he was a good looking older man. He isn't George Clooney, but then there is only one George Clooney, sigh.

"I understand. You had every right to be suspicious of me. I shouldn't have walked up to your house, especially after dark, ring the doorbell, and tell you that I had watched you walk home." He laughed a little under his breath looking down. "You must have thought I was a stalker. I hope I didn't scare you, *much*," (The *much* part was under his breath).

"Of course you didn't scare me, *much*, (under my breath). A woman must take care of herself you know. I did what any other woman would do … (freak out and) call the police," my hands were flipping around like I was drowning in two inches of water.

"By the way, why did you come to my house? Oh, forgive me, but we were never properly introduced." I stuck out my hand and said, "I'm Amy Kayden."

"I'm Joe Elliot," as he cautiously reached out to shake the hand of the person responsible for placing him behind bars even if it was only for a couple of hours. "I wanted to give back your tissue, handkerchief, whatever you call it, that you dropped. I don't have it on me right now, but I could drop it off another time, when you aren't home or when it is light out?" he smirked waiting for me to be embarrassed and humiliated, which I was and just didn't want to look it or admit it either.

"Funny guy, huh." I half smiled with detest in my eyes.

"Oh, of course. I knew it fell out while we were 'walking' and I completely forgot all about it," I was lying through my teeth but didn't want to be caught. "You can drop it off anytime you want or would you rather me pick it up sometime?"

"I'll drop it in the mail, if you don't mind. I know where you live now," he stated curtly.

"That'll be fine, since you know my address. Thanks so much, bye-bye now," Quickly I turned, with a dozen or so cans of mushroom soup in my cart. You never know when you will have a fetish for mushroom soup. I really love the stuff. Really.

Now, I need to do some grocery shopping. One of the clerks was picking up all the rest of the mushroom soup cans that were everywhere, and was placing them back on the display.

I bent down, handing the clerk several cans of soup, "I am so sorry that awful man knocked over all these soup cans. He must really hate mushroom soup." I sprinted down the next aisle as if nothing had happened at all.

∾

I ran into a few other people I knew from the old days. The old days meaning when the kids didn't have their driving licenses, and were busy with school sports. It seems that you only see people, other adults, when your kids are playing the same sport. Now that the kids are all adults (age-wise only that is), those days are gone and so are the friendships we once had. Time to move on, again.

I must have spent at least two hours in the store and filled up the cart until "my cup overfloweth." It actually over flowed. I think mostly with mushroom soup. Wow, I haven't had a cart full of food since, well, since last Christmas.

I made it through the check out line without any hitches, interruptions, embarrassments, or accidents. I loaded the car and headed for home. What a morning. Life can be so embarrassing for people at times. Sometimes, I feel sorry for them.

∾

As I was driving home, I turned the radio on and heard one of John Fogerty's songs, remembering how much Cameron loved his music. I started to sing along and then remembered 'the box' again.

My mind started thinking, *(yes I do that sometimes)*, about the tickets so I put the 'metal to the petal' or is it the 'petal to the metal?' and raced home. Racing for me is going five miles over the speed limit. When I finally reached the house, I closed the garage door and quickly threw all the grocery bags on the kitchen counter. It was a bit noisy with all those soup cans crashing down on the countertop. I ran into my bedroom, Tom and Jerry in tow, and took 'the box' out from under the bed. I placed it on the bed and just stared. Tom and Jerry jumped on the bed, and sniffed the box and started to moan and wonder what I was going to do next. They sniffed the chocolates. They continued to moan knowing there was something edible in there and it wasn't doing them any good in the box.

"C'mon boys. Let's go back into the kitchen to put the groceries away. Then I promise to give you something yummy."

They were excited about all the bags in the kitchen too. They were excited about anything that had food in it. I reached into one of the bags and took out a rawhide bone for each of them. They seem to bury, rather hide, them all over the yard and under the girls' beds. I just don't understand why they don't eat them. They know I didn't make them.

Why are they saving them? A rainy day? Hell to freeze over? What? I just don't get it.

They both wagged their tails, like windshield wipers on a rainy day, and sprinted off in opposite directions of the house for a new secret hiding place. They both seem to think they have the perfect place every time. Whatever.

Everything is put away, the bags are gone and now what? Oh yeah, 'the box.' I ran all the way to my room, without tripping. I sat on the bed. This time I was alone. It was cold and quiet in the house. It was kind of an eerie feeling. No, it is an eerie feeling without the scary music. I could even hear the grandfather clock all the way from the living room ticking away. I opened the box and read the note again. I have no idea who "*The Big Mac Corporation*" is or are. How do I find out? I am not sure what to say or to whom. I took out the candles and smelled them. They are my favorites for this time of year, cinnamon. I placed one of the candles on my nightstand, and the other in the bathroom and lit them both. I just love to take a bath with scent of candles. I feel as if I am at a Spa or a fancy Resort far, far away from everything and everybody. Remember those Calgon commercials … "Calgon, take me away." Only this is much better than Calgon, which was probably just flaky detergent of some sort that would make me scratch and itch after the bath.

I took the chocolates out and opened the box. They are Godiva chocolates, another favorite of mine. How did they know? Who told them? I smelled them, and sighed. Eating one, I danced around the room as if I were in seventh heaven. I closed the box of chocolates and placed them on my nightstand, for later. Oh what the heck, one more won't kill me. Another sacred dance for the chocolate queen, me!

The envelope, with the tickets, was staring at me. I opened it up, took them out, and looked at them. They are for next weekend. There are two tickets, one was for Cameron and the other for me, I assumed, I am hoping that is what they thought. Whom am I going to go with? I won't go. Then the 'Big Mac Corporation' would be upset and find out, maybe. Once again, **who are these people**?

I grabbed the phone. Dialed. Waited two rings.

"Larry, it's Amy. I need to ask you a question. Who is the 'Big Mac Corporation'?" There was silence at the other end. I waited patiently, okay not so patiently. "Larry, are you there or what?"

"Amy, I don't really know. Why?"

"Because I received two packages from them the last couple of days. One was a huge basket the day before Thanksgiving with all sorts of goodies in it, and the other package was a box with chocolates, candles, and concert tickets. I need to know who sent them. "Got any ideas, Lar? The return address is from your building. Now do you know, Larry? Hello, anyone home McFly?"

"Sorry Amy, I can't help you. Enjoy the goodies and concert. Have to run. Call Carol if you are lonely. Bye." Larry was quick to get off the phone for some reason or another. I think it was another.

He sounded like he knew something. I guess I could go down to the office building and check the tenants myself.

I hung up the phone and sat down on the side of my bed where the Godiva Chocolates were whispering to me on the nightstand. Of course, I had to have one more. I turned around. Tom and Jerry are staring at me with those sad eyes, and drooling all over the bed. I shooed them off the bed. Of course, I gave them each a piece of chocolate, dark chocolate. The vet says that any kind of chocolate is bad for dogs, but Tom and Jerry love it as much as I do. What the hell!

I started to think of what I need to do to find out about this "Big Mac" group, and what they know about Cameron and me.

"Let's go boys. We need to go think." We all marched outside, into the beautiful afternoon sun, sat in my rocking chair, and we all started to think. At least that is what I was doing.

"How can I go down to Cameron's office building and just snoop around on each floor? Boys, are you with me here?" They just looked up and turned their heads to the right.

"Okay then, I guess I am on my own for this one boys. I will look in the directory on the main floor and see what I can find. It sounds simple to me so far, right boys?" They just sat there with their tongues hanging out as if they were smiling. "When I find it, what do I do when I get there? Maybe Carol can come up with something. Good thinking boys."

I dialed Carol's phone number. It rang twice before Carol picked up.

"Carol, I'm sitting in the backyard thinking, and I decided that I need you," I said in a demanding way. I waited for a response at the other end of the line. I didn't hear one. I waited a little longer. Finally, I yelled, "Carol!"

Thirty seconds later, Carol came franticly running into the backyard, "You rang my dear," huffing and puffing, with her phone in her hand. "You never know when your phone is going to ring," as she hung it up and placed it in her apron pocket.

"Have a seat. We need to plot," I whispered. I told Carol about the two boxes we received lately and the group that sent them. I also mentioned that Larry might know something too. She lifted one eyebrow and tilted her head. She thought we needed to figure this out as well, and the sooner the better. We sat there for the better part of an hour throwing crazy ideas out. Every time we thought of an idea, Tom and Jerry sat up and their ears perked up too. Then neither Carol nor I decided that it was a great idea, and Tom and Jerry moaned and lay back down again.

"Tis the season to be jolly, don't you think Carol?" I queried. "Maybe we should be little elves and deliver some good cheer." There was a small pause and a puzzling look on Carol's face.

"Maybe one of us could be an elf, and the other could just be jolly." Carol's face didn't look so elf-like right now, or ever for that matter. Remember that Carol is six feet tall.

"Oh yeah," I laughed, hiding behind my coffee mug. "Maybe we should deliver some cookies, but I won't bake them."

Carol tilted her head to the right side now, just like Tom and Jerry. "Okay, then what?"

"We could give them out at the reception desk on their floor, and just make some chitchat. While you're chitchatting, I can look around. What do you think?"

"Sounds interesting," Carol thought out loud. "Go on."

"I will be the snooper," I said. "I am the logical choice of course." Carol frowned as her eyebrows tilted upward.

"OK, then. When do we do this?"

"Let me think. We need to go soon. I have tickets for a concert next weekend that this 'Corporation' sent me. I want to find out about them before the concert. Don't you think I should find out?" Carol shook her head in agreement. "Let's plan on Monday morning?"

"Sounds goods. I suppose I need to be cheery. That will be a tough one on a Monday morning; you know what I'm saying." Carol's eyes were wide as a margarita glass. Okay, make it two glasses.

"I will make some coffee, and we can add whatever you like. But all I have is peppermint schnapps."

"That sounds good. At least I will have fresh breath," Carol smiled with those pearly whites.

"I'll be doing the driving, since I don't usually drink. Be here after you drop the kids off at school." I said with my mind wandering in a million directions thinking, just thinking, and a few evil sounding giggles.

൴

After Carol left, I went into the kitchen to pour myself another cup of coffee.

Still thinking aloud to my boys, "I need to buy some cookies, loads of cookies. What else?"

൴

The days flew by. I spoke to all my children on Sunday afternoon. All the girls are doing well in school, at least that is what they tell me, and Michael is working at a job he will learn to love so he can move up the ladder of success.

൴

Monday morning snuck up on me. The coffee is perking, as I promised Carol, with some peppermint schnapps waiting on the side.

I bought cookies, placed them on decorative plates, and wrapped them up for our little holiday outing today. Carol bounced in the kitchen door.

"Ready or not, tis the season!" Carol danced her way to meet Mr. Coffee. She grabbed a cup and put some Schnapps flavoring in it. "Everyone needs a cup of this on a Monday morning. Oh, what the hell, every morning for that matter."

Off and running we went.

I parked the car in the underground parking, in case we needed to make a quick escape. We went in and looked at the directory. I had been here a thousand, okay only a few times, and I don't think I ever stopped to look at the directory just to see who else is 'wasting' space here. Carol and I looked intently and both saw it! Big Mac Corporation, Third Floor. Thank goodness it isn't too far up, incase we have to head for the stairs for our quick get-away, (plus I am afraid of heights and am a little claustrophobic in elevators).

We cheerfully went into the elevator with a few other people. We smiled and wished everyone happy holidays and good cheer. They rather responded back by mumbling "same to you."

We made our stop and got off on the third floor. My face was already hurting me from smiling too much on the elevator. We went towards the front desk where the receptionist was sitting, looking busy. I didn't say she was busy, just looking. She looked familiar to me, but I couldn't place her.

"Good cheery morning. And how are we this fine holiday morning?" My smile was so big you could slide a pumpkin pie, make that a chocolate cheesecake, in there including the tin.

"Just fine thank you. Can I help you with something?" the young receptionist asked.

"Why yes, of course you can," as I looked next to me, Carol was humming a holiday tune. "I am looking for the president of your corporation please." Looking at her desk and I could see her name was on a block written in script, *JEANINE*. No last name, just Jeanine. Maybe she doesn't have one. Hmm.

"Do you have an appointment?"

"Uh, no. I didn't think I needed one." My eyebrows raised as I tilted my head to one side.

"Well, I am afraid you do. Would you like to make one?"

"No, thank you. All we want to do is spread some holiday cheer and give you some cookies that I made." Carol and I smiled.

"How thoughtful of you ladies. They look so good. We should all have your kind of spirit this time of year. Just a sec. I will get Betsey, uh Elizabeth," as she waddled away.

I started looking around the office and wandered a bit while Carol was on guard at the desk. Carol is going to whistle when they come back. I was trying to find anything with names or pictures to give me a clue as to whom and what they were. I wandered down a little hallway and saw a couple of closed doors. I looked around to see if anyone was watching me. I carefully opened one of the doors and went inside. I closed the door and turned on the light. It was the coffee room with a copy machine and magazines all over a humongous wood block table. I looked at the magazines to look for a name on the address label. It said "Big Mac Corp" only, and the address. Hmm. "That doesn't help me any," I whispered to myself. I snooped around the cabinets. As I opened one of them, a ton of magazines fell out and landed all over the place. *What a mess.* I could hear Carol chitchatting. I heard footsteps coming in my direction. I tried to pick up as many of the magazines as possible before the door opened. It was only Carol. *Whew!*

"What are you doing in here?" she whispered. "I already whistled." She looked at the room, "What the hell happened in here? Oh, my, god." We scrambled to pick up the magazines and shove them back in the cabinet. She raced back out to the front where Jeanine and now Elizabeth were waiting.

"Oh, I was trying to find the ladies room." Carol was quick.

I came running down the hallway and yelled, "Happy Holidays everyone! Let's have some cookies, shall we?" I added, as I raised my hands in the air for joy.

"This is so nice of you ladies. Would you like some coffee?" Elizabeth offered.

"Sounds good to me," Carol's eyes lit up. "Do you have any kind of schnapps to go with that?"

Elizabeth just looked at her with a surprising look on her face.

"Oh, I'm just kidding, it's much too early in the morning for that, right?" Carol gave out a big laugh. Jeanine and Elizabeth led us back to the room we were just in with the copy machine, coffee maker, and all the magazines all over the table.

"Why don't you ladies have a seat and we'll get to know each other a bit over some coffee and those cookies," Elizabeth stated suspiciously. "Come, have a seat. I'll get you a cup of coffee." We all sat at the table. There were a zillion magazines all over the place. Jeanine straightened some of them up by putting them in piles and pushed them to one side of the table.

After we sat down, it became very quiet. We stared at one another, waiting for someone to start a conversation. I just wanted to know who these women were. What kind of business they are running here? How they were associated with my husband. I started to tap my fingers on the table and smiled, becoming very nervous about this situation. I couldn't stand it any longer.

"So ladies, what kind of business do you run here, if I may ask?"

"We, Jeanine, Lynette and I, run a very small business here. We've only been here for nine months or so. We don't know many people," Elizabeth said without divulging too much information.

"What floor do you work on Amy?" Jeanine asked politely.

"Oh, me. Umm, I don't work per se. My husband works on the fifth floor."

"And what does he do?" Jeanine asked.

"My husband is a lawyer on the fifth floor," Carol added quickly to help me. "His name is Larry and he has been with the firm for, who knows how many, years," as she waved her hands in the air. "We just thought we would spread some holiday cheer early. So, happy holidays!"

Carol lifted her cup of coffee and tried to take a bite of it and then tried to sip her cookie. I think I did the same. The other two women just stared at us in utter surprise.

"So, what kind of business is this anyway? It looks like an interesting place to work. I see you have heaps of magazines on the table. Do you run a magazine shop?" I asked chidingly with a big smile.

Jeanine and Elizabeth looked at each other. Elizabeth turned to us, "We run a number of small businesses out of this office. It isn't just one type of business. For instance, Lynette, is out shopping with a client. She takes them to various high-class shops, in and out of town, to help them with their wardrobe and accessories and such. We also offer private classes in etiquette and dating tips," Elizabeth continued. "It has been pretty rewarding for our clients."

"Oh, how nice for them … and for you of course," I turned to look at Carol about what to do next. Carol just raised her eyebrows and smiled. "How did you decide to rent office space here? Do you know someone?" I questioned.

"Actually, there was an attorney who helped us out," Jeanine gladly said. "He was doing us a favor and helped with the lease. We didn't know where else to go for space, and we really couldn't afford it, but he made us a deal we couldn't refuse," she added with a few giggles.

What kind of deal. Why couldn't they refuse? What was in it for them, and what was in it for Cam? How much longer can I hold back my anger, or whatever it is I have building up inside of me.

"Who is this man in shining armor, if I may ask?" I questioned while biting my tongue.

"He passed away a few months ago." Jeanine sadly said. "But he gave us the start that nobody else would give us."

Elizabeth interrupted, "He made us an offer to lease this floor for six months free and build up our business. If we weren't able to start making a profit in six months, we would owe nothing. If we were, which we have, we would owe rent for the next six months.

"Wow that sounds so encouraging. How could he make a deal like that?" Carol asked sincerely.

"It's a really long story, but we met outside this building. I actually bumped into him, literally. We began talking and told each other where we grew up. Both of us grew up in foster homes in the same town. He knew what it was like to be alone, struggle through childhood and teen years," Elizabeth explained clearly.

It was then that I understood it all. Cameron was helping those he could. No one helped him, and maybe he wished someone would have. It all makes sense now. I don't know what I was thinking, rather I do, and yes, I will admit it, I WAS WRONG. That only happens once in a lifetime.

Carol and I wished them well in their endeavors, explaining that we needed to visit the other floors, and left quietly. Tis the season to share joy and be thankful for what you have.

She knew my name was Amy!

Chapter 6

Dog day Afternoon

Carol and I sat motionless in the car, all the way home. If someone placed a nail in one of my tires right now, I would be able to hear the air sizzling out.

"Carol, I don't know what to say."

"You don't have to say a thing. That's what friends are for honey." She patted my shoulder gently. We smiled and had some more coffee back in my kitchen, with a little additive, which I really needed right now, and mostly wanted to drown in it.

∾

That evening, while lying in bed with my boys, watching reruns of Seinfeld, it hit me. I figured it out! I remember seeing these women before. Elizabeth and Jeanine were the 'ladies in red'. They came to my home after the funeral. They were the ones that made the ruckus while snooping around, my humble home. It all makes sense now, sort of. They were thanking Cam by sending the holiday basket and box of gifts to me and my family, (I think it was a thank you for the mess as well. One can only hope that is what they were thinking as well). I can appreciate it now without any odd feelings involved. What do I do now? I have a concert to attend next weekend. I haven't been out with anyone in years, literally. Cam didn't like to go out much, or maybe he didn't want to go out with me. I think I will settle for the first part of the last sentence. He kept to himself, a homebody of sorts.

I don't know where to start looking for a date. A date! What is a date? Sounds like a four letter word to me. I don't want to look for a date. Nathan and Chase are neighbors and friends. I couldn't ask one of them. That wouldn't be right. Hmmm. The decision is clear. I will give Nathan and Chase the tickets. At least a couple would be out on a date (there's that four letter word), and having a good time!

Now I can enjoy the rest of the Godiva chocolates without feeling guilty. So can Tom and Jerry, even though they don't know what guilt is, (But a Jewish mother knows. Oy, veh, does she know). The box was lip-smacking to the very last chocolate. I think the three of us ate the whole box in record time!

Bringing out the lights and decorations for the holiday season is exciting. At least it is exciting for me. It was time to get started with the *hoopla*. I always put the outside lights up first. It takes me several hours to unravel and figure out which bulbs work and which ones need replacements, and then there is the correct strand order of course. You know, the tail bone is connected to the … whatever bone, and so on. What a process it is. Every year I vow that I will remember which end is up. It always turns out that I pick up the wrong end, (No wonder I have to dye my hair the following day to get rid of those new gray hairs). Tom and Jerry enjoy watching me do this timeless chore every year. They stroll outside and find the perfect place to lie in the sun. They watch their mom make a fool of herself, by yelling, tangling up the strands of lights, stepping on some rawhide bones that were cleverly place by you-know-who, shouting out obscenities, and finally coming out with the end result of a perfectly lit house for the season. Well, this year wasn't going to be any different, except that I hope there aren't any hidden rawhide bones waiting for me to step on.

"Come on boys. Let's go outside and get started. It was only one o'clock. We have the whole afternoon to get some lights up."

Once again, I forgot which end of which strand the lights should begin. The strands were tangled. I sat, stood, and held up a tree while trying to untangle them. Then I tried each strand in the plug. Nothing was working and I was starting to sweat. It was hot out there. Either it was really a warm day or those hot flashes are following me around, again. In either instance, the damn lights aren't working. Some of them were flashing and some never lit up at all. I practically tore the skin off my fingers while trying to replace the bulbs. I tried plugging in some of the strands again, but to no avail. I screamed on the top of my lungs. The boys just casually looked up from their afternoon nap, saw that I was okay by ***their*** standards, and quietly laid back down. It was late, according to my clock and the sun is just beginning to set. You know what that means. It's time to go in and lock up the house. At least the boys had a nice, lazy afternoon in the warm sunshine.

"Tomorrow is another day," I declared as we walked on in the front door. I was trying to look like Scarlet O'Hara in "Gone with the Wind." Well, at least sound like her with a southern accent. I know I will never have an 18" waist, and somehow I don't think Vivian Leigh ever did either!

I left the damn lights all over the front yard. I will deal with them later, much later, probably just till tomorrow morning. The three of us marched inside, rather I marched and they 'pranced' into the house, turned on the outside lights, you know the ones that came with the house, and then locked the door and turned on the alarm. "Now we are good for the night boys," I stated confidently and continued to march into the kitchen to make dinner for the three of us. Tom and Jerry will eat whatever I am capable of cooking. They never complain about my cooking, so it can't be that bad, and they are still alive and well, for the time being.

I was actually hungry tonight. I worked in the front yard for hours on end trying to figure out the status of our lighting fixtures for the upcoming holiday season. I may not have gotten very far, but it sure worked up a small appetite.

"Pot pies sound good to me boys. What do you think?" I asked, expecting an answer. They just stared at me. I walked over to the freezer; where I stock a few items, mainly pot pies, lean pockets, and homemade matzo ball soup. Yes, matzo ball soup. I can cook something edible. I pulled out two potpies, one turkey and one chicken. The boys were eyeballing the pot pies.

"Which one do you want, the chicken or turkey?" Tom and Jerry didn't have a preference. I could tell by the looks in their eyes. They actually would prefer both.

"You guys can't seem to decide so I will have to decide for you. Eenie, meany, miney mo. You will have the chicken potpie."

They wagged their tails in delight. Their tongues were hanging out the side of their mouths as if they were smiling back.

I decided to cook in the real oven tonight. The oven is that box right under the stove (the appliance with the four round things on top), with all the clean knobs. I know it will take awhile to cook them both, but we can wait.

We can keep busy while we are waiting. I turned the oven on, waited a few minutes for the preheating to be done, placed the potpies on a shiny cookie tray, which is obviously hardly ever used, and placed the pies in the oven with the timer set.

"I've got a great idea! Why don't we, meaning me, take a nice long bubble bath while we are waiting?" Why am I talking to the dogs? There isn't anyone else to talk to in the house and the dogs don't answer me back. "Let's go guys," as we leisurely walked back to my bedroom and into the master bath.

I turned on the hot water and sprinkled lavender scented bubble bath. Lavender is supposed to be a soothing scent and help people relax. I threw my clothes in the hamper, which is located in the corner of the closet, a place where Cam could never find, even if there was a neon light above it flashing every three seconds, **2 POINTS!** His idea of the hamper was anywhere on the floor making a trail from the bedroom to the bathroom. I guess that way he will always find his way to either place.

The tub filled up quickly with tons of bubbles, which I love. I turned on the cd player, and lit some candles. I ran back to the kitchen to get a glass of red wine, because red wine is good for the heart. Now I am ready for my evening with the "stars" (bubbles). I sat in the tub and stared at the bubbles. They look like millions of night-lights twinkling in the sky, don't you agree? I sat back, took a sip of wine, and just sighed while listening to the '*music of the night*.' The boys were right there with me. The music was soft and soothing, the bubbles were mesmerizing, the wine is relaxing. I must be dreaming because I hear sirens, fire trucks, and the sounds are getting louder and louder. I dozed off in the tub with the wine glass still in my hand.

The boys were going stir crazy. They were jumping around the bathroom and howling. The sirens sounded as if they were out my front door.

"OH MY GOD." I jumped out of the tub and ran through the hallway into the smoke-filled kitchen. Sure enough, the smoke was coming out of the oven and throughout the kitchen, dining room, living room and chimney, so far. There was a bang on the door and the dogs were still running amuck. I ran to the front door and opened it. Then the house alarm sounded off. The sirens and the alarm were all so loud that I could barely make out what the fireman is saying.

"Good evening Mrs. Kayden. We got another phone call from one of your closest neighbors. I see, (laughing under his breath) you and the dogs are okay," the young, perfectly shaped, handsome, fireman said. "May I come in and put out your fire?" He was staring at my body.

I was standing in the doorway stark naked. I forgot about the potpies in the oven. I jumped up and forgot about a towel or bathrobe when the commotion started, yet still holding my wine glass. I couldn't tell you if there was anything in it or not.

Embarrassed at my situation, I quickly covered the important body parts. How humiliating to be totally exposed to the world, at least the world of our local firefighters. I ran to my room either to get a robe, or out of mortification. By the time I came back out, dressed appropriately (covered up to my neck), there were several firefighters all over the house, opening the windows and doors. One of them turned off the oven and then opened it to a flame shooting out. He put it out quickly. The phone rang and it was the alarm company asking me if everything was fine.

"Sure it is. Thank you," I quickly hung up.

Two minutes later two security cars rushed over and literally parked on the grass, where all my holiday lights ***are***, and I am emphasizing ***are.*** The two security men ran inside with their hands on their holsters, and found the firefighters.

One of them looked puzzled, "What is going on in here?" as he stood up straight and put his hand down, along side of his gun.

Then I met the other security man by the front door, "Mrs. Kayden, you didn't give the proper 'code' on the phone."

Here's another embarrassing situation. Cam would be too humiliated to admit that he was married to me if he was still around, but then none of this would have happened if he were around, most likely, because he doesn't like pot pies.

The fire chief slowly walked over to me, with a huge smile, "Mrs. Kayden the potpies won't give you any more trouble."

Of course, he was laughing under his breath, like the rest of his troop. Apparently I put the oven on at 550 instead of 350 (where are those reading glasses when you really need them), forgot about the timer, which was dinging, and to top it all off, I dozed off in the tub for who knows how long.

"Just trying to keep you boys in business," I said without tarnishing my reputation even more.

I then spoke to the security man, and whispered the 'code' in his ear. He shook his head and he and his comrade said good night. They never apologized for parking on my lawn and ruining my holiday lights. They just got into their security cars and popped some more lights on their way out backing away, off the front lawn. The firefighters slowly disappeared as well. Two of them stayed behind and made sure all the smoke was out of the house, and closed all the doors and windows once again. Of course, they told me to be more careful, as usual. I just smiled and shook my head, "as usual," twice.

All the neighbors were out in the street staring. Carol and Larry came into the house, after everyone had left. Carol was in hysterics and practically crying, while Larry was calm as a cucumber.

"Is everything okay Amy, dear? Is anything burnt or broken?"

"Just my pride, (burnt and broken)."

I told Carol and Larry the whole story of what I thought happened. Carol was deeply concerned, while Larry just expected this to happen, as if it was an everyday event in the life of Amy. He even had a bag of pretzels he was eating when he came over, and continued to eat them throughout his visit. He did ask me one question though.

"Got any beer?"

Another day, well done!

Chapter 7

A New Day, a New Season

The next morning, after the 'hot' event last night, I went out into the front yard to see the remains of my holiday lights. What a mess! There were busted Christmas lights all over the yard. I called the yard service that we occasionally used, once in a blue moon. They agreed to help me out for a small fortune (wishing it were in pesos, but with today's economy who knows what is worth more). I was glad to pay it. Jose and his gang did a great job on the clean up.

Jose, probably the only gardener in Southern California, who speaks English said, "We put lights up for people like you, Ms. K."

"What do you mean, people like me?" as I crossed my arms, placing them on my chest, and waited for an explanation. I thought he was going to say 'people who are electrically challenged.'

"Widow People, Ms. K. We put lights up all the time for many. You let me know, Okay?"

I uncrossed my arms. I turned around, looked towards the sky with my hands reaching in the air, and silently blamed it on Cameron. I slowly took a deep breath, and turned back around.

"Well, let me think about that Jose, and I'll let you know."

"Okay, Ms. K. We can put them up for you, for a fee of course," he added, with a smile.

"Of course! I assume it is by the hour. I will call if I need you. Thanks for cleaning up today," as I handed him cash. God forbid people use checks anymore. I turned my head towards the sky one more time and sighed.

ᘓᘐ

Sitting out back, in my safe zone, I can enjoy the peace and quiet, quite different from last night's scene. I was thinking about Christmas this year and how I want this Christmas to be like all the rest, but I know it won't ever be the same.

"I promise I will do my best to make it a memorable Christmas for everyone, whether they like it or not. Sigh."

"I'm going to put the new lights up by myself, just like every year. Don't change what isn't broken, I always say." (That wasn't meant to be a pun in anyway). Well, you know what I mean.

Talking to the only ones who can hear me now, Tom and Jerry, "I will buy all white lights from now on. That way they will be easy to replace, and they won't need to be in a certain order for each strand. Cam was always so strict about the 'color' order on the strands. I can connect any of the strands together and not worry about which one connects to which and such. This will be so easy, I hope."

Later that morning I went shopping for white lights. Shopping this time of year can be exasperating. Everyone is buying lights, gifts, decorations, and partridges for their pear tree, (Have you ever seen a partridge in a pear tree? Honestly). Trying to go down the Christmas section is like being stuck in a traffic jam. No one is moving one way or the other. Maybe their lights aren't working, or maybe someone ran over their lights in the middle of the night. I grabbed what I could of the white twinkling light sets, and made it past the next intersection. I just love 'twinkling' lights.

Candles were next on my agenda. You can't ever have enough candles, you know. I quickly pushed my cart over to the other side of the store to buy scented candles. Of course, now that everyone else grabbed their lights they followed me over to the candle section. Once again, I grabbed what I could. Nathan and Chase were in the candle section as well. They saw me in the crowd.

"Amy, do you need some candles?" Nathan whispered pointing at the cinnamon and spice scented ones. I shook my head yes, and he snatched a few for me and placed them ever so carefully in his cart. Chase was guarding the cart with his life. Everyone wanted the scents of the season. People were grabbing the cinnamon, vanilla, pumpkin, fir tree, and something-berry scented candles. Cam always hated the fruity scented candles, saying they smelled like a restaurant bathroom.

"I will bring them over later," Nathan silently mouthed over the crowd. I shook my head in agreement, smiled at both of the men, and then waved good-bye for now.

Getting through the checkout line was even worse than a traffic jam in rush hour, (not that I know that for a fact, but by seeing it on the news). It was more like a pileup on the freeway. One would think they could possibly open more lanes, instead of having them blocked off… just like a freeway. They kept calling for more checkers, but no one showed up.

"Just let me get out of here in one piece," I whispered under my breath. At least I thought I was whispering until the lady behind me laughed out loud, and shook her head in agreement.

Next on the list is grocery shopping, again. It seems like I am always there and I don't know why. I guess food shopping is always on a weekly schedule. I planned to make several pies for Christmas, (hoping one of them will turn out decent and edible). Every year I try to make pumpkin and apple pies. I don't think ANYONE appreciates my pies.

∞

Home at last. Tommy boy and Jerry greeted me at the garage door, probably wondering what I brought them this time.

"Sorry boys. I didn't bring you goodies, how about some hugs and kisses?" I bent down and greeted my boys. They wagged their tails in delight. They never complain.

Where do I begin? First, I need to put away the groceries. Second, take the light sets outside. Third, I need to get my messages off the phone. The light is blinking like crazy. It's that time of year, when people are inviting everyone to parties and such. I just love parties!

The first message is from Jose, wanting to know what day to come over to put up my lights. He is assuming too much. You know what happens when you assume? I will let you figure it out.

"I'll put up my own lights buddy, muchas gracias," talking to the message machine as if they could hear me on the other end.

Second message is from Carol just saying "hey."

Third message is from my brother, Rich, but I can't understand anything he was saying because his wife, Sara, was yelling at him in the background.

"I will call him back when I feel like it, the bastard. Thanks for checking on me once in awhile big bro." I guess I am a little more than irritated with him. He usually only calls when something is up with Mom and Dad. He could at least ask how I am doing. That damn wife of his, ugh. Don't get me started on her, that wench.

Mom left the next message. "Sweetheart, your father and I would love for you and the family to come here for the holidays."

Whom are they kidding? It is freezing cold in New York around Christmas time, plus the kids have things to do, people to see, places to go, and as for me, well, me too, I hope! I know they are thinking of me, and what they think is best. I have been out west most of my life now. I left freezing cold New York to go to warm, sunny bright California to attend college and never looked back. Cameron and I met in college. We were college 'sweethearts'. At least that is what I thought.

My last, message was from a long lost friend of mine from New York, Joel Fox. We went to elementary school together and lived across the street from one another, and yes, he is of the male gender. How did he get my number? He left his number on my message phone, and said I should call him when I am ready.

"What the hell does that mean? Ready for what?" I figured Mom was up to something, like being a 'Yente' perhaps.

"OH NO, I am not ready for that yet or maybe ever. I will be considerate enough and call him back. That will be as far as it goes. I am sure it is nothing. Who knows what he wants. Maybe he just wants to say Hello. Maybe he and his family are visiting. Maybe my Mom has a bigger mouth than I thought," speaking to the dogs.

While putting the groceries away and talking to Tom and Jerry, the doorbell rang. The boys barked, howled, and trampled over each other on their way to the front door, as usual.

"Who Is It?"

"Tis I, your friendly, good-looking, neighborhood, candle salesman, Chase." I laughed as I opened the front door to a smiling jolly middle-aged man and a bag full of heavenly scented candles that I had ordered straight from Target.

"Come on in Chase." He followed me into the kitchen and placed the bag on the kitchen table.

"Would you like a cup of coffee, with a little schnapps?"

"Don't mind if I do," Chase's eyes lit up said with a huge smile on his face. I gave him a mug and he helped himself to both the coffee and some schnapps.

"Nathan wanted me out of the house so I wouldn't gobble up all the cookies he is baking."

"Oh, you know Nathan loves you and doesn't want you to get any bigger," patting him on the belly. "Besides if you eat them all now you won't be able to fit in your Santa suit for Christmas Eve this year. I know how much you love giving out the candy canes on our street." Chase did have a jolly look about him, especially this time of year. It is both Nathan's and Chase's favorite time of year, not because it is Christmas, but because they met ten years ago during the holiday season. This year is special for them both.

"I didn't know how many candles you wanted, so I just loaded them up. Whatever you don't want, I can either keep or I will take back," Chase said seriously.

"Don't be silly. I want them all! You know I love the scents of the season," as I took a big whiff in the bag. "So, how much do I owe you?"

"Nothing. It's my gift to you, Amy." He put his hand on my hair and stroked it gently.

"Don't be ridiculous. I can't expect you to buy my candles for me," I said with a solemn look on my face. "I want to pay for them Chase. I can afford to pay for a few measly candles."

"Why can't you just accept this as a gift, from me and Nathan?" He just stood there in the kitchen staring at me with a heartbreaking look.

"How can I turn that punim down?" Honestly now, he is only trying to be a good friend and neighbor. "Okay, just this one time though," I whispered and then gave him the biggest hug I have given anyone in a long time.

Chapter 8

Let there be light

Bright, and early the next morning, the three desperados marched outside to the front yard. I brought all the new lights out with me and started setting up camp for the morning.

The lights took all morning to put together. I had the big ladder out and moved it little by little, went up and down the ladder all morning long. It really is a lot of work to put the perfect holiday lights on a house, especially since they have always been perfect every year. This year was no exception.

We, the boys and I, took a lunch break. I decided to make good on my phone messages and call everyone back. Carol first. We chitchatted about nothing in particular.

"Larry is going to put the lights up Saturday. If you want a good laugh, come out on the lawn and take a seat in the front row, along with the kids." Larry is a good lawyer, not any kind of electrician.

Big bro was next. I called his office instead of his home, in case Sara was there, and actually decided to answer the phone. Sara and I had nothing to say to one another. She never called or sent a card after Cameron was gone, and she didn't fly out for the funeral. Who needs a sister-in-law like that? His secretary answered and said he was out of the office for the rest of the day. I asked that she leave a message that his only sister, had returned his call from the previous day.

It was time to call Mom back. Before I start dialing, I need to put on a pot of coffee. Speaking, or rather listening to Mom always makes me thirsty. I feel like I am out in the desert crawling back to civilization. All set and ready to dial, with phone in one hand, coffee mug in the other. I sat outside in my safe zone.

"Mom, it's me." Pause.

"It's Amy. How many other daughters do you have?" looking up at the somber blue sky above, as if God was supposed to figure this one out for her.

"Hello dear. It's good to hear your voice. How are you doing?"

"We are all okay. I'm returning your call from yesterday."

"Did I call you? I don't think I did. Maybe your father did. I'll ask him, just a minute dear." Mom put the phone down and walked into the other room. I could hear her yelling at dad all the way in the other room.

"MOM, it doesn't matter," yelling into the phone. 'Oh my god,' I thought. She is going crazy and taking me along for the ride.

Mom eventually came back to the phone, "Dad said he didn't call you sweetheart, but if you want him to, he will."

"No, that's okay. I'm calling you now. You want to know if we would come and visit for the holidays, right?" taking a big gulp of my coffee, feeling sane for the moment.

"That would be wonderful dear. What a lovely surprise! When can we expect you and the babies?" She still called me her baby, and then my grown children are always going to be babies to her.

"Mom, we can't come. The kids are busy and already making plans and such. Michael is bringing home his girlfriend."

"Is she Jewish?"

"It doesn't matter to me Mom as long as he is happy. Don't you agree?" trying to get her to see that happiness is more important than someone's religious beliefs. My parents are old school and you know how that can be.

"Oh, I don't know. Your brother, well you know," she stopped for a minute. "We really don't know what Cam is, so I decided that he's Jewish. Sara, what a disappointment she is. Thank goodness they didn't have any children."

"Mother, that isn't nice, true, but not nice," giggling under my breath. "Let's just get back to your phone call yesterday. Mom, you and dad should come out here. You can even stay at our house, instead of a hotel. How would that be?"

"You know Cameron wouldn't like that dear. We couldn't impose on you and your family, you know. I don't want to cause any problems Amy dear."

"Mom, Cameron is gone, remember? You were here for the funeral in the beginning of the summer. You brought cheesecake, remember now?" My eyes rolled around. Sometimes getting old doesn't sound very appealing to me.

She paused for a moment. "Oh yes, I brought you cheesecake, I remember. Why did I bring you cheesecake dear? Were you sick?" She sounded worried now.

"No Mom, I wasn't sick. Cameron passed away last summer and you and Dad came out for the funeral," I tried to stay calm.

"So did you like the cheesecake? Do you want me to send you more? It is the best you know, New York Cheesecake." She already forgot about Cameron.

"No, thank you. I don't need any cheesecake. We have cheesecake stores here too. I just called to say hi to you and Dad," I finally stated to get out of the situation.

"I'll tell your father you called dear. Give the children a kiss from their Grandma. Tell them to write me soon," Mom added at the end. Mom doesn't realize that this is the twenty-first century and snail mail is long gone. They don't have a computer, they don't know how to use their cell phone, let alone retrieve messages off the answering machine. Technology, huh?

"Love you Mom. Dad too. Talk to you soon. Bye."

I just sat there, on my rocker, thinking about my parents. I understand they are getting older and they don't remember everything. I wish we lived closer so I could help them a little bit. I can't believe that someday I will be that old, if God lets me live that long, and if my kids don't drive me to suicide!

Now for the phone call of the day. I am not sure how to handle this one yet. My old pal, friend, sometimes enemy, and neighbor from way back called me unexpectedly. I haven't spoken to Joel in ages. We grew up together, learned to swim together, tried smoking together, and we even took his Dad's car when we were13 years old. We had crushes on each other, in high school, but not at the same time. That would have been too convenient for a relationship to occur, even though our parents would have loved a marriage between the families. Our parents talk every now and then, to keep up with each other and our families.

Here goes nothing, as I dialed his number. It rang several times before a message machine picked up. I forgot that there are three hours that separate the coasts, and he is probably at work, at least I hope he works. So I left a message, "I'm calling you back Joel. I guess we can play phone tag, and now you are it. I'm home for the rest of the day now. Call me when you are ready, Amy."

I hung up the phone thinking what a lame message. What was I thinking? It sounded so childish. He probably thinks I'm a nerd. Who knows? Oh my God, maybe I should call back and leave another message.

So I dialed again, let it ring several times, "Hey there, sorry about the last message. I was expecting you to pick up, but I see you still aren't home and I am leaving another lame message. Call me, bye."

I hung up. I forgot to say my name and it sounded so dumb. Let me try one more time.

Third time should be a charm, and hopefully the last time. "Hi again. Sorry about the other two messages. I didn't know what I was saying, or thinking for that matter. I know it sounded silly and I am not a silly person. Actually, right now I don't know what I am. So I will understand if you don't want to call me back because you probably think I'm a nutcase. If you do, I promise I won't act like an idiot and I'll pick up. Whatever you decide will be fine with me. I think I've done enough damage here and I hope you are getting a good laugh at my expense. Talk to you soon, maybe, Amy."

Well, how pathetic was that? I don't think I'll be hearing from Joel, EVER. I think three pitiable phone messages, from the same woman, are more then enough for any man to handle in one day. I paused for a moment after I hung up, took a deep breath, and decided to move on.

Tom, Jerry, and I had lunch outside on the patio. It was such a beautiful afternoon; we couldn't resist enjoying the fresh air and warm sunshine. I sat for a few moments after lunch and closed my eyes. I must have dozed off just for a minute or two.

I dreamt that Cameron was home, during the day, and helping with the decorations for the holidays. We had company over, lots of company, eating, what else, New York Cheesecake. It was a brief dream, and I know it had to be a dream because, first of all Cameron was there during the day, secondly, he was helping with the decorations, thirdly, we had people over, and finally most importantly, he was eating cheesecake, which I know he didn't like. Someday I hope to have a home filled with people enjoying each other's company and eating chocolate cheesecake. You can't blame a woman for dreaming now, can you? At least dreaming is something that no one can take away from a person.

"Let's go boys. We need to put up some more lights," taking in a deep breath. Putting the lights up by my lonesome is my thinking time. I can think about whatever I want and for however long I want, as long as I know what my hands are doing, then I can let my mind wander off.

While I was trying to focus on putting up the lights, the phone rang. It actually rang several times during the afternoon. I didn't bother to take the mobile phone out front with me. My kids get upset when they can't reach me, RIGHT NOW. Sometimes I have to put my foot, rather phone, down.

The afternoon went by swiftly. I put up the holiday lights in the front. I don't know if they will work just yet. I will leave the lighting ceremony for another adventure. It is getting dark now, so we all know what that means…time to go in.

Before retiring for the evening, I felt I just had to try the lights, for my peace of mind. I flipped the switch to the timer. Mission accomplished. I can breathe again. The lights work and it looks illuminating, if I must say so myself. I can't believe this will be the first Christmas without Cameron.

Back in the old fortress, we (Tom, Jerry, and I) locked the doors, and turned on the outside lights for the evening. I wanted to celebrate my 'good' electrical work and barbeque some steaks. Of course I didn't have any that were defrosted. I had to put the steaks in the sink under hot water. Sort of, what I had to do with the Thanksgiving turkey, but not to the extent of the bathtub. God knows I don't want to go through that again for a long time, or ever for that matter.

I felt safe in the backyard at night. The bells I placed on the gate ring when they are disturbed even a twitch, and the motion light detectors go on when there is movement of any kind. I also have Tom and Jerry here to save me, if ever that need should arise. Or should I say, I could save them, which is more likely the case.

I put the BBQ on high to try to let it heat up faster. I placed the two semi-defrosted steaks on the BBQ and closed the lid. I danced into the kitchen. I tried to decide what to eat with the steaks. Salad sounds good, or some green beans with salt and pepper, or both! I was gathering all the ingredients for the salad when I noticed the phone blinking like crazy. Everyone knows how Jewish Princesses love to talk on the phone. I pushed the button to listen to the messages. First, Michael called to yell at me for not answering the phone this afternoon. What a caring son. Second, Mel called to say "hey." Third, Joel called back. **Joel called back**. I played his message.

"Hello Amy. Hey, I know it has been such a long time since we talked. Your Mom gave me your phone number awhile ago. I thought you needed some space and now the time is right. You know, your Mom still thinks we are thirteen years old. She yelled at me for climbing your roof, with my brother, while you were eating dinner. What's that about? We did that over thirty years ago and now she is yelling at me for it. Anyhow, I just thought I would give you a call and let you know that I will be out to the coast next week. Let me know if you will be around. Tag, you're it. Joel." The phone clicked.

I stood there for a moment. I wasn't sure what I heard. I played the message back again. Hmm, what does this mean? Is he coming for business? Are his kids and wife coming too, what? The only way to get my answers is to call him back. I am dialing Joel's phone number back again, actually for the fourth time today.

I should have looked at the clock first. I forgot it's three hours ahead back east. I already dialed and the phone is already ringing. I couldn't stand still. I started my pacing around the kitchen island. I'm not sure what to say.

"Hello," Joel answered in a low quiet tone.

I paused for a moment. Then I thought he must have caller ID. Who doesn't nowadays? I had to answer.

"Hi there. It's me, Amy. I finally got you…on the phone that is," as I scratched my head and bit my lips. I could sense a grin at the other end. (Sometimes words just come out of my mouth and I am not sure how they got in there to begin with. Does that make any sense?)

"So you do, have me on the phone that is. It's good to hear your voice. You sound so much older than thirteen," He laughed, (because men don't giggle). "I hope you finally look older too. As I recall, you were a scrawny little thing."

"I am definitely not scrawny and haven't been for quite some time. You try popping out four children and still looking scrawny. Anyway, I hope I'm not calling too late. I forgot about the time difference. I just walked in the house. I was outside putting the holiday lights up and it was getting late, so I came in, the lights aren't quite finished, but it was getting dark, and the dogs are hungry and so am I. So I decided to start dinner and then realized that the phone messages weren't answered yet, and I am going on and on and you must think I'm a crazy woman or something."

"Just something."

"What?"

"That's okay. I wanted to know if you were going to be around next week. I'm coming out for business. I'm in the hotel business. I am usually out in LA a few times a year. Can we meet for dinner or something?"

"Something sounds good to me. Just kidding."

"You are quick Amy. You always were quick with the wit."

"Sure, dinner sounds great. Let me know your schedule, when you will have free time. Are you bringing your wife and children?"

"I'm not married, anymore. I've been divorced for five years now. And we didn't have any children, thank goodness. I think I was married to one though."

"Oh, I'm sorry. I didn't mean to be so nosy. I just wanted to know if I needed to make plans for you alone, or (I paused for a moment), you alone is good. Of course, we can get together and have dinner. You can call me when you know your schedule and I will make sure to put you on my calendar," I responded with a little too much glee in my voice, (What calendar do I have?)

We started chatting about the old days. I was walking around the house laughing while straightening the picture frames on the wall, from room to room. We were talking, maybe forty-five minutes or so, when the dogs started to go nuts. They started howling like crazy and running all over the house. I tried to hush them up while talking to Joel. I put them in the twins' room to keep them quiet. They started to scratch the door. Then I heard sirens. They were getting louder and louder, and so were the dogs. I opened the door to let Tom and Jerry run. They leaped over me and ran into the backyard where I saw some red lights and firemen, again.

"Oh no, not again," dropping the phone. I ran out but it was too late. The steaks were dead, long gone, charred to nothing with the smoke and flames billowing into the night sky. "I did it again, didn't I Chief?" I sadly and embarrassingly said as he put out the 'deadly' flames.

"Yes you have, Mrs. K. Mrs. Deutsch called us again. I guess she enjoys peering over in your yard every now and then. But we are always glad to see you and the boys, and to know that you are all fine and dandy, and dressed if I may add." The rest of the firefighters were laughing as usual.

"I am sure we'll be seeing you again soon. Not too soon, I hope for your sake. Maybe you should invite us over before you start the BBQ and we will make sure you don't burn up the neighborhood, and have a hot meal. But not too hot," He smiled and waved goodbye for now.

"So long. Sorry. I'll try to be more careful."

"Well, there goes dinner," Looking at Tom and Jerry with my hands on my hips. "Let's lock up and look in the pantry for something else to eat."

Once inside, I locked up again and turned the alarm on. We looked in the refrigerator for a while, and closed it. We looked in the freezer and stared. There was still some New York Cheesecake from last summer.

'New York', 'phone', 'Joel', oh my god. I dropped the phone and ran outside. What must he be thinking? I quickly ran to find the mobile phone. It was on the floor in the hallway. I picked it up.

"Hello." There was no answer. There wasn't even a dial tone.

I ran back to the kitchen and hung up the phone on the receiver. I started pacing back and forth while biting my lips.

"Should I call him back? This is silly. I'll explain it and he'll understand, and then he will think I am a bigger nut then he did before. Here goes nothing."

I dialed back, for the fifth time today. Joel picked up the phone on the first ring and said, "Yes, can I help you?" with a little laugh in his voice.

How embarrassing is this for me, again? "I am so sorry Joel. I don't know what to say or how to explain it," as I paced around the kitchen island.

"That's okay. You don't need to explain. I heard a commotion in the background and I figured it would take a while, so I hung up. I knew you would call back when it was all over."

"I was barbequing in the backyard and I closed the lid and forgot about the steaks. They must have caught on fire while the smoke was everywhere in the backyard. Obviously enough smoke for one of my neighbors to call the fire department again."

"Again?" he questioned.

"I have a habit of leaving things on the fire too long."

"I think I did that with my second wife," Joel added for a good laugh on his end, not expecting me to understand that one or figure it out. But I knew what he meant, I think.

"Well, it's late and I shouldn't be keeping you up. I'm sure you have to go to work tomorrow." "Why don't we touch base again when you're out here? I don't have anything planned and I'll come up with a great place we could meet for dinner. How does that sound?"

"Sounds wonderful, Amy. I look forward to seeing you soon, very soon," Joel said with an optimistic tone in his voice. "Until then, I will bid you farewell, M' lady."

I giggled (because girls do that), and said good night. We both hung up at the same time. I just stood there for a moment. I turned around, looked in the backyard, and screamed. "What's for dinner boys?"

Chapter 9

Just Right, I think

The holiday season is shaping up nicely. The lights look festive and inviting, with a timer attached, of course. Placing lights in the backyard, for the first time, makes my home look so illuminating and homey. I just love twinkling lights, everywhere.

All the rooms are clean and fresh. Candles are set in every room. Three cheers for the fake tree! Cameron always had to have a real fir tree for Christmas. He said it smelled like being in the forest, not that he knew what it was like in the forest since we never went camping, (thank goodness). I prefer the fake, I don't have to pick up the pine needles on an hourly basis or remember to water it everyday. Now it is my way.

Michael is bringing home Liz. She would definitely feel more comfortable in a room to herself, even though I am sure my son may make a visit or two (I don't even want to think about that). Liz can have Melanie's room while she is visiting with us, while Mel bunks in with me.

Mel, my pumpkin, used to do that when she was little. She would wake up in the middle of the night, quietly sneak into our room, and whisper to me, to move over. We would cuddle, and fall asleep together. I miss those days…

There is still a 'to do' list. First I need to start baking pies and freezing them. I said first because in case they don't turn out as I expect;

I will still have time to run to "Marie's" and buy some "homemade" pies. Second, shopping for the kids' presents takes up most of the time. I have to make my lists and check them twice… where have I heard that before? Third, and last, I need to make a dinner reservations at a nice restaurant for when Joel arrives. I hope. It's going to be a wonderful, traditional family Christmas after all.

Everything is working out, just right. I think.

Chapter 10

Here comes something, and it isn't Santa

This time of year is so exciting, for me at least. All the decorations, bright lights, festive music, gifts, and food (even if I make it), creates a memorable time for everyone. My children will be with me for a few days, all under the same roof. That is what makes a holiday special, togetherness. However, sometimes, there can be too much togetherness…

One by one, the kids will be coming home for the holidays. Finals will be over for all the girls and they will be racing home to be with me, at least that is what I want to believe. Michael will be joining us too, for a couple of days. I can hardly wait for all my children to be home for the holidays. I think I'm ready. I hope I'm ready. Well, whatever I forget, we will have to play by ear and do what comes naturally, as always the case.

Joel called when he made it safely to Los Angeles. He has to work Monday through Wednesday, but we could have dinner Wednesday evening, if it works out for me. I made a reservation at a nice quaint restaurant nearby. It isn't a date. Joel is an old friend and we go back to the time of the dinosaurs, (I do remember playing with kids that were the size of some dinosaurs).

The girls made it home safely, but not quietly. They are women you know. We all love to talk. The first night we all had dinner together.

I made spaghetti. It's hard to burn spaghetti, a little over cooked, but edible. It was like old times at the dinner table with all the girls talking. Since Michael wasn't home yet, we had a blast talking up a storm and laughing loudly, and non-stop.

Tom and Jerry were so happy to have their sisters home. They follow them around the house, tongues hanging out, shaking their monstrous bodies from side to side, and wiggling their tails a million miles a minute. Julie and Jenna expressed that they are going to reorganize their room. I don't know why they feel the need to move furniture around, while Mel will just hang out with her friends.

൭൧

"Melanie, you are going to share my room with me when Liz and Michael come home." I smiled and gave my Pumpkin a big hug.

"Mom, why me? Why do I have to? Mom, I need my space you know." Mel pulled away.

"Oh, I know Pumpkin. It will only be for a day or two. Be a good sport. Remember how you used to sneak into my room, and ask me to move over. Wasn't that fun and cozy?"

"Mom, I'm a grown woman now, and I NEED MY SPACE." It wasn't that she was upset with bunking in with me, just that she had to give up her personal space. Remember, everything is about Mel.

"Just think of it as camping out at the Ritz for a night or two. You can take a long hot bubble bath without the others knocking on the door. Wouldn't that be nice?" She loved my bathroom.

Mel shook her head in agreement and walked away quietly to her current assigned quarters.

൭൧

A few mornings later, I announced, "Girls, an old friend of mine is out visiting, rather working in LA for a few days, from New York."

"And?" Jenna stood there with her eyes widened. "Why do you feel the need to announce this Mother?" She sounded so adult-like. It was scary.

"I just thought I would let you know that I am going to dinner with him. You girls will have to make dinner yourselves."

"You mean you have a date?" Julie screamed with excitement.

"It isn't a date. It is just dinner with an old friend."

"I would call that a date, Mom." Julie walked over to get a cup of coffee.

"Whatever." I didn't want to get in an open discussion about what is a date and what isn't. God only knows I would lose against all three of my daughters.

"Melanie, you are in charge of making dinner for all of you tonight." I didn't even look up to see what expression she had on her face. I don't think I want to know.

I know what she plans to do...order a pizza after I leave. They are old enough to decide what they want to eat, as long as there is a vegetable on top of it, then that will be fine with me.

The kids' plans for evenings have always been on the chalkboard by the garage door. This way I keep track of where they all are, and what time everyone will be home. Last one home has to put the alarm on, as always, is the rule in this house.

∾

The day flew by. I slowly walked into my room to get ready for my dinner, not date, tonight. I glared into my closet and just stood there.

"I have absolutely nothing to wear," talking to myself.

The boys were with the twins in their bedroom. They like hanging out with them when they are home. They each get a sister to themselves and love all of their undivided attention.

"Should I look festive, sexy, or nun-like?" Well, sexy is out since I don't think I have ever looked sexy, (At least not according to Cam. He wouldn't allow it). I just stood there with one hand across my mouth and the other holding on my hip. It took me thirty minutes, and at least five different outfits before I decided to wear all black. I look great in black! I put my make-up on and brushed my hair (whatever there is to do with curly, wavy hair). I wore simple jewelry. I didn't want to overdo my outfit, just be simple and elegant, which I think I always am (Cam never would tell me how I look. It would have been nice, once in awhile, to hear I look great or something. However, I guess Hell would have had to freeze over to get a compliment out of him). A little perfume on the neck and wrists, and I am ready to go.

"Mom, are you ready for your date?" One of the girls yelled from the hallway between the bedrooms. I did hear giggling. They want to check me out before I go. I got a couple of whistles and an "ooh la la."

"Girls, don't be ridiculous. It isn't a date. It's just dinner." I did love the attention.

I was opening the garage door when Melanie yelled, "Mom, don't forget to write on the chalkboard. That goes for you too," she laughed. I wrote down dinner and be home by 10ish.

∞

I left early to be at the restaurant before Joel. I ordered a glass of red wine, remembering it is good for the heart, and so I could relax a bit. I sat there waiting, changing my sitting position every thirty seconds or so. Maybe he changed his mind, maybe he got lost, maybe he ran out of gas, or was in an accident. Two minutes later, a bunch of baby pink roses were set in front of me by the waiter. I gave the waiter a funny look.

"The gentleman by the bar sent them over."

"What gentleman? I don't know any gentlemen. Who-," I paused.

Joel came up from behind me, "I would recognize you anywhere." He smiled from ear to ear. We hugged. Gosh, he smelled great!

"You look fantastic Amy. Better than I imagined."

"Thanks. You do too," nervously said. "The roses are beautiful. Sit, sit please."

"I remember you always liked pink roses. I don't know why I remember that, I just do," he came back with. "I'm sorry I was late, I was looking for a flower shop. Luckily for you, I found one."

I didn't know what to say now. We just started to talk; rather I started to talk, about my children. I talked for half an hour before we even ordered any dinner or more drinks.

"You must be starving. We need to order some dinner before they kick us out," I whispered, and laughed at the same time.

Joel and I sat there for a long time reminiscing about the old days, while we were enjoying dinner, red wine, holiday music, and the ambience of the restaurant. He also told me about his ex-wives.

"I have been married twice. The first marriage was when I was 19. We were both so young and foolish. We figured that out and finally had it annulled after six months. My second marriage was with 'the child'. She just wanted to be taken care of, 24/7. I worked and worked while she played and played. When I found out that she was playing, one on one, with each of the tennis and golf pros, the marriage ended. I haven't had a long-term relationship with anyone since." He sighed.

Not knowing what to say or do, "I think I will have another glass of red wine. How about you?"

"No. I am trying to cut back," as he laughed. "It's late in my head. Don't forget the three hour time difference between the coasts."

I usually don't drink more than a glass or two, but this was a special occasion. I am having dinner with an old friend. After I finished the second drink, I realized that I wouldn't be able to drive home, (Usually one drink and I am taking my shoes off and feeling hot under the collar… probably those hot flashes). I had a little buzz, and didn't want to take a chance on the road.

Embarrassed about my condition, which was probably nothing to everyone else in the world, I found it difficult to ask Joel if he would follow me home. After a few uncomfortable quiet moments, I spit it out, not literally.

"Do you think you could follow me home?"

He gave me a puzzling look.

"Oh, that didn't come out right. I didn't mean it that way. I meant because I drank two glasses of wine. I didn't mean for, well, you know, **that**," I shamefully added. "The more I talk, the deeper the foot goes in the mouth."

"No problem. I'd be honored to drive you home. Will that suit you, M' lady?" he said with an honorable voice.

"That would be superb," I shouted with a little too much animation. My arms went flying in the air, and as our waiter walked by, I knocked over a tray of mini desserts that landed on Joel's lap.

"I didn't know if we were staying for dessert or not. I guess we'll try them on for size. Don't worry, it's on me." Joel joked.

The waiter was shaking his head as he was cleaning the mess and apologizing at the same time.

I was so embarrassed. What did I just do? The waiter apologized profusely, even though it was my fault. Joel started to laugh, so I joined along with him, apologizing every two seconds and trying to help him clean up. The manager came out and was astonished at what he saw. He yelled at the waiter and told us dinner was on him, since desserts were on us. We all laughed some more.

At this point in the evening, I didn't care. I was in a happy place. I haven't been in a happy place in a long time.

We walked, rather I waddled, to my car and handed Joel the keys. He helped me in. I put my seatbelt on, sat back with my head resting on the back of the seat, and just sighed. Joel had a hard time getting in, since I have the seat adjusted all the way up to the steering wheel. That happens when you are petite. My son declares that I am short, but what does he know. He is a man.

"Push those buttons over there," as I pointed to the door, somewhat, "to fix the seat."

"Okay. We are good to go then. Where to?"

I assumed he knew where I lived. I forgot to tell him. It was like going through a maze trying to get home. I kept on assuming he knew where to turn. I never know the street names, just the landmarks, like turn right at the big cactus, and make a quick left at the house with the big round fountain. I think we went in circles for a while until I snapped out of my 'buzz' and guided him to my home.

It was still early in the evening and all the girls were out visiting with friends. Michael would be home late, just as he said earlier in the week. I erased my whereabouts from the chalkboard. That way everyone knew I was home. I put the roses in a crystal vase on the dining room table.

I asked Joel, "Would you like to change into something more comfortable? Because of the desserts, that's all. I could wash everything for you in the machine, no problem." I showed Joel my humble home, and into Michael's closet for a change of clothing. I was so nervous. I haven't had a man in my home in a long time. While he was changing his clothes, I walked to the kitchen, opened the fridge, and took out the red wine. I poured myself a glass. I gulped it down out of sheer stress. I yelled down the hallway, "Joel, would you like some wine?" He said sure, and I poured him a glass.

He came out of Michael's room wearing a bathrobe. "I just don't feel right wearing your son's clothes. Sorry. Hope this is okay."

"No problem. I understand. Now give me your clothes and I'll wash them."

I put his shirt and pants in the washing machine. It is a good thing he was wearing jeans and a polo shirt, and not a nice suit.

"Why don't we go sit in the living room, have our wine, a real dessert on a real plate, and we can talk or something." (What the hell did I just say? I said talk or 'something.' I hope he doesn't get the wrong impression. It's probably too late for that now).

While we were waiting for the washing machine to finish the cycles, we sat and stared at one another. I kept on sipping, rather gulping, my wine and definitely feeling the after effects now. We were both speechless. He moved over and sat closer to me. I stiffened up. I started babbling on about the kids, the Christmas tree, and the ornaments.

Joel reached over, and with his hand turned my chin towards his and kissed me. I was still stiff as a board. I think he did it to shut me up. After the three-second kiss (I don't know how I figured it was three-seconds...but then I was always good at math), I kept on talking as if it didn't happen. He laughed, sat a little closer and reached again. This time it lasted a little longer, and I began to feel like jello, along with my legs. That usually happens when I drink, which I normally don't do, but every once in awhile, you know what I mean.

"I think I hear the washing machine," I whispered trying to catch my breath, and backing away while fixing my hair.

Joel smiled and sat back. I really think he was enjoying watching me squirm. I don't know what to do. Is this a date? Are we friends? What are we doing?

"I understand. You aren't comfortable. I realize that I just flew out to California and have already made a move on you, on our first date, and we haven't seen each other in over 30 years," Joel commentated to me. "But I do feel like I've known you forever. You haven't changed one bit Amy."

"Let me go and check the washing machine." I stood up to straighten my clothing, I mean, they were all still on me (what are you thinking?), and walked slowly into the kitchen so I could hear the washing machine when it finished its cycle. Joel followed me into the kitchen.

"This is a date? I ruined your pants and shirt. You had to drive me home, and ..."

"None of that matters. You are too adorable and I can't resist." He reached over and held me close. "We had a wonderful dinner with scintillating conversation. I enjoy your company and would like to continue our date if you don't mind."

"Oh, well. I'm not sure what this is. My girls said it was a date, but I didn't want to believe them. So, I didn't," He stopped me mid-breath and did it again. He kissed me right in the middle of the kitchen. The dogs sat there and wagged their tails.

We kissed for a while, a long while, before I remembered that I had children that might walk in any moment. Then the washing machine buzzer sounded. I broke away and slowly walked backwards to the utility room. As I backed up, I hit my head on the doorframe to the utility room. Who cares?

When I returned, I noticed my wine glass was full again. I became more relaxed as the night went on, because of the red wine, what else. We finished the bottle and he asked if I had another. I showed him where the wine bottles were stored, and he opened a new one. I have never had that much wine in my body at one time in all my life. We all know that red wine is good for the heart. So drink on!

After another glass, or was it two, I felt a little tipsy, *again*, again. I decided that it was hot in the house, or I was having more hot flashes.

"Don't you think it is hot in here?" He just smiled at me.

I opened the French doors to let fresh air in the house. We walked outside and looked up at the stars. The stars were twinkling, and remember that I love twinkling lights. It was breathtaking, and definitely cooler outside then inside. I was looking up at the stars and walking forward and didn't realize how close I was to the pool. It was only a couple of steps away. Remember, I have had more than my quota of red wine this evening.

Joel saw that I was standing too close to the edge of the pool and ran over to grab me. It was too late. I fell first, Joel followed, unknowingly, into the freezing waters below. My mouth was wide open. Tom and Jerry saw their Mommy in distress and jumped in to save me. Joel helped me to the side, and lifted me up to sit on the side. Tom and Jerry were barking and dog paddling to the steps. I was hysterically laughing and then it turned into sobbing.

"I'm so sorry. I don't know how to act in front of you. If you want to leave, I'll understand," as I sat on the side crying my eyes out.

"No, I'm not leaving. I don't have any dry clothes. How could I leave you anyway? I think we both need to change. Let me help you M'lady," Joel said seriously. He jumped out, and lifted me to my feet. We were both shivering, as well as the dogs.

"I always have towels outside. Let me get some."

I gave one to Joel. I wrapped one around my shoulders, and I laid down two other towels for Tom and Jerry. They like to lie on the pavement and rub their backs. Joel and I watched them and laughed. I started shivering.

"You need to get inside and into some dry clothing M'lady."

I didn't disagree as my teeth were chattering away. I quickly headed into my bathroom, took off my dripping wet clothes, and put my bathrobe on. I still had Cam's robe on the back of the bathroom door. I stared at it for a while and then decided it was time to 'use it or lose it.'

"Joel, here is another robe. One that is dry." I threw it out to him.

"Thanks," is all I heard back. We both went back outside to help the boys dry off. We each took one dog (I didn't want any sick dogs for Christmas).

I reiterated what I had said before about ruining the evening. Now I had the pool incident to add on to this evening as well. After the boys were dry, I hung the towels on the chairs by the pool.

"I insist on helping you relax now. Amy, you need to lie down, while I listen for the dryer." He walked me back into my room and made me lay down on the bed to relax.

"I'll go check my clothes in the dryer."

I think I just shook my head in agreement. At least that is the last thing I remember.

∞

Morning came sooner than I had hoped. I woke up with a slight headache. I sat up slowly, looked over to my right and saw that Tom and Jerry were sleeping on top of… Joel!

"AHHHHHHHH!" My heart was beating so hard, I scared myself as I screamed.

Joel jumped up out of my bed.

"You slept here? Did we--"

I didn't get a chance to get another word in before Michael came running down the hallway, opened the door, and shouted, "Mom, who is he? What's going on in here?"

Melanie came running and was shocked. "Mother, how could you," and smiled at Joel. "He's cute." Melanie was supposed to have slept in my room with me, but then Joel was in here. Where did Melanie sleep?

Here come the twins. They just laughed, and giggled. Meanwhile, all my children were in my bedroom. Joel and I were just standing there wearing bathrobes, thank goodness.

"Mom, did you and he?" Melanie asked and made a gesture I don't wish to describe.

"Well, big A, we are waiting," Michael said in a manly tone.

"No, did we?" I turned to Joel and asked.

"Nothing happened here. Your Mom and I didn't do anything. We fell asleep. Wait, that didn't come out right. Your Mom had a couple of drinks and felt a little light-headed, so I put her to bed. She fell asleep before my clothes were dry. We had an accident at the restaurant and in the pool. Let me explain this--"

"Can we all go in the kitchen and talk about this?" I demanded. "We all need to calm down, get dressed, and grab a cup of coffee and just listen. Everyone will meet in the kitchen in ten minutes."

Everyone shook their heads, gabbed under their breath, and went back to their assigned rooms, while Joel ran to the utility room and checked the dryer. Joel was dressed in a flash. I dressed in the bathroom, quickly as well.

I went back to the kitchen barefoot so I could turn on the coffee pot. The girls came in one by one. I completely forgot about Liz. What would she think about her boyfriend's mother?

Back to my bedroom to put my sneakers on, and then on the way out I saw a young woman, assuming it was Liz, come out of Michael's room. I snuck back in my room so she wouldn't see me. Sticking my head out slightly, I wanted to see what was going on out there, like any nosy Jewish Mother. Joel was in the hallway, when Liz almost rammed into Joel. He introduced himself. Michael was right behind her and I could tell he was embarrassed because he didn't say a word, which is unlike any of MY children.

We all made it back to the kitchen and everyone grabbed a mug to hide behind, at least that is what I was doing.

"Who wants to start?" I was looking at Michael.

"Huh? Why are you looking at me Mom?" Michael questioned, really knowing why.

"Let's start by announcing to the household where everyone was last night, shall we? I'll begin," I said with a stern tone. "I slept in my bedroom. There, that wasn't so hard. Who's next?"

Jerry barked. We all laughed under our breaths. Everyone knows where Tom and Jerry sleep.

Joel spoke up, "I slept in your mother's room, but it isn't what you all must be thinking. Let me explain." He took a deep breath. "Last night we went out for a nice dinner. The dessert tray ended up in my lap (all my children looked at me knowing how that could happen). I drove your mother home because she had one too many glasses of wine," (again, they all looked at me, rolled their eyes and shook their heads). Your mom put my dirty clothes in the washer. We walked outside and looked at the stars while we were waiting for my clothes. Your mom took one too many steps towards the pool and fell. I then followed suit, to help your Mom, and then the dogs went in after her," Joel explained and took a breath.

All the kids were staring at me. Then Joel spoke again.

"Let me finish explaining. I jumped in to help her, not that she needed my help. I just wasn't going to stand there and watch. We all got out of the pool freezing to death. Your Mom and I dried the dogs and then went inside to warm ourselves as well, not what you all are thinking either." (Everyone raised their eyebrows and opened their mouths). "We changed into bathrobes. Your Mom was very upset so I made her lie down while I put everything in the dryer. She fell asleep and I didn't want to wake her. I waited in her room, sitting in the rocking chair. I heard all you kids come in LATE last night. I closed her door, so she wouldn't be disturbed. I was almost asleep in the rocking chair, but it just wasn't that comfortable, so I went to lie down on the bed; on top of the covers, I might add, and fell asleep. Tom and Jerry were separating us by sleeping on top of me. Nothing else happened. End of story." Joel was exhausted after that. He took some deep breaths.

All the kids just stared at this man and me, and back and forth a few times more, with their mouths hanging wide open. No one knew what to say or do until Liz stood up.

"Hi, I'm Liz. We haven't met yet Mrs. Kayden." I felt a little off guard by this introduction. We shook hands and sat down. That broke the ice a little for everyone to start talking, especially the girls.

"Okay now. Everyone else tell me where you all slept last night. I think it is your turn Michael," I waited for a response with my eyebrows up and staring right into his eyes.

"You know Mom. I slept in my room, where else?" Michael calmly said while he was shaking one knee under the table.

"Uh huh," I added. "Anyone else want to volunteer their whereabouts last night? Melanie."

"I slept in my room of course!" as Melanie covered her mouth and looked at her brother for help. "I know I was supposed to sleep with you Mom, but I forgot."

"Next … anyone?" I looked around waiting for someone else to speak up. "Okay then. Some of us are clear about our whereabouts, others--"

"I think you and I need to speak alone, now, outside," Joel said calmly. While he pushed me outside, the kids started mumbling under their breath to one another.

"What are you doing here? Are you trying to ruin your relationship with your children? You know where everyone slept and so do your kids. I might add that they are all young adults. Don't bring anything up unless you are prepared for a fight and someone to leave," Joel explained.

We stood there for a moment. I was thinking. "There are rules in my home. It would have been nice if my children followed those rules. Even for just a few nights," I declared.

"This is true. They should know better and I am sure after this so-called coffee klatch meeting they will be more careful, don't you think?" he questioned me. "Don't you think we should go back inside, have a nice breakfast, talk to your kids, enjoy having them around, and then time for me to say good night? It's been the longest date I've ever had. Not that I haven't enjoyed your company. I have, very much so. It's time for you to spend the holidays with your kids." He smiled and put his arm around me and gave me a quick hug, and a light kiss on the top of my head, which hurt from last night.

"How did you get to be so smart? You don't have any kids and you aren't married?"

"I guess it comes naturally. I've been around enough families in the hotel business to see a lot, and learn even more."

I gave him a nudge and smiled as we both walked back in the kitchen together. "Okay, now, who is up for pancakes this morning?" I grabbed the spatula in one hand and the frying pan in the other.

"As long as you aren't cooking them Mom," Melanie said.

"I'll do the cooking. Everyone sit down and enjoy. This will be my gift to you," Joel stated.

We all had a wonderful breakfast. We laughed, talked, and ate a ton of pancakes. I just love to see my kids together, talking, laughing, and eating. Then Joel insisted on leaving. He had to catch his flight back to New York.

I offered to drive him back to the hotel, but he refused and called the hotel. A chauffeur came to pick him up. He said I needed to spend time with my kids.

I walked him out to the limo, clean clothes and all. He said he would keep in touch, but didn't make it sound like a promise. He kissed me on the cheek. The limo left me standing there alone, on Christmas Eve morning.

Now where are my endearing children?

Chapter 11

Tear Drops

Everyone is back to his or her own routines. It was wonderful to have my children home, chaotic at times, but I loved it. Liz got a good taste of what it's like to be a Kayden family member now, if that's what she was thinking, or maybe I was thinking it for her.

The girls are back at school, hopefully studying. Melanie is in her last semester and is so excited about graduating in June. That means she will have to get a real job. I don't think she realizes that yet, being the "Prima Donna" that Cam brought her up to be.

Once the kids went off to college, what they did with their time and schedules was up to them. I consider them adults, and I treat them that way, most of the time. Cam never did. He would constantly badger them with questions about classes, their study habits, when their tests and papers are due and so on.

I insisted on letting them make their own decisions and mistakes, and if they fall, they will have to pick themselves up and keep on going. They have to learn to cope with life's mishaps and learn to move on. Cam disagreed. He didn't think falling and making mistakes was part of the master plan. You had to do it right the first time… at least in his head. I think that is why the kids would secretly talk to me first. I am the calm parent. So far, I think I'm doing okay.

It's time to bring down the lights, and put them away until next year. It was a memorable Christmas. We did talk about Cam, and it was a little easier than it has been the months before. Time heals all wounds, so I hear. It will take a lot of time for us, at least me, to move on without much pain, and just keep the memories

Now it's time to move on with another chapter in my life. It has been almost twenty-five years since I held a job and did something for myself. I do have a Bachelor's in Psychology. I think I would need a few classes to catch up with the rest of the world if I were to pursue that field. So, moving on to other pastures, shall we?

What have I always wanted to be when I grew up, besides five foot three inches tall? I always wanted to be an Astronomer, or CPA, a Singer, and an Artist. Becoming an Astronomer or CPA would take a lot of schooling and I am much too old to start over again, at least in my head. Trying to get my kids through college is more than enough. Singing is out, except in the shower and when I'm in the car. My kids tell me I am no Barbra. I could try my hands on painting. Granted, I am no Michaelangelo, but maybe a close second. It depends on the eye of the beholder.

I loved painting when I was a kid. I am very artistic, even if I have to say so myself. Off to Michael's to buy some paints, canvases and stuff. Looking around the craft store was loads of fun. It brought back memories of something. Do I want to use oil, acrylic, or watercolors? What size canvases do I want? Do I draw it with pencil first? So many decisions to make, I can't remember how to choose.

Walking around my lonesome, I asked one of the women who works there, "Can you help me please? I want to do some painting."

"Why don't you start with our beginner's class on Wednesday nights."

"I don't need any classes. I already know how to paint," laughingly as if I was a pro. She just stared at me as if I was an idiot that just escaped from the looney bin.

"How about starting with a scratch pad and just sketch first?"

"I don't need to do that either." Again, she gave me 'the look'.

"Thank you anyway. I will be fine on my own," as I walked down the next aisle. Some people have a lot of nerve, trying to tell me what to do, and how to do it. Only I do that.

I decided that oil and acrylic were too messy. Watercolors are best. Besides not being messy, it dries quickly, and comes in such beautiful different shades of the rainbow.

Walking to the front of the store to reach for a basket, an old looking, thickset, hairy hand took a hold of the other end of the same basket. It was Joe Elliot. Why do I keep running into him, literally?

"I will let you have this basket if you promise not to run me down one of the aisles?" he smirked.

"Very funny," I let go of the basket.

"I guess this means I better watch my step in here?"

"You better. You never know what is going to happen," grabbing another basket.

Why does this man keep torturing me? I didn't do anything to him…oh, yeah, I did. That doesn't mean he should treat me any differently than anyone else in the neighborhood. Maybe he acts that way to everyone. Moving on…

As I turned around with my basket in hand, I saw the flower aisle. They had hundreds of beautiful flowers. Since Valentine's Day is the next big holiday, the red and pink roses are set in the front. The pink roses look so real with water droplets hanging on them as if they were ready to fall off from the early morning dew. The pink roses Joel gave me were long gone now. They did last over three days, which is good for me, considering I don't have a green thumb.

I haven't heard from Joel since our 'date'. Maybe it was just a dinner and nothing else. Maybe I scared him away. Maybe he will call soon. Maybe, I should stop worrying, and MOVE ON.

I purchased a sketchbook with some watercolor pencils. I also bought some pink roses with the droplets on the petals. I will place them in a little vase at home on the dining room table, where the others had lain before. On my way out of the store, I ran into Joe again.

"Well, I see we made it through the store without a major catastrophe," he laughed.

"Yes, but you haven't made it to your car yet." I smiled and walked casually to my car.

My car was parked a couple of rows over. I stopped behind another car and could see he was checking out all of his tires when he reached his car. Of course, they were fine. He opened his trunk to put his bag in and the trunk hit his head, hard. I started to laugh. He looked around to see if anyone was watching. Then he rubbed his head, yelled an obscenity, and moaned.

"That's what you get for being a smart aleck." I whispered to myself so proudly, so I thought.

He looked up when he heard my voice and the trunk lid hit him again.

∾

Tom and Jerry were sitting on the kitchen floor waiting for me. I thought they were waiting for me. They cried a little and walked back and forth to the laundry room. I asked them what the problem was. Of course I didn't get an answer, just a few cries. I realized I forgot to give them fresh water for their bowls this morning, so they had to drink out of the toilets, which I hate. They usually end up with a stomachache and diarrhea. I could always tell when I came back from a trip if they were "watered" or not by the moans and diarrhea in the backyard.

The phone message machine was blinking. I pushed the button to listen. The first message was from Liz. She said she had a great time at our house and wanted to thank me personally, but that Michael said she didn't have to. The second message was from my Mother, and I have no idea what she said. I don't think she has any idea of what she said either. My last phone message was from Joel. I was surprised to hear from him, (Well, not really surprised. I was wondering when I would hear from him). My heartbeat sped up as if I just finished the half mile race, okay just one lap around the pool.

"Amy, this is Joel. I had a nice time with you and your kids. Is it like that all the time around there?" I could hear a little laughter in his tone. "I don't have your email address, but I will give you mine," which he recited, twice. "Email me your address whenever you are ready."

Ready! Ready for what? I am not sure what that means. I think I am reading too much into everything lately. I need to calm down, later.

I didn't want to seem too anxious about emailing him right away, so I waited an hour. I just jotted down a quick note letting him know I received his message. I must have rewritten it a dozen times or so. I guess that is better than leaving at least three goofy messages on his phone. I also said that things in the Kayden household are always chaotic, but I love it that way, and wouldn't have it any other way. I sent it off into cyberspace. I just hope he gets it sometime this century.

I immediately got a response back. "Wow that was quick. He must be sitting there." Nevertheless, it was just one of those office response emails saying that he is out of the office right now. I guess he gave me his office email and not his personal one. That doesn't sound very promising to me.

ᘏ

I called Carol and asked her what to do with my life, besides breathing every now and then. I told her I am going to start painting. She didn't respond. "Carol, are you there?"

"Yes, I am here, but apparently you really aren't there at all," she yelled through the phone.

"What is that supposed to mean?"

"What I mean is, you are doing something ALONE. You need to be with people, not just Tom and Jerry. I love them too, but you can't live with dogs alone Amy."

"Maybe… I do like painting, I think. I am going to try it anyway, but what else do you think I should do?"

"I think you should go online and find some dates, go on single cruises, work out at the fitness place, get a part-time job, or be a volunteer. That's what you should start doing, instead of sitting around the house waiting for the paint to dry. No pun intended. Go online and look up cruising for singles."

"Okay. I will look. Thanks Carol. Love ya."

ᘏ

My, my, you can do anything online nowadays.

I spent the whole afternoon on the computer. My eyes, hands, back and butt are killing me. It's time to get moving.

"Hey, Tom, Jerry, you want to go for a walk to the park?" They raced into the bedroom, jumped on my bed, jumped off and raced back down the hallway.

"I take it this means YES? Let's go boys."

Once I had the boys secured, unlike a time before if we all think back, we went to the park for a walk. It was a beautiful sunny day with a little chill in the air. There were kids playing at the park. Thank goodness, there wasn't a soccer game going on right now. It was late afternoon, almost dinnertime. I sat on one of the benches and just 'people watched'. Kids were playing on the swings, sandbox (yuck), and monkey bars. Moms were standing together talking and supposedly watching their kids. I saw two couples sitting, one in the grass, and the other under a tree. They were cuddling and holding hands. A kiss here and there, but no heavy petting (and I don't mean the dogs). It is nice to see people together. It made me think of Cam, not that he would ever come to the park with me, or walk the dogs, or even cuddle. It was just the thought of him still being around and knowing he will be next to me every night, so I would feel safe.

The sky is getting ready for a picturesque sunset. I want to be home before dark, because we all know what that means. Yes, time to lock us in! I made dinner for the three of us, something edible for me, and dog food for the boys. We sat and watched a lifetime movie together, and cried together, and it wasn't because of the movie. Those damn hormones! I decided to check my email. There is always a ton of junk mail. The girls are always sending me funny emails that are so cute. I do correspond with a few girlfriends from high school and college as well. We try to keep up with one another at least once a month. I did receive one from Joel. It was a quick response to my email. He said:

> *Received your email address. Now I have you. I am out of town right now on business. I do check my email every evening when I am finished for the day. You are probably wondering why I gave you this email address instead of a personal one. Easy explanation, I don't have a personal*

one. I will let you know when I will be in LA again. Would love to go out for dinner again, this time on you!

Take care, Joel.

"Well, that was nice and impersonal."

What am I thinking? We don't have a relationship of any sort, except friendship. I shouldn't be thinking anything else right now. Time to move on, as I shut down the computer, walked into the dining room, and gazed at my pink roses with teardrops.

Chapter 12

When it rains, it pours

Time to go to the beach! You may ask, 'NOW? Isn't it winter?'

Why yes, it's winter. This is the best time to go to the beach with my canvas and paints. I love the ocean. I love the smells, the sounds, the wind blowing through my hair, and especially the sand between my toes. If I could move right onto the beach, I would do it in a minute. It is so peaceful, beautiful, and serene. The only thing I don't like about the beach is getting wet, and dirty, and stepping on small sharp shells, and maybe a few other things too, but I JUST LOVE THE BEACH!

I packed up my art supplies in the trunk, along with a chair. I thought I would bring Tom and Jerry along too. They love to run on the beach and bark at the waves, run away, and sit by me. There won't be any people there this time of year, so no one will feel threatened if there are two humongous animals running amuck.

The three of us hopped in the car. We are ready for an afternoon at the beach. Tom and Jerry love to go for rides in the car. They each sit in the back by a window. They prefer the window to be open so they can stick their heads out in the wind while their ears fly. I just don't understand why dogs do that. Have you ever tried it? I thought, for *doggone* sake, to try it out, while I was driving on the PCH, (Pacific Coast Highway).

I pushed the button to open my window. I stuck my head out as far as I could, while still operating the vehicle. The wind was pushing my face backwards, towards Jerry's head. I couldn't breathe very well, or see very well for that matter. A car coming towards me went through a huge puddle, as my head stuck all the way out. ***Swish***...my face was soaked with dirty water. *Yuck.* It caught me by surprise. I couldn't catch my breath. I spit out some brown water and gagged. The dogs were barking like crazy. I guess they were trying to tell me to 'BEWARE.' I think they were really laughing at me, not with me, because I certainly wasn't laughing.

"How gross," as I spit again, as much of the mucky water from the street. "How can you boys do this?" They looked at me and tilted their heads. I thought I heard snickering.

I have had my 'shower' for the day. I need a towel. I always keep a towel or two in the trunk. Cam always thought it was silly to have towels in the car. Boy was he wrong. We arrived at Will Rogers State Beach and there were quite a few cars.

I let the dogs out first, since they were pushing and barking to get out. I gathered up my belongings: the canvas, paints, blanket, and chair. What a handful I have. The wind was blowing like the north wind just came down from Alaska, and it was cold. I figured it would warm up once we were out there, and settled in a spot.

I walked out with all the stuff, tripping along the way. I decided to do it in shifts. I can't carry everything at once. I left the canvas by the walkway. I continued to walk onto the sand and found a location in the middle of the beach, between the lonely snack bar and roaring ocean. I spread the blanket, and opened the chair. I walked back and picked up the canvas. Tom and Jerry followed me back and forth each time. They were so happy to be here. They wagged their tails and trotted in the sand.

Once I had set everything in place, I sat for a moment because I was exhausted. I took a few deep breaths and just enjoyed the scenery and sounds of the ocean. It was breathtaking and so relaxing. First I am going to take Tom and Jerry for a little walk along the beach while the tide was low, before I get started. I won't take them too far so I won't forget where we are located.

The wind was picking up a bit. I saw a gang of surfers way out yonder. They must be nuts to be out there. The tide started to come in now. The waves were getting a little bigger, the wind was picking up speed, and it was getting tough to keep my footing in the sand. There were a few people walking by, and asked if they could pet the dogs. I said they love attention, any kind of attention.

One man was walking by himself. He looked familiar to me, but I was afraid to make a fool of myself and start talking to him. I don't know why. I have made a fool of myself many times before. However, the man walked up to me, "Amy, is that you?"

I was in shock. My eyes popped open as well as my mouth.

"Who are you? Do I know you?" I was a little nervous that he knew my name and there aren't many people out there that I could turn too, except that gang of surfers went out yonder.

"I didn't think you would recognize me. I kind of lost a little hair on top," he laughed. "We went to high school together. It's me, David, from the baseball team. I've been out in California since I graduated. Do you remember me?"

"Of course I do. We went out once, didn't we? Of course I remember you. What a small world." I reached over to give him a little hug, but he backed up. Now I felt like an idiot.

"So what brings you here David?" Standing there with my arms crossed now, and the dogs pacing in the sand, I didn't know what else to say or do.

"I come here almost every day. I walk along the beach for hours and just think. My wife loved to take walks along the beach. She died a few months ago, and my son is living in New York," he nervously laughed.

"I'm sorry about your wife." I didn't want to get stuck on the subject of death. Can you blame me?

"So, what do you do David?" I know I didn't want to talk about Cam right now, especially with someone I haven't seen in over three decades.

"I am semi-retired. I used to be a stockbroker. When Susan became ill, a few years back, I cut back my hours and spent more time with her. Then when she became bed-ridden, I worked out of the house so I could be with her night and day."

"Oh. I'm sorry David," I switched positions of my arms and moved my feet in the sand. I felt very uncomfortable. Now I know how others feel when they are talking, or rather listening, to me.

"You know, maybe we should have lunch sometime, and talk about the old days?"

He looked excited there for a moment. "Okay, how about tomorrow? How about we have lunch right here at noon?" He was quick to jump on lunch. He must be very lonely these days.

I wasn't sure how to respond, "Alright, I guess."

"I'll take care of it; just bring you, and the dogs. I will bring Daisy, Susan's dog. She hasn't been to the beach, since before Susan passed. I think Sue decided she didn't like the beach anymore once she became ill and couldn't see the ocean, smell the air, or feel the wind." David looked down and then out into the wide ocean.

It was a little awkward at that moment. "Sounds okay to me, and the boys I am sure."

David then turned to head back, waved and said, "Well, I guess I will be seeing you tomorrow."

I walked back down the beach slowly with Tom and Jerry. They were having a blast barking at the waves, which were getting bigger and stronger. The wind was also picking up in strength, and it was getting colder. When we reached our little area, all my possessions were scattered. My chair was pushed over, the blanket looked like someone had stepped all over it with lots of sand in it, and my paints were thrown all over within a few feet of the blanket. I wasn't sure if someone had done this and was looking for money, or the wind did it. I will say the wind did it. I still felt a little uneasy, and maybe someone was watching me (I know I'm paranoid at times). I packed up, and put it all back in the car. I may not have done any painting, but I had the chance to go to the beach, which I don't do very often.

*

While driving home, I was thinking about David. I don't really know him. For all I know he could be a mass murderer hiding out on the beach or something. Or maybe he is really a beach bum. Maybe he really killed his wife, maybe his son left because he killed his wife, and then he killed his son too, or maybe I need to stop thinking for a while and just make it home in one piece with Tom and Jerry sitting in the back seat with their heads out the window.

൬൭

Home again, home again. I unloaded the mess in the back, and I am not talking about the dogs. I shook everything out in the driveway before taking it into the house. Carol came cruising up the driveway with her apron on and phone in hand. "I have been trying to call you for hours. Where in hell's name have you been?"

"Well sorry *Mom* for not calling or leaving you a message. I just took the boys to the beach to do some walking and try painting."

"What have I told you? You need to be around people, not just the dogs," she scolded me with her hands on her hips ready to attack me again at any moment.

"Listen, you can't just mope around day after day." She took a deep breath. "Let's make some plans for a girl's weekend. Doesn't that sound great? You, me, and a couple of friends could all go for a long weekend somewhere, a resort and spa?" Carol sounded so excited now.

"Actually, that does sound good. A get-a-way somewhere at a spa would be great. I haven't had a vacation in years, literally. You know how Cam would never take time off for vacation. I think that would be great!" Now I was excited and couldn't wait to make some plans.

"Good! Do you want me to find a place or should we do it together?" Carol had the look of a nine year old in her eyes, and probably drooling a bit too.

"Let's plan it together. We can look on the internet," I suggested.

"How about we look tomorrow afternoon?"

"I have a date at the beach tomorrow for lunch." I looked into Carol's eyes to see her reaction.

Carol's mouth opened big, her eyes widened to the size of golf balls and there was a big grin.

"So, you have a date do you? And who is this with, if I may be so bold to ask?"

"I ran into an old friend from high school. I went out with him, once, when he was on the baseball team our senior year." (And I think

ONCE, is the key word here). "He has been living out here since graduation. His wife just died and…"

"Uh oh," Carol interrupted. Her eyebrows raised and she tilted her head to one side.

"What?" I looked at Carol not knowing what was going through her head. Sometimes I didn't know what was going through my own, let alone someone else's.

"That could mean trouble. When a man's wife has recently passed away, he is usually looking for a replacement. You know what I mean."

"Oh, you have been watching too many Dr. Phil shows. I don't think so. He sounded okay to me. He certainly didn't sound desperate, (or maybe he did). He did ask me quickly to have lunch for tomorrow?" I started thinking. Was I too quick to say yes?

"Just be careful. Take your cell phone and call me if you need me. Not to change the subject but, we can do the internet thing when you get home, okay sweetie?" Carol whispered as she held my hand.

"It's getting late hon. I need to get back to my kitchen. I think a Tornado named Adam may hit it soon." Carol turned and started to head back out of my driveway.

"Why don't you come over for dinner tonight? Larry is working late. He has to be in court tomorrow and wants to be over prepared, as usual."

"No thanks Carol. I need to get the boys cleaned up from the beach and then I want to take a long, hot, bubble bath, and have a glass of wine. You know that red wine is good for the heart! I'll call you tomorrow. Thanks anyway. You know I love you."

Carol shook her head and she swiftly walked home.

"It's getting late boys. It's that time." They barked a little, as if they knew what I meant. I closed the garage door, locked us in for night, turned the outside lights on and then the alarm. This is the routine I've had since we bought this house twenty-two years ago, when I was pregnant with Melanie. It makes me feel safe, and sound. I think the boys do too.

~

After my long, hot, bubble bath, I checked my email. There was a funny joke from Melanie. The twins sent me quick hellos. I keep asking them for their last semester grades and they keep telling me they don't have them yet. I find that hard to believe. Then there is always a bunch of junk mail. I keep deleting all the way down until those are gone. There was an email from an old girlfriend from college. The last email was from Joel. He actually sent me a picture of himself in Paris, by the Eiffel Tower. He noted that he was out of the country right now, but was thinking about me.

"Isn't that nice boys," I said, in a sarcastic tone. "Do I remind him of the Eiffel tower, small at the top and big at the bottom?"

I had some hot soup and toast with a piece of American cheese in the middle. That is my version of a grilled cheese sandwich. The last couple of evenings have been pretty cold and windy. I wonder if we are in for a storm. I lit a couple of candles in my room and made sure the flashlight was within reach.

Off to bed we go. I ran down the hall to turn off the computer, and made myself a cup of hot cocoa and brought two doggie biscuits back with me (not for me), to my bedroom. I turned the TV on and watched reruns of my favorite sitcoms. Tom and Jerry hopped up on the bed waiting for their evening treat. We all fell asleep together with the TV on, and one of my candles sizzled out during the night, (Not sure how to interpret that).

The next morning was cloudy and cool. The clouds were a dark gray and very dreary looking. I thought about my date for lunch. I guess I will show up, without the dogs though, but definitely with an umbrella.

I waited at home as long as I could, that maybe David would figure out my phone number somehow. I realized I didn't tell him my last name.

I drove down to the beach in the cold wind and mustiness in the air. I brought a blanket and my umbrella. It was drizzling out, but not bad enough to cancel a lunch. After all, everyone has to eat lunch. I locked my car, and brought the blanket and umbrella out onto the beach area.

There wasn't a soul in sight. The waves were rough and very thunderous. The wind was approaching mach speed as I sat there chilling, and not in the good sense of the word. I spread the blanket down, sat and looked around. I kept on looking at my watch, watching the second hand. We were supposed to meet at noon right here on the spot where we met yesterday. I sat there for thirty minutes, and now it started to rain a little. I opened my umbrella and sat there like a homeless woman, in the rain. I sat there until 12:45 PM when it started to thunder and lightening. The rain was pouring down, and I was soaked. Not only was I soaked to the skin, so was the blanket and the rest of the beach. No wonder no one was here.

I've never been stood up before in my life (Not that I have had so many lunch dates in my life). I ran back to my car, drenched from the torrential rains. Remember, I always carry towels in the car and I definitely needed one. Cam always thought it was a dumb idea to have towels in the car, but I have proved him wrong again, not that it matters now.

I dried myself off as best as I could. My hair is a disaster. When it gets wet, it looks like I stuck my finger in a socket. I brushed it back, with my fingers, as best as I could for the time being. I'll fix it at home, if it hasn't steamed itself too much from my anger.

This drive home was the longest ever. I don't know if I hit every single red light, but I know I hit most of them, plus with the rain coming down like cats and dogs, it made the roads even slower. I thought I might need a water rescue if I didn't make it home soon.

I pulled in the garage and the dogs were barking like crazy. It was a downpour now, with thunder and lightening. I know my boys are afraid of all that, me too. I closed the garage and locked us in.

"Mommy is home." I gave Tom and Jerry hugs and kisses. "Everything will be okay now. Let's go." During this kind of weather, I am usually afraid the electricity will go out, so I lit a few candles all over the house, even though it was still early in the afternoon. I just have to remember to blow them out later on in the evening, otherwise my good friends, from the fire department, may show up. I also made sure I had my cell phone and a flashlight. The boys followed me from room to room, as usual.

I went into the kitchen to make a cup of hot cocoa and saw my message machine blinking. I pushed the button to hear the messages and there were three. The first one was blank. It had no message, just air. The second one was the same. I thought that was strange until I heard the third message. Surprise, surprise, it was from David. He must have called my mom in New York to get my phone number.

"Sorry Amy. I know I was supposed to meet you today. It is too soon for me to be 'out' just yet. I apologize. Maybe we can get together some other time. I hope you didn't go down to the beach. The weather is just awful."

"Well boys, what do you make of that? I am standing here soaked to the skin. He could have called earlier, at least early enough before I left for the beach." I dried off and put on my warm, comfortable robe.

Making lunch was a necessity now, since I missed it earlier. Just as I sat down at the kitchen table with a bowl of cream of mushroom soup, the phone rang. I decided that I wasn't going to answer it, incase it was HIM. I certainly didn't want to talk to David right now. Instead, it was Carol. She called to see if I was okay. She knows I'm afraid of the dark, thunderstorms and a lot of other stuff too. I ran to pick it up and caught her in time.

"I'm here Carol."

"Is everything okay? I bet your date was cancelled because of the weather, huh?"

"OH, it was cancelled alright. Don't ask." I took a deep breath and sighed loudly.

"Do you still want me to come over this afternoon? The kids are home from school early, probably because of the 'hurricane,' and are watching movies. I could use a little outing," Carol asked.

"Only if you really want to come over in this weather, Carol. It's bad out there right now. You may want some time to yourself. You could take a bath, all by yourself with bubbles," I suggested.

"Nah, I'm good. I'll be over in a few."

I put on a pot of coffee while waiting for Carol to arrive at the kitchen door. I also put out some peppermint schnapps for both of us. I turned off the alarm and unlocked the door. I went into the freezer, took out two slices of New York Chocolate Cheesecake (because it's the best), and placed them on paper plates to thaw. Carol came sprinting into the kitchen, with her apron on, and umbrella open. She placed the open umbrella on the floor in the laundry room. She had her phone in her apron pocket. That's Carol, have phone will travel!

"I brought the computer into the kitchen so we both could sit and look."

We decided that we needed a spa resort of some kind, that isn't located in sunny California. We picked sunny Arizona. There are so many different locations in Arizona. We pinpointed either Phoenix or Sedona. We could either fly or drive, depending on the location of the spa. We looked for an hour or so, and then took a coffee and cheesecake break.

Carol's phone rang in her pocket. She picked it up and it was one of the kids.

"What the hell is going on over there?"

Jodi had pushed Sarah off the couch and now they think her arm is broken. Carol dashed out of the house, telephone in hand, apron on, and left her umbrella.

"Call me if you need any help." She shook her head and ran down the street in the rain.

"I guess I'm on my own boys."

After I locked the kitchen door and put the alarm back on, I sat back down at my computer. The rain was still coming down, but not as vigorous as it was earlier. There was still loud thunder and lightening all around as well, but the boys and I are okay, for now. As I was searching the internet, I received an IM. It was from Melanie. I wrote back, "Hey Pumpkin, what's up?"

"Just doing some research and I noticed you were online Mom. What are you doing?"

"Checking out some spas in Arizona."

"Let me know when and where we are going," Melanie hinted.

"I will tell you already, ***you*** aren't going. You have school. It is going to be Carol and me. She says I need a vacation away from here."

"You should go Mom. You need to get away. Dad never took you anywhere, so you deserve to go somewhere. Who's going to take care of Tom and Jerry?"

"I haven't gotten that far yet. I'm sure Nathan and Chase probably can. I'm not going to worry about it just yet. We haven't figured out which spa and when yet."

"Need to run Mom. Need to do some WORK! Love you."

"Love you to Pumpkin. Kiss, kiss. TTYL. Mom"

Right after I ended my conversation with Melanie, another IM popped up on my computer. This one said, "Hey Big A." I knew it was Michael. He knows I don't like it when he calls me that.

"What is it, little m?"

"I'm here at work and saw you online. You usually aren't on during the day."

"Well I am today. Carol and I were looking up some spas in Arizona. Has your station ever done any pieces on spas anywhere?"

"I wouldn't know that Big A. I am not interested in finding out either." I didn't think he would know or be interested, but it couldn't hurt to ask!

"Okay then. Signing off," just as I was signing off for the day, another IM came up, but it was too late. I couldn't see who it was and by the time I was back online, whoever it was, was gone.

Later that evening I called Carol. "Carol, is everyone okay?"

"Sarah is just fine; she needed some TLC from her Mom."

"Aw. Just wanted to make sure everything is okay."

Chase called after I hung up with Carol. He remembers that I don't like being alone in storms and offered to come over with Nathan. I told him that I'd be fine, that the boys are with me, and I'll call if I become too scared.

I made some popcorn, fat free of course, and watched a DVD in my room. I picked a comedy, *Something's Gotta Give,* with Diane Keaton and Jack Nicholson. I think it is hilarious and that would help me get my mind off the weather.

KABOOM! I jumped ten feet in the air. Tom and Jerry did too. I don't know if I startled them or the thunderstorm startled them. The rain didn't seem to want to stop. It was as if the clouds were crying, and crying.

It is two in the morning and I am scared to death. I know the alarm is on, I blew out the candles before going to bed, all the doors are locked, the outside lights are on, and the boys are with me.
KABOOM! KABOOM! I am shaking and breathing heavily under

my safe comforter. Should I call Carol, Nathan and Chase, Michael, Melanie, or the twins?

I took deep breaths and told myself that everything will be just fine. It's only a storm and nothing else. I'm safe in my home, in my bed, with Tom and Jerry. My heart is beating so loudly it could wake the dead, if there were any nearby, (I hope not). I told the boys that they can never die on me.

Chapter 13

Fine and Dandy

Thank goodness, I can see sunlight streaming through the French doors in my bedroom. I sat up and yelled.

"We did it boys. We made it through the night."

I'm sure they had no idea what I was talking about and they probably didn't really care right now. They laid their heads back down on the pillows and tried to go back to sleep.

I jumped out of bed, went into the bathroom, and looked at myself in the mirror. I was smiling from ear to ear.

"I did it! I made it through the night. This was my first storm, all by myself."

I danced around with my hands up in the air. I looked back in the mirror and suddenly, I was alone. Sometimes, it was lonely when Cam was here too. Somehow, just his presence in the house made everything just fine and dandy.

"Today is the first day of the rest of my life. I am going to get out there, meet people, go places, do things, and enjoy life."

I took a nice, long, hot shower to start my day. I put on a pot of coffee, fed the dogs, and made some oatmeal. I'm going to eat right, exercise, and take care of me for a change. I don't know why it has taken so long for me to realize that **me, myself, and I,** am the most important people in my life, besides my kids and 'boys' of course.

I called Carol.

"Today is the day I pick a Spa. I am going to make reservations and see who wants to go."

"Good for you hon. Count me in, whenever it is. I will tell Larry we have a girls' weekend to attend for our health and well-being. He knows I need a get-a-way as well as you. You sound different. Is everything okay?"

"Everything is fine and dandy. I need to take care of me now. I'm going to start by exercising, eat right, read more, go places, and meet people."

"Well, it's about time Amy. I'm glad you are coming to your senses and realize that you are important. Let me know if you need anything or just want to chat, hon."

"Will do. Right now, I need to go on the computer and figure this all out. Talk to you later."

I hung up the phone and went into the kitchen to eat and turn on the computer. I sat there with Tom and Jerry on each side of the chair. I had my oatmeal, coffee and positive attitude working for me this morning. Nothing could go wrong.

Twenty minutes went by and I was surfing the web. The Camelback Inn in Phoenix looks very inviting. It is centrally located, not too far from Scottsdale, Carefree, just a little ways from Sedona, and hidden behind Camelback Mountain, which is where I assume they came up with the name 'The Camelback Inn.'

The pictures of the resort make it look so nice, peaceful and picturesque. This is the place for a girls' weekend. Now I just need to pick the date and check the airlines. I think flying would be best. We can rent a car when we get there. I spent the next hour or so making plans. It isn't easy making plans for a little vacation. I forgot how much time and effort it takes to plan everything. I also want to make appointments for a massage or two, facials, mud baths and more. I am going to enjoy this outing, even if it kills me. I deserve it.

I emailed the hotel with some questions and just as I pushed send, I received an IM. It was from Joel. He said he tried to IM me the other night, but I must have signed off before it reached me.

I IM'd him back, "Yes, I saw someone (I didn't know it was you though), but it was too late. My computer signed me off, and it took a long time to sign back on again and by the time I was back online, you were gone."

"No problemo. How is everything? I'm in Greece now. I travel a lot in my business. That is probably why my second marriage didn't last," he jotted down.

"Well, Greece sounds exciting to me. I have never been abroad. I would love to travel to Europe sometime or anywhere abroad, before I die, LOL," I noted.

"It isn't much fun seeing it solo, so pretty much I stick to my job and why I am here. So, how have you been? Going out to restaurants? Swimming? I am just kidding. I had a great time with you. It rather reminded me of when we were younger growing up in New York. Our families would have dinners together. Remember the fights I had with my brothers, and Rich? It was like one big family. Those were the days," Joel jotted down.

"Sounds like you enjoyed the good old days. Me too. We didn't have to worry about anything in the world. Our parents did it for us," I wrote. "Those were fun times and memorable ones too. I remember a lot. Now I am blushing because of what I am thinking."

"And what is it that you are thinking about?" Joel typed cautiously.

"Just stuff. Embarrassing stuff. Remember when your brother ran around the backyard with only his boots? That was funny. I also remember when your dad had to pick up your aunt at the airport and your brother, my brother, you and I went along for the ride. Do you remember what we did in the backseat? Now remember we were only eight years old at the time. Remember when we used to play Batman and Robin? You were always playing Batman and I was Batgirl or Catwoman? Just good times."

"Yeah, I remember. All too well. Do you remember when I pinned you on the couch? I wanted to kiss you but you didn't want to kiss me?" he added.

"I remember that very well. You were trying to take advantage of a helpless young, inexperienced girl. I couldn't move." I laughed as I typed it. "Well, I don't want to keep you from your work. So I will let you go for now," I added.

"**You can keep me as long as you want**. No problems there," Joel typed in bold letters. "You must have other things to do. I'll talk to you again soon. I should be back to the states soon, and back to California in March sometime. Hopefully we can have dinner on me, not literally though."

"Okay. It's a deal. I won't eat until then," I typed back laughing.

"You're a funny lady Amy. Bye for now," he wrote and signed off.

"Sigh."

Now where was I? Oh yes, arranging for my trip. I decided to go the weekend before Valentine's Day. I set up the resort and made tentative arrangements for the airlines. I called Carol to see if that weekend would work for her. I also emailed a couple of girlfriends from college to see who would be interested in joining us. I don't think that too many of them will be able to come on such short notice. It can't hurt to try. If it just ends up with just Carol and me, that will be okay. Carol and I are the best of friends. Spending a nice, quiet long weekend with her to just eat, chat, and relax will be wonderful for us both. The massages and facials will be great too.

Now I need to do some shopping. I haven't bought a bathing suit or travel clothes in years. I don't even know if I want to be seen wearing a bathing suit. I don't have any nice luggage either.

The end of January is the best time to shop. No one is around. Christmas is over and so are all the returns from Christmas. I need to shop around and buy some luggage. I don't think Cam and I ever bought luggage together in our twenty-five years of marriage. We used what we had and really didn't go anywhere that needed a big piece or two. I am treating myself and buying a matching set. I promise myself I will use them and get them very dirty.

I guess I spoke too soon…

I was walking out to the car with my new luggage dragging behind me. I bought luggage with wheels. What a concept! It was about five o'clock. It is getting close to lock up hour. I was trying to hurry and cross the crosswalk when **HE** drove up behind me and beeped the horn loudly. It scared the crap out of me and I dropped my luggage in a big puddle. Well it got dirty sooner than I had hoped. Joe Elliot saw what had just happened and started laughing behind the wheel of his car. Is he spying on me, or what? Why is it that I run into him all the time? Is God punishing me for something?

After I caught my breath, I grabbed my new, wet, dirty luggage and kept on walking. I ignored him, and walked even faster to hide my humiliation. He followed me down the parking lot aisle and parked a few cars beyond my car, which meant he has to pass me to get into the store. I tried to pretend I didn't see him, but it was somewhat hard not to as he was laughing as he got out of his car. I placed my new luggage in the trunk and closed it. I got in the car and started to back out. He didn't stop so I could get out of my parking spot. I saw him approaching the same puddle that my luggage found and I raced to go through it just as he was crossing the crosswalk. Now who has the last laugh?

I made the airline reservations for Carol and myself, a reservation at 'The Camelback Inn' to stay for a few days, appointments for a massage and facial for both Carol and myself, and a reservation for a car at the Airport when we arrive in Phoenix.

I think things are turning in the right direction now. I am looking forward to having a great long weekend in the Arizona desert with a few good friends. We will sightsee, eat, sleep, eat, drink, get a facial and a massage, eat some more, drink some more, relax, and just enjoy the scenery and each other's company, whether we are talking or just being together quietly.

Carol has always been like a sister to me. The sister I never had. She never had one either, so we have each other. Everything is turning out just fine and dandy.

Chapter 14

Arizona Bound

February is here and my trip is nearing. I told all the kids that I would be gone for the weekend. Of course the first question the girls asked was, "Can we come too?" The second question was, "Who is going to take care of Tom and Jerry?" None of them seem too concerned about me having a good time.

"None of you girls are invited. This is a Mom's trip only. Nathan and Chase have agreed to take care of Tom and Jerry." I repeated myself three times to all three girls on the phone.

Michael didn't ask and probably didn't care. He just said, "See ya."

It turns out that it will be just Carol and me. My other girlfriends from college can't attend because; they have younger kids, or work, or both, not enough notice, or their husbands said 'NO WAY'. I see it as their loss because we are going to have a nice relaxing mini-vacation in the sunny and warm Arizona desert.

I cleaned my luggage after I got home from Macy's. It looks almost new again; rather, it looks a little used, which is better. That way it looks like I am a 'traveling Mama'. I packed about a week before we were leaving. That is how excited I am.

Nathan and Chase came over the day before my flight.

"Hey guys. Here is the spare key and spare garage door opener. Let me remind you how to use the alarm." We marched over to the front door and I told them the code. Now let me show you which lights should be on in which room, and make sure the boys have fresh water each morning, and …"

"We know Amy. We will make sure the house is secure, and the dogs eat. You know us. We love Tom and Jerry too," Chase whispered.

"I can't thank you enough guys."

"Oh yes you can. Just have a great time," as Nathan leaned over and gave me a hug. Chase too. "It will be our pleasure and don't even think about calling."

I gave them each a big hug goodbye and thanked them over, and over again, even when they were walking down the driveway back to their home.

I had a hard time falling asleep, but I managed to find some slumber around two in the morning. Better late than never.

Our flight was leaving around two in the afternoon, so we had to leave for the airport around noon. In addition, we're losing an hour with daylight savings. We took my car to the airport. I didn't want to impose on Nathan and Chase to take us. It is always so hectic at LAX and Nathan and Chase don't do well in chaotic situations.

We managed to find a parking lot after looking for twenty minutes or so, practically back at my house. It's amazing about how full these lots are. Where are the people who own them? Where are they all going?

"We should have just taken a cab." I was a little annoyed but didn't want it to get in the way of our trip.

Once we checked our luggage and our ID's, we started to walk to the gate. It was pretty crowded in the airport and we kept on bumping into people right and left. I had my purse in one hand and a carry-on piece in the other, plus my book (which is mainly for looks because I can't read while I am in a plane or car, or any moving vehicle), and my pills. Yes, my pills. I need valium so I won't freak out during the flight. I am not too keen on the take-off or the descending. I am not fond of the middle either, which leaves absolutely nothing else.

Just a little further to the gate. Of course, it is the last one in the terminal. From the looks of things, this flight was going to be packed. We were looking for a couple of seats while we were waiting for our flight. Both Carol and I were looking everywhere. Finally, I saw two seats and ran over to them. I placed my bag in one and flagged down

Carol with a big wave in the air. Just as I was about to sit in the other seat, **HE** sat down.

"Oh, my God. It can't be." I sadly said looking down at him. My whole body posture just shortened me about two inches.

"Don't tell me you are on this flight?" Joe Elliott said in a low, not so enthusiastic tone.

"Yes I am," I proudly said. "What are you doing here?"

"If you must know, I am going to watch my oldest daughter play in a soccer tournament." Joe announced to the whole group sitting around us. "Why are you going to Arizona?"

"If YOU must know, I am going on a vacation with my friend," I casually pronounced and pointed her out to him in the crowd.

"Well, I knew it couldn't be a man." He snickered to himself. "I hope you aren't sitting anywhere near me. I certainly don't need a headache in the air," Joe said laughing loudly.

"I don't see why it should bother you. You are an 'airhead.'" Now who was smiling?

I paused for a moment to think, "You've got some nerve," I said loud enough to embarrass him in front of a bunch of strangers. I grabbed my carry-on bag, the one I had placed in the chair, and turned quickly. I hit him smack in the shoulder, and hard. I walked away quickly to where Carol was standing and waving. She had found two seats a couple of rows away.

Right before we were about to board, I took two valium (a low dosage of course), with my bottled water. As soon as we were seated (first class baby), I asked for a real drink.

"Some red wine would be nice about now," I said smiling at the flight attendant. Remember that red wine is good for the heart. He said it would be a minute or two.

"That'll be just fine."

It probably isn't the best idea to drink and take valium, but Carol is here and will make sure I'll be okay for the flight. After all, I don't fly very well without any of them (valium, wine, Carol…)!

I drank it quickly so I would be relaxed for take-off, and boy was I relaxed. Between the drink and valium, I was in heaven (not intended to be a pun because we were flying). Carol had a Bloody Mary as well. We finished off the drinks before we even left the gate. I was very thirsty.

"Are we there yet Carol?"

"No, not yet hon, almost, pretty soon. You will be fine." Carol reached over to hold my hand. That's what friends are for.

Once when we're finally airborne and somewhat leveled off, the steward came around asking if we wanted more drinks.

"Of course, we will have a second round. How could I say no? We are on vacation."

Before I received my second drink, I had to excuse myself and use the little 'girls' room. I climbed out of my seat and over Carol. I found my way to the back of the plane and visited the facilities, (I know they have a facility for first class flyers in the front, but I needed to stretch my legs and walk around a bit).

"Oh, much better." I was talking to myself after I closed the door to the bathroom.

On my way back to my seat, the pilot turned on the 'Please be seated' sign.

"We are having some turbulence."

Of course that made me nervous as hell. I hate turbulence. My legs started to feel weak and my heart was pounding hard. I tried quickly to get back to my seat. It seemed so far away, so I saw an empty seat and sat down just for a minute until the plane stopped shaking so much, (or was it me that was shaking?). I took a deep breath, got up, and tried to run back to my seat. We hit an air pocket or two and I smacked a man's hand holding a glass of red wine. The wine spilled all over his white polo sweater.

"I am so sorry," I said to the man. "Let me help you there."

I looked down at the man with the red stain on his white sweater. It was Joe Elliott. I changed my tune and couldn't be in a better mood now.

"No I'm not sorry," and laughed all the way back to my seat. I sat there chuckling to myself. The rest of the trip went smoothly. Red wine is really good for the heart!

"Welcome to Phoenix folks," I heard on the intercom from the pilot. He told us the weather was perfect and to have a safe trip wherever our final destination will be today. Isn't that sweet? He told us to have a nice trip.

My being a little tipsy, Carol had to drive the rental to the Camelback Inn. It is so beautiful with the palm trees, golf course, mountains, cactus and most important, the SPA. We walked around the resort for quite some time, (I needed to get my legs back, if you know what I mean).

Dinnertime at a nearby restaurant was on the agenda tonight. There is an old, quaint, Spanish-style, house that is now a restaurant within walking distance to the resort. We sat outside near the fireplace, and there were some portable heaters all around to keep everyone warm. I ordered the beef stroganoff. It is to die for. We ordered some martinis before our meal. I had a choco-martini (chocolate hmm), while Carol had a pomegranate martini. Scrumptious!

The weather is a bit chilly, but the ambiance of the restaurant made up for it. There's quite a crowd, mainly couples, especially since Valentine's Day isn't far off the calendar. A woman is selling red and pink single roses from a basket on the other side of the restaurant. They smell so good I could eat one, if it were made of chocolate.

Carol and I enjoyed our quiet dinner, just the two of us. We hardly, or rather ever, get to spend time with just us. Moving on to desserts, Carol and I looked at the menu again.

"I can't decide. Everything looks delish. What do you think Carol?"

When I put my menu down, the 'rose' lady put a pink rose in front of me.

"No thank you. Not right now," and smiled at her nicely.

"It is already paid for miss."

"What? By whom? I don't know anyone here," as I looked around. Carol's eyebrows lifted as she covered her mouth.

The 'rose' lady pointed to a dark-haired (actually pepper), man wearing a light gray sweater and dark gray pants. He was looking right at me. I smiled.

"I'll be right back Carol. Order me a dessert please. Anything with chocolate will be perfect."

Leisurely walking over to the gentleman, who was sitting alone, I made myself at home by sitting down across from him. He was looking at the menu.

"Joel, what are you doing here? Are you following me?" I laughed a flirty laugh.

"I just happen to be here in town on business, came to dinner, and saw you. Really. I said once before Amy, I would know you anywhere. What are you doing here?"

"My friend, Carol, and I are here for a mini-vacation." I pointed to Carol and she waved back. "We just arrived this afternoon and we are staying at the Camelback Inn. What about you? What are your plans?" I leaned forward to show him I was more than interested.

Just as I was waiting for an answer, a young woman was standing behind me. She said, "Excuse me Mam, but you are sitting in my seat."

Embarrassed and mortified, I jumped up out of the seat. I stumbled on my shoes, nothing unusual for me.

"I'm so sorry. I didn't know you were on a date, Joel," as I looked right into his eyes. "Forgive me please. Thanks for the rose." I nodded to the young woman, and then marched away as fast as I could without further embarrassment. I certainly wasn't smiling now.

"Who is that?" Carol looked back and forth from me to the table across the way.

"That is Joel. Remember, I have told you about him millions of times. He was my neighbor in New York growing up. He was visiting LA right before Christmas," I explained in a low mono-toned voice. "I'll explain everything after we leave, which is right now."

I signaled the waitress, with my hand waving frantically in the air, so I could pay the bill. I could have put out a candle twenty yards away with the way I was thrashing my hand.

"What about dessert? I already ordered," Carol was confused.

"We will have it wrapped up and take it with us, okay?" I said in a louder voice now.

I didn't check the bill, just threw some cash onto the table, and made like a Tazmanian devil. However, I did grab the dessert, plate and all.

I did leave the pink rose.

Carol and I returned to our room quietly. I practically threw the desserts on the little coffee table by the window looking out at the beautiful mountains.

"Do you want to go in the Jacuzzi for a dip? I need to do something, anything right now."

"No hon. I think you need some 'alone' time right now. You go ahead. I am going to get in my pj's, check in with Larry and the kids, and turn on the TV."

I shimmied into my constricting swimsuit and a robe, and sat in the Jacuzzi all by myself. I did take the robe off before I got in the water. Thank goodness, no one else was around to see me in my suit (No one should have to witness that but me).

I had some thinking to do. I don't know why I was upset. I shouldn't be. Joel isn't my boyfriend. WE only went out once, and what a date that was. We are friends, if we are still friends, and he can go out with whomever he pleases, even if she is young enough to be his daughter. Was I upset because I saw him on a date, or because she was young, or because he didn't call me when he returned to the states? Probably all three. Everyone knows bad luck comes in threes.

I tried not to think about it while I was relaxing in the nice, warm, bubbly, hot water. I did sit there too long because I began to look like a raisin in twenty minutes. I got out, put my robe back on, and walked slowly back to our room. I was relaxed now and felt a whole lot better than an hour ago.

Carol was watching TV. She turned the TV sound way down.

"So, are you ready to talk now?" She sounded so concerned.

"I was upset and probably had no right to be, but I just needed some thinking time alone. Now I feel a little better. I have come to my senses knowing that we aren't "dating" or "going out" and, I have no right to tell Joel who and who not to go out with, right?"

"That is correct. I understand completely. Amy, you shouldn't be upset or angry. He is just a friend. If it were anything else, he would have let you know by now. Do you want it to be more than just friends?"

"I don't know. He lives so far away and maybe it is too soon to be involved with someone just yet. You know, Cameron hasn't even been gone a year yet. I don't know. I just don't know what to think anymore."

We talked for a couple of hours while watching a movie, and indulging into our desserts.

~

No matter whatever happens, never leave a chocolate dessert standing alone.

Chapter 15

Two Cashew Chickens Please

The next morning looked breathtaking out here in the desert. I opened the curtains to see the vibrant mountains in front of me. It was such a beautiful site to see. It was so peaceful, calm, and serene. I felt like I could reach out and touch them. By golly gee, I probably could if I opened the front door. The air was a cool crisp with a slight wind coming from the west, (like I know which way that is right now). I certainly don't see this every day. Carol and I had breakfast brought to the room, something we never get at home, not even on Mother's Day. It was fun to be able to eat in our pajamas, outside on our private patio, overlooking the picturesque mountains.

We had a schedule to keep today. In the morning, Carol and I are having Swedish massages. Then we will take it easy by the pool, or in the Jacuzzi, or both. Lunch at the Spa, then a nap, while in the late afternoon we have facials scheduled. How relaxing does that sound? It will be so soothing and unwinding. Just what we both need, want. We won't have to talk or make chitchat. It will be a comforting and tranquil day at the Spa!

"Ready to roll Carol?"

"I am indeed, shall we?" as she opened the door leading the way to paradise for the day.

We sauntered over to the Spa and signed in. We took a tour of the facilities. Soothing low tone music played in the ceilings and walls, and the lights were dim everywhere, behind some pretty shades of peach and beiges all around. It looked so inviting and peaceful. The music was entrancing and calming. A bathrobe and slippers were waiting for each of us. We could spend the entire day here doing absolutely nothing. That sounds too good to be true. They will even feed you when you are hungry. Now this is my kind of heaven. No one ever 'waits' on me at home.

My massage was unconditionally the best massage I have ever had (maybe even better than sex, but who remembers). I floated over to the pool area. Carol floated over to me when she was finished. She looked drunk. Her hair was a total mess. She walked funny and had a different smile on her face than usual. She plopped down in the lounge chair next to me and just sighed.

It seemed like hours by the time we had a leisurely lunch outside by the pool, along with some mango daiquiris on the side. All I know is that they will find us for our next appointment.

We strolled inside to the sauna for a little taste of the desert heat. We managed to stay in there for about ten minutes before Carol screamed, "It's like a desert in there. How can anyone stand to live in that all year long?"

"People do it every day and have been for thousands of years. Remember our ancestors Carol, and how they walked through the desert for forty days and forty nights, so they say."

We grabbed some towels and headed for the Jacuzzi. The water felt wonderful. It was uplifting and I felt light as a feather, considering where I was. I guess the Moon would be another option for that as well. The music continued throughout the facility and was soft and peaceful, like moving in slow motion. I never want to leave.

I heard an angel call my name. It was time for my facial. I grabbed my towel and robe. A nice young woman showed me to my room. Another hour of pampering, sigh.

I went back into the quiet room after my facial to relax on a lounge chair, waiting just for me. Carol was already in there. She said she wasn't feeling so well and just wanted to lie down and relax, (maybe the daiquiris got to her head). I brought her some lemon water. She drank the whole cup right away.

"Slow down there. Sip it slowly." I brought her another.

"I'll be fine in a little bit. Don't worry about me. Go relax on a lounge. I am okay."

It was almost six o'clock when I awoke from yet another needed nap. I looked around and didn't see Carol. She must have gone back to the room. When I reached the room and opened the door, Carol was lying on the bed with her robe still on.

"Carol, how do you feel? Do you need something, water, crackers, a drink, medicine, what?"

"No thanks hon. I think I am coming down with a cold. Who knows?" As she waved her hands in the air-conditioned room, I noticed it was freezing.

"Carol, its so cold in here. Why is the air on so cold?"

"What are you talking about? I am hot as hell. It's almost as bad as being in that sauna earlier. I really don't know how people can live here." She clutched her robe tighter to her body.

I went over and turned the air off, well not off, but to a comfortable zone for both of us.

"We are supposed to have dinner downtown tonight. Do you want me to order in from the hotel instead?" She didn't answer me.

"Carol, do you want me to get you something to eat, like some dry toast maybe, or tea?"

I felt awful right now. Carol didn't feel well and I didn't know how to help her. Not to be selfish or anything, but it was vacation time! I didn't want her to get sick now. Later, maybe, after we get home. Then at least I could make her some matzo ball soup.

"Actually there is something you can do for me that would make me feel a whole lot better. Go get dressed up, and go out to dinner without me tonight."

"What? How could I go without you? You're my friend, you aren't feeling well, and I am not going to leave you here alone while you are sick, (or go out by myself)."

"Okay, how about you get dressed, go to one of the restaurants we talked about, and bring back some dinner? Would that make YOU feel better?"

"Well, a little bit better. What do you think you'll be able to eat? How about some soup? Godiva is always good no matter how you feel," trying to cheer her up. Carol did smile.

"How about you call me on the cell when you get to a restaurant you like, and let me know what's on the menu?" Carol's eyes lit up with the suggestion.

"That's a great idea. That's what I'll do." I turned to the bathroom to freshen up and get dressed. I put some clothes on, nothing too showy of course. Just my basic black, (I always look good wearing black). I put on a little makeup. I don't want to look dead walking around anywhere, not even in our hotel room.

Right before I left, I checked on Carol. She had dozed off. I didn't want to disturb her so I jotted down the time I left, put the phone number in my cell, and closed the door ever so quietly. Just as I was turning around, a big shadow appeared right behind me. I jumped ten feet in the air and screamed.

"Aaaaaaaah!"

"Hold on there M'Lady. I am not here to hurt you," a man said in a low voice, as he took a couple of steps closer to me.

"You scared the hell out of me. How did you find me?"

I was shaking all over, especially my legs. Didn't I mention that my legs get weak when I am scared? They felt like jello right now.

"I need to sit down for a minute." I sat down on a bench about twenty feet from my room.

Joel laughed.

"It was easy to find you. You told me at the restaurant that you were staying here. I am in the hotel business, you know. I called last night, but, uh, you weren't in your room. So I thought I would drop by now instead and see if you and Carol would be interested in having dinner with me tonight. Are you headed somewhere in particular M' lady?" he queried.

"You caught me off guard. I am still shaking. Just a sec." I was trying not to look at him, as I sat there holding my heart in my stomach (how did he know Carol's name?).

"You left so abruptly last night that you didn't give me a chance to introduce you to one of my new assistants. Her name is Kelly. She isn't my girlfriend, and she wasn't a date. It was more of a dinner meeting than anything else really," Joel explained.

I just sat there and didn't say a word. I didn't know what to say or what to do. I was still trying to get over my initial shock of him sneaking up behind and scaring the living daylights out of me.

"I came over to pick you and Carol up for dinner tonight. You must be hungry," tilting his head and eyebrows up.

"Well, a little. Carol isn't feeling well. She may be catching a cold, and I told her I would be right back with something for her to eat."

"How about this, now just listen. I'll talk to a manager at the hotel, call room service, make up a nice simple dinner with hot tea and honey included, and send it down to your room for Carol. Then I'll take you out for a nice dinner in town on me, and not literally. Then we can walk around and do whatever you women like to do? What do you think Amy?" He had the face of a little boy ready to go to an amusement park. How could I say no to that punim.

I did blush. "I guess that sounds fine. I was going to try and let Carol rest, while I walk around before ordering some take-out. However, this sounds a little better," I nonchalantly said. It sounded a lot better. What am I thinking? Poor Carol doesn't feel well and I am reaping the benefits of it.

"Great. Let's head over to the hotel. You can sit and be comfortable in the lobby while I take care of Carol's dinner. Then we'll be on our way."

I shook my head in agreement. We quietly walked over and I sat down for maybe five minutes before Joel was ready to go.

"Our limo is waiting M'lady," he so humbly announced as he bowed down in front of me.

I had to smile, and blush some more. He extended his right arm and I gladly took it. Don't get me wrong, I was still embarrassed about dinner the night before. At this point in my life, it just doesn't matter. Embarrass away!

The mild-mannered limo driver took us to one of my favorite places to eat. Chinese, what else? We drove right up to the front door of ***PF Changs***. Apparently, Joel must have an 'in' at restaurants too. Instead of having to wait, they led us to a quiet table in the back corner. There was a single baby pink rose lying on the table.

"What the ..." I turned around with my mouth hanging wide open.

"I took a chance." He smiled from ear to ear. He had surprised me again. I just love surprises.

"I had this planned, and was hoping you would agree to go out with me tonight. Sit please. I spoke with Carol last night, when you went out for a walk," (That explains how he knew her name). "She is like a mother hen when it comes to you," he laughed. "She asked me a million questions: about my intentions; what I do for a living; and more. She is a funny lady and cares about you." There was a pause. His eyes met mine.

"So do I." He leaned over and gave me a soft kiss on the cheek.

I was speechless, for a change. I was actually 'stuck in a corner," How ironic is that?

"How sweet. I don't know what to say. First I embarrass you in a restaurant in California, then in my home, and then in another restaurant, here in Arizona. What's a girl to do?" I felt a hot flash starting, but its so dark in the restaurant, he won't be able to tell.

"You can work your way to the East Coast," he said with a laugh. "I think it is charming in a quirky sort of way. I actually think it means you like me."

"Oh, maybe. I'm just not used to dating, men, or going out. It's different for me. I was married for over twenty-five years, and now I feel lost. It's hard to explain."

I completely forgot to thank him for the lovely rose. I went on and on about me, myself and I.

"And thank you for the rose. I love pink roses." I held it close to me so I could smell its aroma.

"You are most welcome," as Joel bent down as if he were bowing to me. "I will always remember that you love pink roses. Ready for dinner?"

"I love Cashew Chicken." We both said in unison and then laughed. We decided to have two orders.

We had a very amusing dinner, even though I could hardly eat a thing. I talked, and talked instead of eating. I usually do that when I am nervous.

"Do you remember when we were little my father would read the tea leaves at the bottom of our cups? He would also make up a story with the fortune cookie and we actually believed it."

"As a matter of fact I do now that you mention it." Joel laughed. "I remember one time when I was fighting with my brother before going out to eat with your family. I can't remember what we were fighting about, probably nothing as usual. At the dinner table your father read the leaves and told me that someday I will get in deep trouble if I kept on antagonizing people. I didn't pick on my brother much after that, at least not until I was bigger than him." We both laughed now.

"Do you remember reading the fortune first before eating the cookie? Your dad said it was bad luck and the fortune wouldn't come true." Joel was sitting back in the chair enjoying our conversation. So was I.

"Yeah, I remember that too. I still eat the cookie first. At least that is what I would like to believe. I never want to be jinxed."

Two seconds later, the fortune cookies arrived on a small white shiny plate. We laughed and stared at the cookies. We each took one, opened the wrapper and ate the cookie before reading the fortunes aloud.

"Ladies first."

"**YOU WILL SOON CREATE A FAVORABLE IMPRESSION ON SOMEONE**." We laughed again. I wonder what that means?

It was Joel's turn.

"FROM THE FLOORS OF THE OCEAN TO THE WAVES OF THE TIDE, A VACATION AWAITS YOU FAR AND WIDE." He just sat there and read it again.

"I wonder what that means? Too bad your dad isn't here to interpret for us." I smiled thinking of my father. "Those days were fun, weren't they?" I shook my head in agreement.

After dinner, we strolled around in the early evening of a winter night in Arizona. I felt a little chill and shivered. Without saying a word, Joel took his black leather jacket and placed it on my shoulders.

"Thanks."

He was wearing a white button down shirt with a gray and white argyle sweater to keep him warm while we were strolling.

Arizona has so many unique shops. It was fun to just walk and talk. I started to feel more comfortable as time went on. Just walking around and reminiscing about the old days is just what I needed. I think he enjoyed it as well. There are times when I wish we could go back and 'play' the memories over, and over again. But we all must move on.

Joel made a quick call and the shiny black limo seemed to appear in front of us in no time at all.

"At your service, M'lady." I smiled and gladly got in, out of the cool winter air of the desert.

The drive back to the Camelback Inn was quiet. "Would you like to stop in for a 'nightcap' before I take you back to your room?"

"I guess just one drink won't hurt me. Do you have red wine, because red wine is good for the heart you know? I promise I will only have one glass, because we know what happens when I drink at least two."

We laughed. "You may have however many drinks you desire."

Then my thought was, so he could have his way with me? So I wouldn't remember what happened? Because I wasn't driving? (a logical thought). Thank goodness all of these thoughts are all in my head, and not 'out there.'

We arrived in front of his suite. He helped me out. Coincidentally he was staying at the Camelback Inn as well, or he moved over there just for tonight, (Is that another thought I just had?). I'm not sure. Nevertheless, I don't mind. We slowly walked to the double doors that led to the suite. Before Joel opened it, he turned to me, tilted my head upwards and kissed me softly on the lips. It wasn't red wine or chocolate, but it was good and I wouldn't mind seconds or even thirds!

The door opened. It was like walking into a dream. The suite was lovely. Music was playing in the background, vanilla scented candles are lit everywhere, a captivating fire in the fireplace, a silver platter of chocolate covered strawberries, a bottle of champagne chilling, and last but not least, a dozen pink roses in a beautiful crystal vase. Now this has to be heaven, and I don't think I ever want to leave.

"Oh My God. This is …," I was speechless, again. He took the black leather jacket off my shoulders and laid it down on a chair.

"This is …" My eyes started to swell with water. I didn't want to cry. I felt choked up. Did he do this just for me? Why?

I turned to him suddenly, "Are you expecting something unusual in return?" I felt like I woke up out of my dream.

"I just wanted to do something special for you, especially after last night's scene." He came closer to me. "Would you like a glass of champagne? It isn't red wine, but a close second."

I took the glass, a sip, and walked around the suite. It was spectacular. The bathroom alone was as big as my living room. The colors were warm and inviting with peaches and beiges all around, just like the Spa environment. What a cool place.

When I came back into the living room area, there he was, sitting on a couch (waiting for me?).

"Come and sit for awhile. Have a chocolate covered strawberry. I ordered especially for you. I know how much you love chocolate."

"You did all this for me? How did you know I would go out with you tonight? What makes you so sure of yourself?"

"I took a chance. We go back Amy, over forty years. How many people can say that? As I said before, you haven't changed a bit. I was stupid back then, and just a kid. I have matured over the years, and I know what I want. I loved you then, and I love you now. In fact, I never stopped loving you. I just never knew how to keep you near me. We were so young back then. When we saw each other in California, I knew I had to get you back into my life again. "

Joel inched closer to me. I didn't expect a confession like this or any confession at all.

"It must be the champagne talking. You don't mean it." I was puzzled right now. "This is only the 'second' date we have had in decades. Of course, the first date lasted overnight and all, and I ruined your clothes, and there I go again, babbling on."

"I do mean it. I have always loved you, since we were kids. I knew it back then, and when I saw you again in California, it only proved it to me. I have always cared for you Amy. I don't want to push you into a relationship. I will take a step back if you want me to." He relaxed and sat back on the couch.

I drank the whole glass of champagne and stuck my glass out for a refill, which he gladly did.

"Don't step back." He stood up and helped me stand up, put his warm, strong arms around me and kissed me ever so gently, not once, not twice, but until I was breathless.

"Now what do we do?"

"Whatever you want M' lady," he whispered in my ear and caressed it with passion until I melted to the floor. He took my hand and walked me over towards the bed (was I too heavy to be carried?). He held me tight, kissed me, and then kissed my neck. I closed my eyes and I knew this had to be heaven.

Chapter 16

Cloudy skies ahead

Saturday morning could have been better, but doubtful. The sun was shining, the birds were singing, and the temperature outside at The Camelback Inn was perfect. I had a happy face on all night, and all morning. I think I slept with a happy face, if that is possible. Carol sat up in bed and stared at me for a long time. She was feeling fine now, and smiling as if she knew something, but wasn't going to reveal a thing. She wouldn't stop grinning.

"What is wrong with you?" I was getting out of bed and trying not to look so jovial.

"You know." She was smiling, teeth showing from ear to ear, and still staring at me with those great big blues. "So, are you going to tell me or not?"

"Tell you what or not?" As if I didn't know.

"You know very well what I am talking about Amy Kayden," Carol's eyebrows were twitching up and down a few times with the biggest grin on her face.

"Don't you dare leave out any little detail. I want to hear everything from the beginning all the way till you just woke up this morning, and took a breath," She sat up in bed as if she were a child, getting ready to hear a Christmas story, (kind of funny for two Jewish girls from New York).

"CAROL, was this all set up?" I was shocked, really I was.

"Sort of, not really, but maybe, some of it," she snickered. "Hey, I'm starving to death. Let's go have breakfast and you can tell me all about your date last night."

"You did know, and you helped. No wonder Joel knew your name before I told him. The two of you were in cahoots, were you not, Carol?" Now my eyebrows were twitching up and down.

Carol giggled like a small child, jumped out of bed towards the bathroom, grabbed her toothbrush, laughed a little, and then started to brush her teeth. I followed her in there and we both brushed away at the same time, and were smiling and laughing with each other, as if we were back in camp and placed our counselor's bra up the flagpole.

We dressed quickly and set off for the dining room for breakfast. The view on the terrace is so picturesque. We sat at a table overlooking the desert surrounding us. We were reading the menu when a pair of 'man hands' covered my eyes.

"Guess who?" Joel gave me a quick morning hug and walked over to Carol.

"Good morning. I'm Joel, you must be Carol." She smiled as they shook hands. "May I join the most beautiful women in town for breakfast?"

Before I could say a word, Carol spoke up.

"Of course you may. It's nice to finally meet you in person." Carol's eyes lit up as if she was lighting up the sky for the sunniest day in the desert. "Hey, just the most beautiful in town? What happened to the most beautiful in the world, or universe?"

As Joel sat down, he uttered, "Of course. How foolish of me. May I sit down with the most beautiful women in the Universe?"

I sat there as quiet as a mouse. Not moving, just staring at the two of them. I wasn't sure what to say to either of them. Should I be mad at them both for the scheme they pulled off, or thank them? Maybe I was still on cloud nine and didn't care.

We had a charming, delightful breakfast together. Carol enjoyed it immensely. Just watching her, watch me, was a sight to see. It was like a mother hen watching her child at play. "Ladies, I hate to eat and run but I must depart. My plane won't wait for me, but I hope you do," as he kissed my hand and his eyes made me melt right into my chair.

Poof, he was gone.

Carol and I sat at the table staring at each other for the longest time before I posed a question.

"More Coffee?" Certainly not the typical question one would ask after a scene like this.

"Pour on, as long as I hear every detail, right down to "the last drop." She grinned, and held her cup next to the coffee pot. I told her the whole story, well maybe not everything. I think we sat there for an hour or so before realizing that we needed to hit the road. Today's agenda was traveling up to Sedona to see red rock country.

൴

Sedona is a beautiful, tranquil, calm, almost too quiet, place to visit. I don't think I would ever want to live there though. I think the red rocks would get to me after awhile. Just thinking about them falling down gives me the 'quakes.' Plus, there are too many curves in the road, uphill, downhill, this way and that. It was a sight to see and worth the two hour drive north through the desert.

On the way back, we stopped at the outlet stores to do what every woman loves to do, **SHOP UNTIL YOU DROP.** Carol and I bought so much that we had to buy a piece of luggage just so we would be able to get it back home on the plane. Of course, there was a chocolate store, and of course, I had to buy some. I knew that wasn't going in the luggage. Besides, how else would I get by today?

Chocolate everyday keeps Amy a happy girl!

൴

Nighttime and all is well in the Valley of the Sun. We were exhausted from our adventurous day up north. We took a dip in the Jacuzzi and then headed out to dinner. Every restaurant had a long waiting list, but we weren't in a hurry so we, what else, shopped around while waiting for our reservation.

~

Let me tell you, Sunday morning came too early for me. We should have booked a late afternoon flight.

"Carol, get up and start packing."

"What? Why don't we try and get a later flight?"

"It's probably a pain in the neck to figure it out."

She gave me a look. You know the look of a child in a candy store begging for anything. I walked over to the concierge and asked them if they could help us out. As soon as I told him my name, he literally jumped. I didn't understand why until later. He said he would send an updated itinerary to the room when it is all finished. By the time I got back to the room, the concierge had already called and left a message saying everything is taken care of and we will be on the 6:30 PM flight back to L.A. (Now don't forget that this time of year Arizona is one hour ahead of California. This means that we will be getting in LA pretty much the time we leave Arizona. Does that make sense or what?).

"That was quick. Wow! I don't know who you have to know in this town to get things done, or maybe I still have what it takes." I doubt the latter though.

"I know who you know," Carol snickered to herself.

Carol and I relaxed by the pool for a few hours before having to go back to the room to pack for real this time. The weather was perfect. There wasn't a cloud in the sky, at least not until we got to the airport, where there were cloudy skies ahead towards California…

~

I returned the car to the rental agency while Carol checked in our bags and we met up at the gate. There was a crowd returning to L.A. this late on Sunday. They started to board early. We were the first ones onboard. How fun!

Just before we were about to leave the gate for take-off, the pilot announced that we had to wait for a late passenger. He was on his way to the gate.

"Oh great," I was disgusted. I thought we were going to slide in early and get home without any snags. "Can't people get here on time?"

Apparently, this passenger was in a wheelchair. I saw the chair and the steward was having a hard time wheeling it onboard. It took the steward a good ten minutes to figure how to get the chair onboard. There was a full cast on the left leg of the person sitting in the chair. That was all I saw. Then they had to pick the person up and help him into the first seat of first class. They placed him in first class, probably out of convenience. What a nuisance for everyone waiting on him. Now we'll be late and probably have to wait in the air before we can land when we get to L.A. I hate that. I slapped through the pages of the onboard airline magazine. I don't even know what I was looking at.

Once airborne, the pilot turned off the seatbelt sign, and people started to get up and walk around. It wasn't as crowded as I thought. I was in a better mood now, and I even forgot to take my valium. I must be feeling good. I was thinking about *him*. I felt like I was in heaven, well, closer then most people right now, literally.

I wanted to see the person who held us up. I casually stood up. Carol and I were seated a couple of rows behind the "handicapped" man, so I couldn't see his face at any angle. I walked towards the front of the plane to ask the steward for a Tylenol. I didn't have a headache but I had to make up something to see the person who put my life on hold. Sometimes I can be nosy… okay, all the time.

As the steward was looking in the medicine bag, I turned around to see who was sitting in the front row with a huge cast on his leg. It was Joe Elliot. I had to laugh under my breath. Oh, what the heck, I laughed loudly. He looked up at me and shook his head in embarrassment. I have never seen anyone turn such a shade of red before in my life.

"So, you think this is funny, do you Ms. Kayden?" he was humiliated. He face turned the darkest red I have ever seen. He just looked down in his lap at the magazine the steward handed him earlier. Little did he realize that it was upside down, which made this whole situation so amusing, (for me at least).

"So sorry for laughing, so loudly, but YES, I do think this is humorous. You held us up you know. I'm sure others were upset about that. But, this is good, real good," as I continued to laugh my head off.

"What the hell happened to you and how did we get on the same flight again?"

"I kinda got in a fight," He looked around as he whispered.

"What? I didn't quite hear you correctly. Could you repeat that?" I shook my head side to side knowing very well what he said the first time.

"I was in a fight with a dad from the other team. His kid knocked my kid over. I ran out there to yell, then he ran out there, then we pushed a little and that led to this," he explained in a low tone voice as quietly as he could.

"I see. You were acting like a child. That's a great impression you left on your daughter, don't you think? Well, I guess you learned a lesson then, huh?"

"And what lesson is that Ms. Kayden?" said in a sarcastic tone.

"Well, you should know," I hesitated. I really didn't know, but thought someone should. I also thought he would tell me what the great lesson is, but he didn't. He must be in a real bad mood right now. I took the Tylenol from the steward, thanked him, and quickly went back to my seat.

Now I really did have a headache. The Tylenol came in handy. I decided I might as well take a valium too. I can see the rest of the trip is going to be cloudy and bumpy, all the back to L.A.

No doubt about it, it was.

Chapter 17

Alone Again

The plane made it safely (with a few bumps in between), back on the ground in California. I can't see the stars in the sky, but when can you in L.A.? It's cold and damp outside. It looks like it may have rained while we were gone.

Carol and I made it home before eight in the evening. The boys went nuts when they heard the garage door go up. They started howling and jumping on the door as they practically knocked me over when I walked in. I sat on the floor with them for a little bit before I checked out the rest of the house.

Joel. Why is my mind wandering towards him?

I could tell Nathan and Chase were in my home. The place was immaculate. They turned on the outside lights and left a few lights on inside the house as well. The house smells great, like someone else was cooking in my kitchen. There was a note left by the phone, and the red blinker going nuts ready for me to retrieve my messages.

Nathan wrote that the boys behaved. They went for walks and ate well (I am sure they ate very well. By looking at Chase would tell you that). They left me some stew in a Tupperware bowl to heat up tonight.

"They are so sweet," talking to Tom and Jerry. "Did you boys have fun with them while I was gone?" I didn't really expect an answer, just some slobbery kisses, which I did get.

I was exhausted and wanted to take a bath. I decided to jump in the tub with some bubbles, soft music, candles burning, and a glass of red wine. I wanted the vacation to last one more night. I relaxed and was unwinding when the phone rang. I let it ring. Peace and quiet is what I wanted right now, (and Joel). The machine picked up, but I couldn't hear the message from my bathroom. I would have to have supersonic ears to do that. We all know that Moms have selective hearing, so the message will just have to wait.

Thirty minutes later, I was relaxed, not from the wine, but from my bathtub extravaganza. The three of us went into the kitchen to listen to the phone messages and have some dinner. I know the boys already ate, but what the heck; they could eat again, no harm in eating dinner twice.

I heated up the stew, and made some hot cocoa too. Then I pushed the message button to listen. All my girls had called and said they hoped I had a great time. Next time they would like the option of coming along.

"Funny how they all said the same thing, with three different phone messages, huh boys." Michael called to say 'hey'. David called to say that ***maybe*** he's ready to go out.

"Not with me. He sounded too needy, don't you think boys?" Tom and Jerry wagged their tails as if their tails were the second hand of a clock ticking away.

My Mom's neighbor called. She was talking in a hurry and didn't seem to make any sense. She said something about my Mom and Dad. It is much too late to call now. It's almost midnight back east. I started pacing up and down and around the island.

"I'll call Rich. I don't care what time it is in their house."

It rang several times before the answering machine was about to start. Then Sara picked up the phone.

"Hello," she sounded like I woke her up from her beauty sleep, which we all know she desperately needs.

"Sara? Where's Rich?" waiting impatiently for an answer.

"Who is this?" (As if she didn't know).

"It's me, Amy, who else would be calling in the middle of the night asking for Rich, besides Mom or Dad?" I said it with disgust in my voice. How could she not know it was me?

"Oh. He's with them somewhere."

"Where?" I demanded to know.

"The hospital I think."

"What hospital and why?"

"I don't know. Call Rich's cell phone," and then she hung up.

What a B-I-T-C-H, (Sorry, I just can't say the word). I can't believe that she doesn't know where or why or with whom or anything. I can't believe she is asleep while Rich is out there with my parents. Some compassion she has. Why did he ever marry her to begin with, none of us will ever know.

It was now after midnight back there when I dialed. It rang and rang. Rich didn't answer so I left a message.

"Rich. It's Amy. Call me as soon as you get this message no matter what time it is and let me know what is going on with Mom and Dad." I am a nervous wreck and don't know what to do, or who to call or anything. HELP!

My relaxing mood is now definitely gone. My stew is getting cold. I'm frantic. I don't want to alarm the kids, so I won't call any of them. None of them can do anything. I don't want to call Carol now. I'm sure she has her hands full at home. Nathan and Chase are dears but I don't want to bother them now. They have already done enough for me, especially taking care of my babies.

"Cam, where are you? I need you now. I don't know what to do."

I kept on pacing around the island in the kitchen. I was trying to think, as I walked faster and faster. I need to sit for a moment since I am making myself dizzy going in circles. Once I sat down my legs started to shake and my mind's going in a million directions.

"Why isn't Rich calling me back?" I was talking to myself. "I could call Joel. Now that's a thought." I started to dial his number.

"No, I can't bother him. I don't want him to think I **need** him, right boys?"

Joel. Stop that. Stop thinking about him.

It's late. Much too late to call him, besides, how could he help? He couldn't. I started to pace faster and faster again, (I guess I won't need to take my walk in the neighborhood in the morning).

"He could call all the hospitals in the city," Tom and Jerry perked their ears up while lying down on the kitchen tile. "Oh, who am I kidding? There are too many to call. I can't expect him to figure that out. We aren't really dating or anything. What are we?"

I stopped pacing and tried to think about what our relationship really is right now. Without even thinking, I started pacing again, thinking about my parents. I was getting dizzy again. I changed my 'flight plan' and made a track into the hallway and down towards the bedrooms to make my route longer, and more straightforward.

When I reached the kitchen for the fiftieth time, I put on a pot of coffee. I figured this is going to be a long night. By the time the coffee was ready, the phone was still silent. I was hoping if I stared at it long enough it would ring. It never did, at least not until three in the morning, my time. Unbelievably, I paced for hours. I didn't realize how late it was until the phone rang, finally. It was Rich.

"What is going on over there? Why didn't you call me back as soon as you got my message? Why doesn't Sara know where you are? Do you know what you put me through these last few hours? Are you going to answer any of my questions?" I just yelled at Rich, while crying at the same time.

He was silent for a moment, trying to catch his breath and everything I just threw at him.

"Amy, I'm sorry I didn't call sooner but the cell phones don't work inside very well. I thought I had left a message, but I guess it didn't get through. I didn't know you called until a few minutes ago when I stepped outside. Sara knew where I was and she was supposed to have called you to let you know what was happening. I am so sorry she didn't call you earlier tonight."

"Tonight? What do you mean earlier tonight? It is night time," I was puzzled now and needed to know everything in sequence.

"Amy, take a deep breath and sit down, please. I have bad news. Mom and Dad are gone." The phone went silent for the longest time. It seemed like an eternity. I waited for Rich to explain what the hell he was talking about.

I sat down but couldn't breathe. I tried but nothing came out. I felt like I was in a dream where you can't move or talk, which is actually a nightmare and you have no control over anything.

"What do you mean 'gone'?" I barely got the words out, while feeling queasy.

"Mom and Dad have left this world together," Rich said in a low monotone voice as if he was talking to his children, which he has none.

"I am not a child or a retard. You mean they are dead. Why can't you tell me that? Why? What happened?" I had huge tears started rolling down my cheeks and into my coffee mug.

"They died in their sleep. Mom must have been cooking, baking, or something and left the gas on the stove. There must have been a leak. One of the neighbors thought she smelled something funny from their place and called the fire department. They came over, and had to knock the door down. You know how Mom felt about safety, and having seven locks on the door," (he gave a nervous chuckle). "The ambulance rushed them both to the hospital but couldn't revive either one of them, honey," Rich explained. "They're gone."

There was silence again. I couldn't speak. I felt sick and dizzy.

I can only picture Mom and Dad in my mind, lying on the bed next to each other, peacefully. Now they are gone and they left me alone.

All alone.

Chapter 18

The Sky's the Limit

"Ladies and Gentlemen, I hope you are enjoying the scenic view over our beautiful Rocky Mountains. It seems like you could reach out your window and touch the pristine white snow peaks, but refrain from doing so. Keep your hands and feet inside the cabin at all times. I don't want to have to make any heroic rescues today. We are experiencing a little turbulence over the Rocky Mountains. We still plan to arrive in New York as scheduled. Enjoy the rest of the flight," announced the pilot.

My brain started to wander again about New York, my parents, Rich, (*and Joel*). Stop.

I'm not even halfway to New York and I have had a valium or two, and a drink or two as well. Who's counting. I don't need any more commotion, or motion, in my life right now. Carol is taking care of my boys and the house. The kids know about their grandparents, and I'm on my way.

It's midmorning, afternoon, or something somewhere in the United States and I haven't slept since the night before last, back in Phoenix, Arizona. I packed quickly and ran out on the first flight I could get to New York.

This all seems like a dream, a blur to me. Maybe I'm having a nightmare and I'll wake up soon. WAKE UP. Wake up already. Am I still in Phoenix with Joel? Stop thinking about him.

I can't sleep. I can't eat. I can't think. Is this what it's like to be totally dependent on yourself? I don't know how people do it. How do they survive? How do you move on? How do you learn to deal with what God has dealt you today or any day? How do you do it alone?

The flight seemed to take forever, as if we were just circling around the globe forever till we run out of gas, or I blow a gasket! All I know is that Rich will be waiting to pick me up at the airport when I arrive. I just brought one carry-on piece so I can get out quickly.

Rich was waiting outside the terminal, just as he promised (Rich, my big brother, my only brother, my only sibling). He ran towards me and we hugged. We cried. We stood there holding each other in silence, not paying attention to the honking cars, taxi cab drivers swerving, or buses driving by. What else do you expect at a New York airport? He threw my luggage in the trunk and we sped off to his home in New Jersey.

"I know I should have flown into Newark Rich, but I couldn't get a flight until tonight if I had."

"That's okay Amy. I understand. Sorry Sara didn't come with me. You know how she is." He doesn't need to apologize for Sara anymore. We all know how she is.

"I have taken care of everything for the temple tomorrow. All we have to do is go through the apartment. You can have whatever your heart desires. I would like Dad's watch that's been passed down over the generations. That's all. You and the kids can have everything of Mom's, her jewelry and stuff. Sara doesn't need or want anything."

Sara doesn't deserve anything, I thought to myself.

"Thanks Rich. I know the girls would each like something of Mom's, and me too. Michael would appreciate something of Dad's. We'll look through everything together. Will that be okay with you?" I looked at my brother with tears streaming down my face.

He put his hand on mine.

"That'll be fine. We'll be together for the next few days. WE are all we have now" (I wasn't sure what he meant by that). We both sat in silence the rest of the trip.

Sara decided to leave for the evening and go out with some girlfriends, so my brother and I could be alone (in our sorrows). Rich and I talked half the night. We laughed. We cried. We reminisced about the good ole days. As kids, we would leave in the morning on a Saturday or Sunday. We wouldn't come back until dark. Those were the days when parents didn't have to worry about where their kids were, what they were doing, and with whom they were with. We didn't have cell phones, computers, Ipods, walkmans, DVD's or other electronic gadgets. We used our imaginations. Those were the days…

∞

Morning came too quickly, (doesn't it always?). Getting up early today, especially with the coastal time change, is difficult. Sara claimed she wasn't feeling well. Gee, what else is new? I remember hearing that one when Cameron died too. I think Rich was expecting that and he didn't even speak to her before we left for the temple.

I forgot how bad the traffic could be driving into New York on a cold, windy, and rainy day in February. Of course it was raining. It was a funeral, right? You have to have rain. I just hope we won't need a boat or canoe to paddle our way around Manhattan.

All of my parent's friends and some old, and I mean old, relatives filled the seats in the Temple, (How do people find out so quickly when someone dies?). Jewish people are buried within forty-eight hours of their death. It all seemed like a blur to me. Everyone coming up to say they're sorry. I stood and shook my head. I just wanted this day to be done. I wanted to go home, my home in California, where I would be safe. I can call my kids and know they are safe. I will know Tom and Jerry are fine and I would be home, in the tub, listening to music and relaxing.

Instead of going back to Rich's home, one of my parent's neighbors, Louis and Selma Susman, had the (after funeral) luncheon in their home. It was more convenient for everyone, especially for Rich. Louis and Selma were great friends with our parents.

So many people were coming into the Susman home. I wasn't paying any attention, just like at Cameron's funeral. Joel's parents came as well. They came over and hugged me. We talked for awhile, or rather they talked for awhile. I have no idea what we, rather they, talked about. I felt like blending into the wallpaper, once again. I don't know how to feel. I will have to mourn another day.

Then I saw Joel. My heart jumped. I don't know why. He hugged me. He didn't say anything.

I couldn't speak. He stayed the whole afternoon while I was in another world. He handed me his card with his cell number, in case I needed him. I just shook my head, and gave him a hug. He left.

"I want to go to Mom and Dad's tonight for a while, Rich."

He agreed. "Might as well start tonight."

~

Rich and I walked into our parent's home. It was cold, dark, and quiet. Rich turned the heat on and a few lights. Selma came over with us, just because.

"If you want me dears, for anything, just walk over. I am right here for you." She gave us each a hug. Rich thanked her for everything and she left.

There we were, just Rich and I. We walked around into each cold, dark room. I guess neither of us knew where to begin. We both just started to open drawers and look around. We started talking and reminiscing with each other from room to room. We were laughing and crying. I have never been as close with my brother as I am right now. Isn't that awful? It takes a funeral to get close to your own siblings. After an hour or two, we found the important things. At least the things we thought were important, like jewelry, pictures, heirlooms, bank accounts, and stocks.

"Amy, we need to sit and talk." He sounded upset. "I need to tell you some things I never told you, or Mom and Dad."

My mind started wondering… Maybe he is gay, and that is why he doesn't have any kids. Maybe Sara is gay and that is why they don't have any kids. Maybe he secretly had an affair and he has kids! Maybe I better stop wondering and listen for a change.

He paused for a moment before he began. I think he was just trying to find the right words.

"Sara and I haven't been getting along now for quite some time."

"Really now. I wouldn't know. Why are you telling me? Has she spent all your money?"

"Let me explain. Before Mom and Dad died, I felt like I was their babysitter, sort of, at least for the last ten years or so."

I started to get a little fidgety, thinking he would blame this on me. "I know you were too far away to help. You have your own family to bring up, and that is fine. I understand completely. I never expected you to fly over every time something happened with them. I have been here for them. Sara has always been frustrated with my taking care of them. Now that they are gone, I feel I can now move on with my own life." What is Rich getting at?

"I've realized how selfish Sara is and we have strayed from one another. I am going to divorce her. She doesn't know yet. I need some time before telling her. I need to settle a few things first." Rich stated this with great confidence, and looked at me straight in the eyes.

"It's about time!" I smiled and gave him a little nudge.

"Yeah, I know. It has been coming for quite some time now. She doesn't love me and I don't love her. As a matter of fact," he paused and started to pace the living room. "There is someone else."

I was silent and shocked. Why is he telling me and why now? I just sat on the couch and waited for an explanation.

"Well, are you going to tell me or what?"

Rich smiled and paced some more. "I have been seeing one of the other lawyers in my firm. She's never been married, and a little younger than me. She wants to get married and have children." Rich waited for my reaction.

"And, what would you like? You aren't too old to have a family you know."

"I always wanted to have children, but obviously, not with Sara. Sara is in her own world, just spending my money in her world. However, I need some favors from you," Rich stared at me.

"Whatever you need from me Rich, you got it! Whatever it takes."

"That's what I was hoping you'd say. I need to put everything of Mom and Dad's in your name. If Sara sees any of this, it will be over my dead body. I also need to put my stocks and other accounts in your name, at least until this whole divorce thing is over. This is going to take some time as well."

"No problem Rich. You are the lawyer here. You owe it to yourself. Just tell me what to do. Hey, when do I get meet this new lady in your life?"

"Actually you did today. You just didn't know it." He smiled. "She was here for a while but was very discreet and didn't stay very long."

"Today was such a blur, (I don't remember much of anything, except *Joel*). I'm sorry."

"Don't worry about it. I have an idea. I arranged for the three of us to go out for a nice, quiet dinner tomorrow night so you can officially meet one another. How does that sound? I know you don't have any plans yet, or do you, my dear little sister? I did notice Joel here today for a long time. Is there anything I should know? Or am I butting in?"

Thinking and now talking about Joel, again.

"I don't know. I feel like maybe there is, but then, maybe it is too soon." I looked down at my ring finger on my left hand and sighed, (I actually never took off my wedding band, come to think of it). "I think he wants something from me. I just don't know what yet."

"We aren't getting younger Amy. Cameron is gone, almost a year. You need to move on. You need someone. I know I haven't been a good big brother. I'm sorry I haven't been around for you."

"I figured Sara had to be the villain all these years. It is just too bad you felt you needed to wait for Mom and Dad to die before you decided to get rid of her. I guess it is a wake-up call," I thought aloud. "But I understand and I want you to finally be happy."

Rich and I talked for hours. I felt so good about our time together. I felt close to him again. It's nice to have my big brother back. I hope it lasts a lifetime.

We stayed in the spare bedrooms at Mom's for the night. She always kept the two extra bedrooms ready for us all the time. She had spare clothing for all of us too.

ꕥ

The next morning was cold, dark, and cloudy. "I guess there must be a funeral somewhere in the city today." I glanced out the window looking downtown.

Selma knocked on the door. As I opened it, she said, "I brought some fresh bagels, cream cheese, lox and some fresh brewed coffee for you kids."

"How sweet of you. Thank you so much. Come and sit with us for awhile." I brought her into the kitchen. She told us stories about our parents and the fun times they had living next door. I asked her if there was anything of my Mom and Dad's that she would like. She said no thank you. I made her take a photo of them. Her eyes started to well with water. I could see she was touched.

"Thank you dear." Once again, she offered her help anytime we needed her.

ꕥ

Rich and I took the rooms by storm. We made piles to give away (mainly clothes), piles to keep (pictures, jewelry and such), and a small pile to be kept secret (the accounts and stocks). Rich went to buy boxes while I kept on clearing through. My cell phone rang in the middle. I ran for it. I thought something happened to one of the kids. It was only Joel. I didn't mean it like that.

"I'm feeling better than yesterday, if that means anything."

"Glad to hear it. I know it isn't good timing and all, but how often do you come back to New York? Would you like to have dinner with me tonight? I know this great Italian restaurant not too far from the apartment?"

"I'm having dinner with Rich and a friend of his tonight." I paused and started pacing. "I don't think I should change his plans."

"Whatever you think is best. Remember if there is anything I can do for you, please let me know. I'll talk to you later." he sounded disappointed. I was disappointed too.

Moments later Rich arrived with a bunch of boxes and tape. I didn't tell him that Joel called. We were busy through lunch and forgot to eat. I wasn't hungry anyway, besides I could always stand to lose a pound or two. I always wanted to look svelte like Carol.

It was almost three in the afternoon. We were exhausted from packing up stuff, making decisions, and just thinking. I made some hot cocoa, like Mom used to when we were kids. Mom always kept the good stuff around, even when we weren't. We sat in the kitchen, drank hot cocoa, and relaxed.

"Why don't you go lie down for awhile Amy. You look beat," Rich looked beat as well.

"Only if you do. You don't look so hot yourself," I rebutted back. "I am a little tired. I'll take a short nap before dinner tonight, so I don't look half dead meeting...what is her name by the way? You never told me?"

"That's right. Her name is Carolyn. You'll like her. She is like the younger sister YOU never had. I already have one and a good one," Rich smiled and pushed me to my bedroom for a nap.

I stretched out on the bed and put one of my Mom's beautiful, handmade quilts over me. It smelled like Mom. I felt like Mom was in the next room. It didn't take long for my eyes to close.

I was so comfortable when Rich woke me at six-thirty.

"I can't believe I slept so long. Why didn't you wake me sooner? Now I'll be up all night long."

"Well, to tell you the truth, once I saw that you were asleep, I left."

"What? Where did you go? I thought you were lying down in the next room."

"I thought we needed some fresh clothes and our own things. I drove home and packed up some of my things. I packed up your stuff, and brought them over. I just hope I didn't forget anything of yours. This way we can both take showers and feel fresh. We're meeting Carolyn at the restaurant at eight, so there is still plenty of time."

"Rich, you didn't have to do that. But, I am glad you did. What Mom kept in here is ancient. I would feel better taking a shower and wearing my own clothes. Thanks."

෴

"Fifteen minutes Amy," Rich shouted. "We need to get going."

"Just a second." I'm actually excited to meet the new woman in Rich's life. After Sara as a sister-in-law, anyone else is a plus, (including men too). I mean that in a good way.

We arrived in front of the restaurant at eight on the nose. Carolyn was waiting anxiously. Rich introduced us and we moved closer to shake hands. Instead, I just gave her a hug.

"It's so nice to finally meet someone that makes my brother happy. That sounds weird? Why don't I just open my mouth and insert my foot."

I think she was shocked, but laughed instead.

"I have heard so much about you, Amy. I'm glad we are finally able to meet."

"Me too" I then turned to Rich, "Rich, it's freezing out here, can we please go in?"

He laughed and escorted us both into ***Patsy's***. It's a quaint Italian restaurant with delicious food, great service, and quiet tables. Turns out it was one of Frank Sinatra's favorite restaurants.

We had a wonderful dinner, served with red wine. We all know that red wine is good for the heart. We talked for hours; at least it seemed liked hours.

We were just about to have some dessert and coffee brought to us when a pink rose arrived in front of me. I looked around, but no one was there. Then the waiter brought me a note. It was from Joel. How did he know I was here? The note said:

Amy … I'll always remember pink roses. I know you must be going through a hard time right now. I'm here if you need me. All you have to do is call.

Joel

He wrote his cell number on the bottom of the card. Rich and Carolyn smiled.

"You knew about this didn't you?"

"Why yes, I did. I saw Joel's card by your cell phone earlier today. I called him to thank him for coming yesterday and asked him what his intentions were with you, since I noticed a twinkle in his eye, and yours for that matter. Then I invited him to dinner with us, but he declined. I told him where and when we were having dinner and if he changed his mind, he would be more than welcome."

"You should have asked me first," I whispered. "I told you before I don't know what our relationship is just yet or where it may go. I don't want to push it or be pushed, Rich," as I looked around.

"I didn't think you would mind. I actually thought that maybe you would be glad if he showed up tonight. I think you need someone to lean on, especially now Amy."

"Well, I will be the judge of that when I am good and ready. This isn't the right time or place. My God, Rich, Mom and Dad haven't even been gone a week, Cameron has been gone less than a year. Don't you think I need a little time by myself before jumping into a new relationship? I feel overwhelmed right now. I need a little time to myself to think." (Another hot flash coming)

"She's right Rich. I understand completely," Carolyn affirmed. "Amy, you need to keep your feet on the ground, stand up straight, and move forward with your head held high."

"Thank you Carolyn. Now if you two don't mind, I'm going to catch a cab and head back to the apartment. You stay and enjoy some coffee and dessert, and pay the bill Rich." I giggled. "I will see you later Rich." I stood up to leave, took my pink rose, and gave each of them a hug.

"Carolyn, it was so nice to meet you. Please don't be a stranger. I am sure I will be seeing you again soon. And thanks for sticking up for me." We both laughed.

"At least let me call a cab for you, Amy," Rich said and led the way to the front door.

"I'm a big girl, Rich. I can handle getting a cab. Go back and enjoy the rest of the evening. I'll see you when I see you. Good night big brother." I kissed him on the cheek. I turned toward the door, stumbled on the fold of the carpet on my way out, and caught the door before I fell.

"*God damn it.* I'm okay, go on," I instructed Rich. He laughed and shook his head at me.

I walked out into the cold, dreary, damp evening of New York City. I thought about walking back to the apartment, but I'm a chicken. It's night and it's dark outside (we all know what that means to Amy Kayden). I know NYC is the city that never sleeps, and people are always walking around. What kind of people walk around in the middle of the night? I just got the shivers. Better than those hot flashes lately.

I held my purse close to me. I looked into the street to find a cab. I didn't look too hard though. I just stood leaning against the front door of the restaurant for the longest time. At least it seemed like an eternity to me, but probably was only a couple of minutes at the most.

A shiny, new, black limousine pulled up in front of the restaurant right in front of me, the window went down, and a voice came from inside the car.

"Get in before you catch a cold."

I recognized that voice. After the door opened, a man came out of the car to help me. Joel moved closer to me and gave me a hug. He helped me into the car.

"What makes you think I couldn't get a cab? I wasn't ready just yet. I was trying to find my wallet so I could pay the driver when I flagged one down."

"Sure. It's okay Amy. You do need rescuing you know. I'm your knight, and here is my shining armor," as he pointed to the car.

"I never said I needed rescuing or a knight in shining armor. What makes you so sure about everything?"

"I just know." Joel signaled the driver to drive around for a while.

"I know you're afraid of the dark. I also know you don't like to be alone. I remember that you're afraid of thunderstorms, and you don't like ferris wheels or merry-go-rounds," he added. "And first and foremost, you love pink roses." He saw that I was holding the one he sent.

I was quiet. I didn't want to admit that he was right about any of it, rather all of it. I need to be able to handle life's 'ups and downs' by myself. I know it isn't all fun, but I have to learn to be able to handle some matters by myself. Apparently, Joel doesn't think so. Neither did Cam.

God damn it. What do I do now?

I sat back in the seat and just sighed (really for relief that I didn't have to get in a cab in New York City in the middle of the night all by myself, which I don't know if I would have done and now I don't need to find out).

"Where to M' lady?"

"I was planning on going back to my Mom's place, unless you have a suggestion?"

"Yes I have several suggestions. First, how about a nightcap? I know a fantastic hotel that has a superb bar." He put his hands in the air waiting for a positive response.

"Oh, okay. Only one drink for me. You know what more than one will do to me."

"I remember. I end up with food in my lap, or all washed up," as he laughed.

"That isn't what I meant. And you know that." I said without trying to laugh too.

"My place then," he told the driver. "Don't worry; I'll be a gentleman, as always. I want to be here for you," as he moved closer in the backseat.

The driver dropped us off at the entrance to this beautiful hotel in midtown Manhattan. Joel helped me out, then had a few words with the driver and the car sped off.

"Shall we then?" he took my arm and led me into the hotel's bar.

Several people acknowledged him with a nod or a short wave. We sat down at a table in the corner and a waiter came over and asked what I would like, and if Joel would like his usual?

"The lady will have a glass of your best red wine and yes, I will have my usual."

Not five minutes went by and the waiter returned with two red wines. "You see, I know that red wine is good for the heart. Especially mine," Joel lifted his glass for a taste, and acknowledged the waiter to leave.

I smiled and took a couple of sips of my red wine. We sat there in silence just listening to the music of the night. NO, we weren't listening to "Phantom of the Opera," (that is a great musical though).

"How are you doing Amy? Do you need anything? Is there something I can do for you?" as he put his strong hand on top of mine, covering my left ring finger.

"I'm doing okay, I guess. Rich is the one that has done everything. I'm worried about how he's taking all of this, and how I can help him. Does that make any sense?"

"Sure it does. I know he's a big boy and can handle it. He's a lawyer. They can handle just about anything, except their own divorces," he quietly added as he laughed under his breath.

We sat in silence, taking a few more sips of wine and continuing to listen to the jazz music that was playing in the background. It's nice not having to make chitchat. I finished off my glass of wine.

"One drink is enough for me. I don't want to fall asleep on you, again," I laughed remembering what happened before.

"Are you sure? I can sit here all night and just gaze at you." Just as he spoke, one of the young and pretty bartenders walked by our table and smiled. He acknowledged her with a smile.

"I don't want to hold you up from anything, like a 'late date' or something like that," I noticed the way he looked at her. "I am willing to take a cab back by myself."

"What? A late date? Who with?"

"You don't have to be here on account of me. I'm a little older compared to these girls. I understand that men have needs and such."

"Needs? What are you babbling about? I'll wait for you till the end of the earth, if that's what it takes." He sat a little closer to me, placed his arm around my shoulder, and gave me a little nudge. "I'm not going anywhere."

I'm still new at this thing called 'dating.' Again, we sat there in silence. He made a quick call and by the time we were outside the hotel the limo was waiting, right on cue. As I was getting into the car, my shoe stuck in a crack on the curb.

"*God damn it.* Those damn New York curbs."

I tripped and actually fell into the car, face down, minus one shoe. I started to laugh and sat up. I went to reach for my shoe but it was too late. Joel already had it in his hand and offered to put it on my foot (just like Cinderella).

"A perfect fit M' lady," he said with a beautiful smile and twinkling hazel eyes (remember how I like things that twinkle).

It was a short ride to the apartment. I sat for a moment while he went to open the car door. When he did, we stood there for a few minutes. I gave him a hug.

"Thanks for understanding, I think."

He walked me into the lobby. "Do you want me to take you up the elevator?"

"I don't know what to think right now. You don't have to take me door to door. I can let myself in from here (I think)," I wasn't so sure though.

He gave me a nice, long, warm, hug and a soft kiss on the lips.

"Good night M'lady." He started to walk away as I pushed the elevator button.

"Wait," I shouted and turned toward the lobby door.

"Would you come up with me? Just until Rich comes back?" (I think he is coming back tonight). I smiled the innocent smile.

"One second. I'll be right back." He ran out the door for a minute and came back in a flash.

"All set. I'll escort you to your abode," as he bowed down with a smile.

I did feel a little better now. In fact, a lot better. I'm afraid to be alone, but that wasn't it.

Joel followed me into the elevator and from there the sky's the limit.

Going up!

Chapter 19

If it's not one Coast, it's the other

I waved good-bye to Rich and Carolyn after they dropped me off at La Guardia Airport to catch my morning flight back to sunny California. Right now, the sky in New York is a beautiful blue and the air is calm. I don't think I'll need my valium for this flight home.

While I was waiting for my flight to take me from one coast to the other, I went through the papers Rich had given me to make sure I remembered what I'm supposed to do with each of them when I arrived home. I needed to go to my bank and safety deposit box ASAP. I needed to call the kids and let them know I'm home (safely) and have some heirlooms for them. I needed to call Larry to ask him to help me with some of the paper work on this end for Rich. I needed to thank Carol for watching my babies for me. I needed to call Joel to let him know I made it safely. What?

Finally, I can't wait to hug my babies a big hello when I get home. That might take up the rest of the day, and then some.

∾

I did it! I didn't fall apart while I was in New York. I didn't take any drugs on the flight. I made it back home safe and sound. I walked into the house. Tom and Jerry went nuts. They were howling and baying, and running up and down the hallway. They practically knocked me over and licked me to death. I was just as excited to see them, but I wasn't going to lick them, just give big hugs and kisses.

It's great to be home, playing in our own backyard, and smelling our fresh California air. I feel comfortable here, at home. Home is where the heart is. Home is where my kids come back to. Home is my safety zone. There's no place like home (de ja vu').

I called Larry at the office and asked for his help. I phoned Carol and she came running over, with her apron on and phone in hand, to give me a hug.

"So, how was everything? You okay? Rich okay? Everything okay?"

I answered each question, one at a time, slowly, while I made us some coffee. We sat for awhile in my cozy, comfortable kitchen.

"Well, I must unpack, do some laundry, settle some matters, you know."

"I know hon. Call me." Carol gave me a big hug, then left, with her phone in the apron pocket.

I emailed all the kids to let them know I was home and to call me tonight. I checked my phone messages, but there weren't any, from Joel. Was I expecting one, or maybe two? Am I jumping to conclusions? I did receive another call from David asking if we can see each other. I know that's not going to happen.

For a quick moment, I thought there would be a message from my parents. Then it hit me. They're gone. They're really gone. They aren't coming back and I won't be getting anymore 'funny' phone calls from them. I'll miss that. I'll miss them very much. I already do. I have the memories in my mind and all the love in my heart so they will never leave me, ever. They will always be a part of me and no one can take that away.

∾

While I was cleaning up and doing some laundry, the kids called one by one. The twins told me they were coming home this weekend for a visit, and probably to see what I brought them. Mel is working part-time and is getting more excited about her upcoming graduation. She has been sending out her resume everywhere. Michael is busy working and hanging out with Liz.

Larry came over after work. I discussed everything with him and gave him Rich's cell number so he could call him in the morning and discuss whatever lawyers discuss. Then I'll do whatever I am supposed to do at the bank. Once he left for the evening, I felt exhausted. It was a very long day, especially waking up in New York and ending up in California in the evening. I definitely wouldn't be a good commuter if I had to do this on a regular basis.

Turning on the hot water to take a nice, long, hot, lavender bubble bath is just what I needed. Remember how I love an evening with the 'stars.' I lit some candles, turned on the radio, and just sunk into the tub for a relaxing evening. I was thinking about my parents and shed a few tears. The tears ran into the tub and blended in with the bubbles.

I was upset and distraught to finalize the fact that I'll never see them again (I hope my kids cry when it's my turn to go. But then again, I'm not going anywhere). I was just about to doze off for a minute or two when the phone rang. I jumped out of the tub, literally, and ran for the phone. I picked it up, stark naked, just in time before the answering machine started. It was Joel.

"Hello," I tried to be calm and cool. I was also trying to hide my body. I don't know why. No one can see you over the phone, or can they? It is a little on the chilly side not having a towel.

"Hey, you made it." he said in a low tone. "Everything okay at the A.K. Corral?"

"Everything is fine here, and the boys are happy to see me. All my kids called and left messages. I have a bunch of errands to run tomorrow and need to straighten some things out," also in a low tone. "You sound like you are sick." His voice sounded sad, as I waited for a response.

"I'm sick as a puppy dog." He paws-ed (oops).

There was silence. I was waiting for him to tell me what was wrong. Did he have a cold or the flu or what?

"I really miss you."

"Oh." I laughed, but it was a nervous laugh. I stood there naked, not knowing what to do. "I haven't had time to sit and think about myself too much the past few days. I do find myself thinking about you, sometimes. In fact, I was hoping there would have been a message or two from you on my answering machine when I came home. I was disappointed that there wasn't any, if that means anything to you."

"Why it means a lot to me. The part that you are thinking about me means something. At least it's a start. I love it! What about the part of me that misses you, Amy?"

"How could you miss me? You just saw me in New York," I said nervously and now pacing, forgetting that I am naked and freezing my tush off.

"I didn't realize how much I would miss you until you left. To tell you the truth, I have thought about you everyday, since high school. Like I said before, I loved you then, and I haven't stopped. I don't want to lose you twice in a lifetime. I want to see you more. How do you feel about that?"

"Would you like me to send you a picture?" I flippantly said. "Kidding aside, it would be a little difficult to see you more often, seeing that you live there and I live here."

"This is true. I guess I may have to compromise. What do you suggest?"

"I'm not sure if there is an answer. I think it would be quite costly for you to fly out here just for a date or two. Don't you?" I wasn't sure what I wanted to hear.

"I happen to think you are worth it, Amy Kayden. I can arrange to be in California next week. I could call you when I arrive and ask you out on a proper date. You say yes, we go out for dinner. If that works out well, according to M'lady, then another date would be in order. How am I doing so far?"

"That sounds good so far. Don't tell me what happens next. I want to be surprised. So, are you definitely planning on coming out? I would love to go out with you, Sir." I giggled softly to myself.

"I didn't call and ask you out yet. You are jumping the gun here. I'm starting to think that you kind of like me. Am I assuming too much?" he laughed. I laughed too.

"Would that be so bad? Besides, I have always liked you." I was being truthful and honest. "I did have a crush on you when we were eight you know. Who said I still don't have a crush on you now?"

I shivered, trying not to let Joel know that I have been out of the tub for more than a fleeting moment, and am now pacing around the house, naked, trying to warm up.

"Oh yeah, I remember. We won't go into details right now," he laughed. "Are you okay? You sound like you are cold."

"I am shivering. I am freezing my buns off, literally. I was in the tub when the phone rang. I jumped out and ran to answer it. I could tell by the ring that it was you, so I hurried."

"You are a funny lady. You have had a very long day. It's very late here, and getting later there, and I need to get some sleep so I can make my arrangements to see you soon. I'll let you get back into your tub so you can relax and enjoy the rest of your evening with the other 'boys' in your life."

"Okay then. I will wait to hear from you." We hung up at the same time, I think. I placed the mobile back on the 'holder thing.' "Well that sounded weird. What was I thinking? Hopefully Joel didn't notice how silly I sounded." I stood there **freezing**. I have been standing here naked for quite some time. I need to get back into the tub to warm up. I had the mobile phone from the kitchen. Why didn't I just take it back to the bathroom with me? Am I falling for him or what?

I started to head back to the tub, then turned around and fetched the mobile phone, just in case. I don't want to be caught naked again, at least not standing in my kitchen.

A couple of days went by and I didn't hear from Joel. Julie and Jenna were on their way home for the weekend. I made their favorite meals: Baked Ziti, macaroni and cheese, and believe it or not, my homemade matzo ball soup! I'm so excited to see them.

The boys heard the girls' car engine humming into the garage. They were scratching away at the door. They couldn't wait for me to let them out so they could give the girls a proper greeting. I opened the door and they went charging out. The girls screamed with joy. They came running in, gave me a hug and kiss, then asked what I brought them from New York. Typical princesses.

The three of us had a fantastic, mother-daughter(s) evening. We ate dinner, watched a movie, and talked about the good times and funny times we had with their grandparents. Eleven in the evening and I am dog-tired (thought that was a cute word). The girls were just getting a second wind. I gave them each a hug and kiss, and said good night. They waited until I was in my pajamas, and lying in bed with Tom and Jerry before they threw a bomb at me.

"Mom, can we come in?" Julie asked. They were both standing at the doorway, staring at each other, waiting for an invitation.

"Of course you can. What's up?" They both looked a little embarrassed about something. That 'something' was about to be revealed.

They looked at each other waiting for the other to speak up first. Finally, Jenna spit it out.

"Mom we didn't do so good last semester in school. We are on probation with the school …

"And the sorority," Julie finally added her two cents worth.

"You mean you didn't do so well. I'm assuming one of those classes is English." They shook their heads.

"I see."

I took a deep breath and sighed loudly.

"What would you like from me? Affirmation that it's okay, because it isn't in my book. Why didn't you girls tell me before, when you knew you were in trouble?"

I sat up in bed now with my arms crossing my chest. I was awake now. Wide awake, maybe even awake enough to wake the dead if I scolded loud enough.

"We figured we could handle it without you getting all worried," Jenna said. "We didn't want to upset you anymore. We know it must be hard without Dad, and now Grandma and Grandpa, and we didn't want to burden you."

"I see," and took another deep breath and sighed. "Well, I think I need to sleep on this one. I think you girls do too because I'm pretty sure you haven't yet, if you catch my drift." They looked at each other and shook their heads in agreement.

"Let's discuss this in the morning. We'll figure it out together." I gave each of them another hug and kiss and sent them off to bed. "I love you girls, no matter what. Just remember that."

"We love you too Mom. Good night," they both said in unison.

I think Julie and Jenna felt a little relief that they told me their problem. I felt disappointed in my girls, and I'm sure they felt as if their problems are off their shoulders and onto mine. Now how am I going to get to sleep tonight?

Joel.

Chapter 20

Sweets for the sweet

Morning came too early for the girls. I am very confident in that statement. They weren't quite sure what they were in for today. I was up early, from tossing and turning all night long, thanks to the wonderful news they broadcasted late last night. Fresh brewed coffee will wake me up a bit and keep my wits about me as I went to sit in my thinking chair outside. Nine o'clock sharp the girls were sitting in the kitchen looking worried.

I heard them talking and saw them pour coffee into their mugs. I walked into the kitchen and sat. Everyone is fidgeting with either their legs, fingers, tapping the spoons and so on, including me.

"Who wants to start first girls?" Looking at them both back and forth, wondering who would be brave enough to begin the discussion.

They looked at each other and couldn't figure out what I was asking either of them.

"I don't get it Mom. You are supposed to tell us what to do?" Julie said all confused.

"I'm not going to tell you what to do. I'm here to listen and together, we'll figure out the next step. You're both adults and need to think like adults. What do you suppose you need to start doing?"

"Study." Julie said while fidgeting in her chair trying to get in a comfortable position, I guess.

"Good answer. What else?" I posed, looking at both of them waiting for more answers.

"Not going out so much," Jenna added, also squirming around in her chair and her feet swaying back and forth underneath the table.

"Or waste our time and start going to class more often?" she added. Now they were getting the hang of it. I just hope they remember it all and put it into action. We talked, rather they talked while I listened. They knew what to do but just needed another pair of ears, I hope.

"Okay, now we're getting somewhere. You girls need to write down what it is you need to do, how much time per day and per week it will take. Don't wait to do a paper, start it as soon as you get the assignment. Go see tutors if needed. Go visit your professors as well. Set a schedule and stick to it. Then at the end of the week, if everything is accomplished, then reward yourself," I repeated for them.

"Thanks Mom," the girls said at the same time. They started to get up from the table with a sigh of relief on their faces.

"Where are you going? We aren't finished here. Go get some paper and pens so you'll start right now. I want to see a schedule made out before you leave this table this morning. Then you're going to put it on a spreadsheet on the computer and make a few copies for yourself and one for me. After a few weeks of following a schedule, we will discuss the progress you have both been making and continue for the rest of the semester. This is all going to take some time. Now, what would you girls like for breakfast?" I inquired with a big smile on my face, knowing I am doing the right thing for my girls.

∾

The girls were working on their schedules, while I was attempting to make waffles. You really can't ruin waffles, can you? I was doing pretty good when the doorbell rang. I didn't want the girls to get out of their 'thinking' mode, so I dashed to the front door with the boys at my feet. It was the florist. I could tell because the delivery boy was holding a huge vase with a dozen pink gorgeous roses in them with an enormous pink ribbon tied around a crystal vase.

I opened the door and he practically threw them on me.

"Delivery."

"I didn't realize deliveries were done so early in the morning," making conversation.

"Well, yeah. That **is** what we do Mam, deliver flowers." His sarcasm popped right out of his mouth along with a huge wad of bubble gum.

"Oops. Sorry bout that Mam. I'll get it." As he proceeded to pick it up off the ground , put it back in his mouth, and he snapped it every five seconds for everyone in the neighborhood to hear.

"Yeah, that's okay. I keep the floor very clean, most of the time. If you are waiting for a tip, forget it." I slowly walked into the house and turned quickly back to the delivery boy.

"The only tip I will give you is to keep your mouth closed, with or without the wad of gum." I proceeded to close the door.

I brought the flowers into the kitchen. They were breathtaking. I didn't want to take my eyes off them. I haven't even looked at the card yet, but I think I know who sent them.

The girls looked up as their eyes lit up.

"Wow Mom, who sent us those?" Jenna asked.

"Excuse me. Who sent **us** the flowers? I think they're for me, not **us** dear." The girls wanted to open **my** card.

"Wait a minute. This is **my** house, **my** kitchen, **my** roses. I will open **my** card."

I opened **my** card. Even the envelope had pink roses on it. The girls were waiting. **My** card said:

It's only Saturday and I can't wait,
to pick you up on Tuesday for our date.
Six o'clock in the eve will be the right time,
Dinner, maybe a movie, and you'll be mine.
Pink roses are beautiful, just like you,
Place them on a table in everyone's view.
Relax and enjoy them until I'm there,
Because you know, I really do care.

See you soon, me

I thought the poem was so sweet. The girls were trying to peek at the card. I stood there and beamed. I held the card close to my heart, just thinking about how thoughtful he is to send roses and write this cute little poem, (I wonder how long it took him to write that).

"Okay, okay girls. You may read **my** card." I showed it to them and they both laughed.

"Who sent them Mom? Come on, who?"

Of course, I knew who sent them. "Oh, just one of my many admirers." They didn't like that answer in the least. They bugged me all morning about it.

"If you girls finish your schedules, print them out, make a nice lunch and serve it outside on the patio for the three of us, then I will tell you who my admirer is."

They went for it. I get a 'free' lunch sitting outside. I wonder who gets to clean up the kitchen when they are finished making a mess. Any guesses.

I'm going to enjoy the rest of my morning: first, by finishing the waffles (the one that was in there when the delivery boy showed up is burnt now), second, cleaning up the kitchen, and last but not least, by taking **my** beautiful pink roses outside. It is such a pleasant day and I want to take advantage of it, and the girls. Tom and Jerry followed me as usual. They decided to roll in the grass and grab some sunshine.

A few hours went by rather quickly. The girls brought out lunch, which consisted of cream of mushroom soup, and some Kaiser rolls for dipping purposes (I taught them that). "Did someone go to the store, actually drive to the store, besides me, and buy fresh rolls?"

"Yes Mother. As a matter of fact, we both did. We also bought some dessert!" Jenna announced proudly. They put the bowls and rolls (that rhymes), on the table and then went back in for the utensils, napkins, and some hot cocoa. The three of us, rather five of us, including Tom and Jerry, sat outside eating lunch quietly, enjoying the scenery, weather, birds singing, and the roses on the table. After the fifteen minutes of silence was up, I asked the sixty-four thousand dollar question.

"Do you have your schedules done? I would like to look them over with you?" I put my spoon down next to the soup bowl, and used my napkin.

"Just about Mom. We need to check it before we print them out. But we do have one right here," which Julie produced. We looked it over together.

"You girls need to agree to actually follow this now." They agreed. We'll see...

"Now tell us Mom. Who is admiring you?" Jenna sat closer.

"He isn't a secret. An admirer, yes, I guess." (There I go again, rhyming).

They looked at each other like maybe the other one knew.

"He has been here before, as a matter of fact, he was here right before Christmas. You both met him. The circumstances were a little awkward but he met all of you kids."

"You mean Joel?" Jenna sounding surprised. "I didn't think he would ever call you again."

"Well thanks a lot. Give me more credit than that, and give him more credit too. I also saw him in Phoenix." The girls looked shocked. Their mouths were hanging wide open and their eyes almost popped out of their heads.

"I didn't meet him there on purpose. We didn't have a rendezvous. We happen to be at the same restaurant at the same time." I don't think they accepted my explanation.

"Are you sure Mom? Maybe he knew you were there?" Jenna shook her head in agreement with her sister.

I never thought of that. How would he know? I guess it is possible.

"Don't be ridiculous girls. Why would a man fly all around the country just to have dinner with me?" I questioned myself on that one. Now I really had to think about this. I'm not saying I'm not worth flying around the country for, just that I couldn't see any man doing that just to see me. Cameron never did anything like that for me. He just brought boxes home for me.

"I also saw him in New York after Grandma and Grandpa died. He came to the funeral. I did see him the day after or the day after that day. I don't really remember what day was what." I tried to convince the girls.

"Sure Mom." They eyed each other. I tried to ignore it. "We're glad you're dating someone, Mom. Really we are." Jenna laughed. Julie joined right on in with her.

We sat there in the beautiful southern California sunshine finishing our lunch. I was just about full and wasn't sure if I had room for dessert.

"So, what's for dessert? I hope it's chocolate."

A woman always has room for chocolate.

Chapter 21

Monday, Monday

It's time to start cleaning the house. Monday morning has arrived, again. Seems like Mondays come around often these days. I feel like I have a ton of energy for some reason. Another reason being, I am expecting company tomorrow night and I want the house to look clean. Not clean, but super duper clean. The girls' rooms were first, then Michael's room. I gave it the ultra-super-duper cleanup. I lit candles in my bathroom and bedroom to spread out the vanilla scent in both rooms. As I was finishing, the phone rang. I walked briskly over to pick it up in the kitchen, so I could get a Fresca at the same time. Might as well kill two birds with one stone.

"Hello."

"Hey there girl." It was Nathan. "I was about to go do a little shopping and wanted to know if you wanted to go along? I need a break from writing jingles all weekend long. I need to get music out of my head for awhile."

"Oh, thanks Nathan, but I'm cleaning right now. I want it to be super clean by tonight." I didn't explain further, and somehow I don't think I needed to.

"I see. Expecting some company tonight, are we dear?" Nathan said teasingly.

"Not tonight, tomorrow actually. I want the house to be ready so I can relax tomorrow."

"I know you won't be relaxing tomorrow at all. You will be a wreck." He laughed. "Chase and I will need to keep you busy tomorrow for a while. We should do lunch at the new French restaurant that just opened up around the corner. How does that sound? It looks like it has great soups, breads, **and** desserts. I am sure they have something with chocolate in it."

"Sounds great. Ok. Lunch tomorrow then."

"Before I hang up, is there anything you need while I am out today?"

"Actually there is something you can buy for me. I need a couple of bottles of red wine. I am down to one lone bottle that is already opened in the refrigerator."

"Consider it done Honey. I'll bring them over later this afternoon. Chase is home working on his computer, so I'm off and running. If you need anything you can call either of us, you know that right?"

"Of course I do. I appreciate it too. What would I do without you guys. I'll see you in a few then. Have fun shopping."

"Okay, dear." Nathan quickly hung up.

The living room needs some sprucing, as well as the kitchen. I need to trim the rose bushes out front and back. Trimming the rose bushes is the best therapy I can give myself. It is the best thinking time while I also beautify my home inside, with some fresh cut roses and the aroma throughout the house, and outside for the clean look. Then I need to bake something: maybe a cake, brownies, or something. I will think about it while I'm cleaning some more. Back to my main man for today, Mr. Clean!

I turned some music on to help me get through the cleaning. Singing along with the Beach Boys, or Beatles, is just what I need while I clean.

I was in the living room and dining room, cleaning them both simultaneously. Those two rooms are easy since they are hardly ever used. The phone rang again and I ran into the kitchen to pick it up. This time it was my brother.

"Hey Rich, what's up?"

"Carolyn and I are planning a trip. It's a business trip to L.A. Do you have any ideas on where to stay?"

"Of course. You are going to stay here. I wouldn't have it any other way and you know that," I giggled. "By the way, what's going on with Sara? Have you told her yet?"

"Not yet. I need to finalize a few more situations here. That is one reason why we are coming out. I want to open an account out in California under Carolyn's name. It's hard to explain but don't worry, everything is going to work out fine."

"Just let me know when you're coming and I can pick the two of you up at the airport."

"That's okay. We're going to rent a car. We need to attend a meeting for the Bar Association. That's one of the reasons for the visit as well. We both need a few write-offs for the first quarter and this will give us, Carolyn and me, a chance to be out on our own, so to speak. Catch my drift?"

"Well then, I would think you would rather stay in a hotel than with me." I waited for a response. I walked over to the refrigerator and took a sip of my Fresca.

"We plan on doing both actually. Carolyn and I will attend the meetings and stay at the hotel, and then we will visit with you, if that is okay with you?"

"That sounds fine. It'll be nice to have you both here. You haven't been here since, since I can't even remember the last time you visited. As a matter of fact, I don't think you ever did. Sara wouldn't let you, would she?" I laughed.

"That's probably true. However, times are changing. I will email you our itinerary for the meetings and such. It'll be next month. Isn't the weather nice in L.A. then?"

"Sometimes it is, and sometimes it isn't. You never know what you are going to get." I was casually pacing the kitchen island now with my Fresca in hand.

"I better get back to work. Talk to you soon. Bye." Then Rich hung up before I could say or ask anything else.

Thoughts about cleaning the kitchen is on my mind. It looked like it needed some help. I needed to eat as well, since I skipped breakfast. The boys need to go for a **w-a-l-k** too. What to do, what to do!

I made myself a quick bologna and cheese sandwich and checked my emails. Mel sent some funny jokes. The twins told me they were following the schedule they made, and are very proud of themselves. It has only been a day. Whatever… I also received an email from Joel asking if I received the flowers on Saturday. I forgot to thank him, so I sent an email back saying thanks. Finishing up my sandwich I thought about taking the boys to the park, and trimming up the rose bushes before tackling the kitchen, later today. Oh, I have so much energy today.

൭൭

Four o'clock and all is well in the Kayden household. I took the boys for a needed walk, and aired out my thoughts at the same time. I trimmed up the bushes outside. Now it's time for the kitchen cleanup. I turned the music back on and started my usual routine of cleaning. The phone rang, again.

"*Stupid phone.* Doesn't anyone know that I am trying to clean around here? Hello."

"Well hello there M' lady, and how are we this lovely afternoon?" Joel said in a romantic tone.

I tried to fix myself up before answering him. I took off my cleaning gloves, straightened my shirt and touched my hair up a bit. I don't know why, he can't see me through the phone.

"Well, hello there. I didn't expect to hear from you today. As a matter of fact, I just sent you an email thanking you for the beautiful roses," I toned down as if I received roses from men all the time.

"I'm glad you received them and I'm sure they are as lovely as you. I just thought I would give you a call while I am on a break."

"That is so sweet. I'm just cleaning up a bit. You know, just straightening up and doing some baking." (I ran into the pantry and **stared** at the cake box, hoping it would bake itself).

"I just wanted to hear your voice because I couldn't wait until tomorrow evening." Joel is a romanticist. I just love that.

"Aw, how sweet." I sighed under my breath. "I'm just tidying up here. I am sure you need to go back to a meeting." I don't know why I am so nervous. He's just a guy.

"Yes, I do. Until we meet again."

He hung up, and I stood there just smiling for the longest time, still holding the phone close to my heart. Tom and Jerry were just staring at me as if I'm a nut case, which I probably am.

Thank goodness for Betty Crocker and all of her mixes. I don't think I ever made anything from scratch, and I am not going to start now. I made sure I put the right temperature on, and the timer is right for sure. But just in case, I will stay in the kitchen, cleaning. This way I am sure the cake won't burn. This is a form of multi-tasking, I hope. My children would be proud. I also fed the dogs and gave them fresh water. The time just flew by when the buzzer went off and I took out the cake, clean as a whistle, no burn marks or anything smelling funny.

I would like to thank Betty Crocker for the 'plastic tub' of frosting. I can't imagine making frosting from scratch, even though I hear rumors about people doing it all the time. *Those peasants.*

The cleaning is done, at least for today. Everything looks sparkling fresh and smells even better with the aroma of all the candles lit around the house. Candles…I need to blow them all out, NOW before I hear from the Fire Chief.

൭൭

Bath time for me. I know there's a nice, hot, soothing tub ready for me to relax in before I tackle dinner, which will probably consist of some cream of mushroom soup. I just love the stuff! Besides, I bought a zillion cans before Christmas, remember?

It's dark out and we all know what that means, time to lock up the house. I locked the doors, turned on the alarm and the outside lights. Safe and sound inside my abode with my buddies.

The boys followed me into the bathroom, as usual. I put some music on, lit some vanilla candles, and threw in lavender bubble bath in the tub. A nice long bath is all I need right now. I ran back into the kitchen, naked, to pour myself a glass of red wine. Everyone knows that red wine is good for the heart!

"Ahh. This tub is just what I needed," as I slowly sunk to the bottom up to my chin.

The doorbell rang. *"God damn it."*

"Can't I even take a quiet bath around here without the phone or doorbell ringing?"

I reached for my terrycloth robe. Tom and Jerry were barking and running down the hallway to the front door. I forgot about Nathan bringing the wine over. That's probably who it is. I looked outside, sure enough it was Nathan. I turned the alarm off, unlocked and opened the door to let him in the front door with a bag under his arm.

"Sorry I am so late Amy. I forgot the wine and just ran back to the store for you." He apologized with so much sincerity. I forgot too. I gave him some money I had left out to pay for the wine earlier in the day, smiled and said good night.

I locked the door again, turned the alarm back on, hopped back in the tub, grabbed my wine glass, and maybe three minutes went by before the doorbell rang again. *"God damn it."*

"He probably forgot something or decided that I gave him too much money," as I grabbed my robe while still standing in the tub.

The dogs went barking and running down the hallway again. I sighed and slowly walked down towards the front door, turned off the alarm, unlocked the door and opened it. It was our neighborhood girl scout selling her cookies.

"Isn't it a little late for you to be out selling cookies hon?" I wasn't annoyed at her, but at her mother who was sitting in the car with the door open.

"Sorry Mrs. Kayden. I need to collect the money by tomorrow." (Nothing like waiting for the last minute Didn't your Mom's Mother teach her anything?).

"That's okay dear. How much do I owe you?" I remembered that I had ordered a couple of boxes. Usually about two dozen, but no one is home to eat them anymore but me, so I just ordered two boxes of my favorite, 'peanut butter patties.' I know they call them something else now, but to me they will always be 'peanut butter patties.'

"Eight dollars," as she turned to look to make sure her Mom was still running the engine.

"Be right back hon." I ran in the kitchen for my purse, and tripped over my own feet.

"*God damn it.!*" Why me? I reached into my purse and only had a ten-dollar bill.

"Oh, what the heck." I ran back to the door and handed her the money.

"I don't have the exact amount, so keep the change dear," and she ran back to the car.

She didn't even say thank you. Some manners her mother taught her. We will see how many boxes I buy from her next year.

I closed and locked the door again, turned the alarm back on again, placed the cookie boxes on the kitchen counter, walked back to the tub again, took my robe off again, and got back into the now lukewarm water. I let some of the cool water out and turned on the hot water. Then I sat back and took a deep breath.

The phone rang.

"*Oh, My, God.* Can I get some peace and quiet around here?"

Again the dogs went nuts running and barking. It was only the phone for God's sake. I told them to hush up. I didn't even have my wine glass in my hand yet. I climbed out of the tub again, put my robe on again, and grabbed the phone that is in my bedroom.

"Good evening Mam. May I ask you to take a quick survey?"

"NO." I hung up and walked slowly back into the bathroom again, threw my robe across the room, now that it's all wet. Back into the tub, I held my wine glass close to my heart (maybe osmosis will work with wine since I can't seem to be in here long enough to sip it myself), and tried to relax. All I could think about was the phone ringing again, the doorbell, or something else disturbing my relaxation time for the evening. Maybe an air-raid will be next. You never know.

This time the bath was going to last. If the phone or the doorbell rings, I am not going to answer either of them. This way I could just sit and relax. I was in the tub for about five minutes, really only five minutes, when the doorbell rang once again.

I sighed and decided to ignore it. The boys were running up and down the hallway barking like crazy. Whoever is there, isn't giving up because they rang it again, and a third time for good measures.

"I can't get a moment to myself."

I took a dry towel and wrapped it around me, slowly went to the door and peeked outside. I didn't see anyone. They must have given up and gone away.

"Of course. Give up when I come to the door. Why not." Instead of getting upset (too late for that), I just grabbed the open bottle of red wine that was in the frig, took a whopper of a sip, and I hurried back down the hallway to my homemade spa with cold water.

As I started to walk back for the fourth or fifth time, who remembers anymore, the motion lights went on out back. I stepped back and glanced through the French doors in the kitchen to get a peek. I whispered for Tom and Jerry to come over to me, but they were still barking at the front door. Some guard dogs they are.

"Come here, NOW," I signaled. They still didn't listen. I bent downward in the kitchen so no one could see me if they are out in the backyard. I placed the wine bottle on the floor and bent down onto my hands and knees, slowly crawled, in my towel, to try to reach the mobile phone. Then I heard a knock on the backdoor. I screamed and the phone came down and hit me in the head. My towel came unwrapped and the dogs came crashing in and were now jumping on the French doors leading to the backyard. My legs were becoming numb (that's what happens when I get really scared. Usually it happens in my dreams and I can't move). My heart felt like it was going to jump out of my chest, while I was motionless. I didn't want to look and see who was there, so I grabbed the phone, now on the floor after hitting me, and dialed 9-1-1, with my shaky hands.

"There's someone sneaking around in my backyard. I can't see who, but my motion lights went on." I was shaking like crazy.

"Are you okay?"

"So far."

"What is your name and address. We'll send a car right over."

I faintly heard a voice from out back. It was a man's voice. He spoke softly and said hi to the dogs, by name. He knows my dogs' names, I thought. That's it. They all make sure they know the pets' names to give them treats so they won't bark. I sat still on the floor shaking and freezing now that I am out of the tub again, and pretty much naked without my towel holding me up. I slowly crawled around the corner, grabbing my towel, to peek out the doors. I barely saw a glimpse of a man with his back to the door now. He was holding something in each hand. *Oh. My God*, I thought. *He is going to break the door open with whatever he has in his hands.*

I stood up, not remembering that I am naked, and yelled.

"NO!"

I must have scared the man as he jumped backward, and threw a box into the pool. He lost his footing and then fell backwards into the pool himself. I grabbed my towel and put it around me. I stood there holding the phone. I turned the alarm off and let the dogs out back. I closed the door and locked it. Flashing lights appearing suddenly, thank goodness, you know the red and blue ones. I felt safer now. One of the officers rang the doorbell and then another officer went through the backyard where the motion lights went on again. All hell was breaking loose. I ran to the front door and opened it. The first officer came in and told me that a second officer went around the back to check it out.

We both heard a commotion out back and went through the kitchen to see what was going on. The officer commanded the man in the pool to get out and lay on the pavement, face down. I still couldn't see who it was. I was shaking from frostbite now, but stood at the backdoor.

"Please wait inside miss, and put something on, PLEASE."

Embarrassment isn't the right word right now, and I will be damned if I can think of a better one. I ran into Mel's room and put her bathrobe on, since mine was wet and my room was a lot further towards the back of the house.

When I returned, I heard several voices. One of them sounded so familiar. *OH MY GOD*, it was Joel lying on the pavement trying to convince the police that he knows me.

"I came through the back to surprise her. She knows me, really she does. She didn't expect me tonight, but it's a surprise." Joel was shaking from the cold, wet winter water of the pool. His eyes didn't look so happy to see me right now.

I ran outside, embarrassed as can be, and apologized.

"I'm so, so, so, sorry. I didn't know it was you."

I turned to apologize to the officers. "I am so sorry. I do know this man." I profusely apologized to Joel and the police officers several times.

They accepted my apologies, I think.

"We know Mrs. Kayden, we know." The police left, laughing as usual, as Joel stood outside shaking in his wet cold clothes and gave me the evil eye without saying a word. I ran over and gave him a couple of towels, also without saying a word. He bowed and retrieved the soaking wet pizza box from the pool. There was a bottle of red wine placed by the door.

"I thought I would surprise you and bring a bottle of red wine and pizza over. I finished early."

"You sure did. I didn't know it was you ringing the bell and then sneaking into the backyard. You scared the crap out of me. I was in the tub, and I am so sorry. How can I ever tell you how sorry I am? I didn't know what else to do except call the police. I was cold, naked, crawling around on the kitchen floor (*freezing my buns off*), and the dogs weren't listening to me. I hit myself in the head with the phone and it hurts now." I was shaking all over out of fear (*and cold*). "What else should I have done?"

"You're right." He started to smile. "I shouldn't have come over without giving you a full report of my whereabouts and my intentions. I apologize." He came close to me, kissed the bump on my head, and hugged me. "Now how about we both change into something a little more comforting? This sounds familiar doesn't it?" he laughed now. I did too.

I ran into my bathroom and gave him Cam's blue terrycloth bathrobe that I left hanging on the back of the door from the last time Joel was here.

"I guess the pizza is a little washed up," as he laid it on the kitchen counter.

"At least we have red wine," I announced. "I'm sure we can find something to eat."

"Well, I know what else we can do besides drinking wine that will keep us warm." as he slowly walked over to me. There I go again, backing away, (I need to stop that).

"I made a cake we can eat." I jumped over to the table where I placed it earlier.

Joel followed me and held me from behind. He whispered in my ear, "How about we just go warm up for now? We can always find something to eat later, when we're hungry for food," (*I caught that one).*

I slowly turned around, held his hand, walked him back to my room, and closed the door.

Just another typical Monday.

Chapter 22

And let there be light

Tuesday morning came much too early for everyone. I always get up early as it is, but getting up at four in the morning is a little ridiculous. It isn't even light out yet. Joel had an early meeting this morning. He is still on New York time, which is now seven in the morning and time to get going for the day. He quietly took a shower and was dressed in a flash. He thought he was being very quiet, and he was, however, I get up whenever there is movement in my room, the bathroom, or anywhere within a mile radius of my home. I started to get up for the day.

"Don't get up on my account. Go back to sleep. I'm on New York time."

"Why are you whispering? It's just me and you here," I said in a normal tone. I continued to get up, put my robe and slippers on anyway.

"You're right. I'm just used to being very quiet in the morning. Sorry about that," he apologized as he continued to whisper.

"I'll go put on some coffee for you before you leave," I offered and walked slowly into the kitchen with my eyes somewhat closed. I guess I could do it blindfolded since it is my house and I have been living here for over twenty years.

I sat down at the table looking at the untouched cake. I was so tired. I, we, didn't get to sleep until.... late. I closed my eyes for just a moment. Joel came in all ready to go.

"How about a cup of coffee, and something to eat for breakfast?" I asked with much concern, since we didn't have any dinner last night.

"Thanks Amy, but we usually have coffee at our early morning meetings," he explained.

"Well at least sit down for a moment or two." He was fidgeting with his clothes and hair so it didn't look like he was out all night, I presume.

"I wish I could, but I can't this morning. But I will definitely take a rain check," as he bent over and kissed my head (again, right where the phone hit me last night). "My driver should be here any moment. I called right before I got into the shower this morning, and I told him I would wait outside. I don't want to wake up the whole neighborhood."

I went to the front door with him. I turned off the alarm and opened the French door so he could see if the limousine was here yet. He saw some lights down the street coming toward the house.

"I'll see you later my sweet, be ready for a date to remember." He walked quietly down the flagstone walkway to the street.

"I love you," he whispered, as he climbed into the limo, and was gone in a flash.

I smiled and just waved. Do I love him? Am I just on the rebound of losing my husband of twenty-five years? Is it too early to be interested in him? It has been less than a year. Am I supposed to wait a certain amount of time? Is he the only man that has taken an interest in me lately, or ever for that matter? Are the butterflies in my stomach any indication of anything? Am I crazy to fall in love so quickly? Am I asking myself too many dog gone questions?

It's too early and too dark to think about all this right now. I need to get some sleep. I need to go back to bed, before the morning light appears. I locked the house up again, turned the alarm back on again, and slowly strolled back to my bedroom. I sat for a moment before getting back into bed with Tom and Jerry. I stared at my left hand. I stared at my ring finger, you know the one with the wedding band still on it. I tugged at it and it flew off. I placed it under my pillow for no apparently reason. Maybe when the sun rises, it will show me the light.

Chapter 23

My Chariot Awaits

I fell back asleep as quickly as if I was having a Swedish massage at a spa, done by Sven. Little did I know that Tom and Jerry were back to back in bed with me and that **was** the massage. It felt good even if it wasn't Sven.

I woke up around eight, which is late for me. I slept soundly for a few hours. I haven't done that in years. I felt refreshed and alive! Did you hear that? I feel alive.

Walking into the bathroom and looking in the mirror, I saw a stranger. Not really a stranger, but someone I hadn't seen in what seems like years.

"Oh My God, it's me! It really is me." I smiled from ear to ear. I could see my pearly whites, and they were dazzling white, if I must say so myself. I couldn't stop smiling, even while I was brushing my teeth. I started to laugh. The toothpaste foamed around my mouth and fell into the sink because I was laughing so hard. Tom and Jerry came in to see what is so funny. I turned to look at them and gave them each a big kiss right on their mouths, because they don't have lips, or do they? I don't think they enjoyed the toothpaste, but they did smile back. I can tell. A mother always does…

Into the shower I went. I still had a big grin on my face. I was singing and having a great time because no one was there to tell me that

I am not Diana Ross or Barbra Streisand. The boys just sat there on the rug and watched their Mommy take a shower.

Dressed and ready for my day, I walked into the kitchen to sip a nice hot cup of coffee that I had made earlier this morning. It tasted great! I made some oatmeal. It tasted great! I covered the cake that I had made yesterday. It looked great! Everything was just so great!

The day is young. The weather looks great! The house looks clean which is great! I fed the dogs, and checked my email. I walked around the house making sure everything is 'just so.' I went out back to sit in my thinking chair with the beautiful sunshine streaming down on the earth below. The air smelled great! The sunshine felt great! Everything is great! Why is that?

Running back into the bathroom, I wanted to see if that strange person was still there. Yes, she is, and still smiling from ear to ear. I cleaned up the bathroom, and decided to do a load of laundry, what little there was, just to do something. I had so much energy. What to do, what to do.

Walking back to my room, I touched my hand, my naked left hand. My ring. Where is my ring? I remembered that I had taken it off last night and placed it under my pillow. Is it still there? Did I move it? I reached under the pillows and grasped the little yellow gold ring with a big diamond in the middle. Whew. I felt relieved and then placed it back on my finger. It didn't feel right anymore. It actually felt uncomfortable. Why? I sat for a few moments deciding what to do about this situation. I took some deep breaths, reached over to my left hand, and touched the ring. I slowly took the ring off, placed it in the fingers of both my hands, and stared. I slowly stood up, walked slowly over to my jewelry box, and placed it down, ever so gently. It is where it belongs. I closed the lid and walked away.

~

I went out back again, and sat in my comfy chair. The air was still fresh and I could smell the light flowery scent from the roses that are just about to bloom. The birds were chirping, the sun felt wonderful, and I feel like I am on cloud nine, (*If there was such a thing as cloud ten, I would be on it in a flash, and not a hot flash).* The phone rang and brought me, somewhat, back down to earth. I ran into the kitchen to pick it up.

"Hello," as I was floating on my magic carpet ride.

"Well, good morning M' lady. I hope I didn't keep you up too late."

"Oh, no, of course you didn't. I stay up late all the time," (lying through my pearly whites and slowly wandered around the kitchen island with my eyes rolling and hand in the air).

"I hope we're still on for later today? I promise I won't sneak up on you, walk through your backyard, or throw food or wine on you."

"Of course we are. What would give you any idea we wouldn't be?" I stood still and held the counter with my left hand. I kept on staring at it. I quickly looked away. What am I thinking? I took the ring off and it is staying off. Oh, stop thinking for a change.

"Just be ready at four-thirty this afternoon. I need to take a nap early this afternoon, so I can be refreshed. I didn't sleep much last night. Must have been the mattress," Joel laughed loudly. I could feel his smile through the phone.

"Must have been. Those hotels can have lumpy mattresses you know. Sometimes your hotel neighbors can be noisy as well. What should I wear?"

"Anything your heart desires, as long as it's a pair of jeans, a sweater, and sneakers. Just be ready." He hung up quickly.

"Ok, then. I guess I'll have to be ready," singing to Tom and Jerry.

It was still early in the day, before noon. I stood there contemplating going back outside or not. I circled around the island.

"I'll bake some cookies!" Tom and Jerry started wagging their tails. I know they don't understand what I am saying, but they understand my tone and excitement. And yes, I know, baking isn't what I do best. I'm not sure what I do best. I went to my 'cooking' bookshelf (*that is always so lonely*), and looked at the **family** recipes (*a book which has never been touched by human hands*). I found one for chocolate chip cookies. It isn't your ordinary recipe from the back of the Tollhouse bag. It is a little more complicated than that. However, there are too many directions, and too many ingredients.

"Well, forget this one boys. I guess homemade cookies are out." I put that recipe down to rest. I need something a lot less complicated. I made the cookies from, what else, the pouch of a cookie mix that only needs water. Simple enough for me.

I stayed in the kitchen while the cookies were in the oven. I ate a few as well, so did Tom and Jerry. We just had to taste them. Of course, I felt sick, not from my baking, just from eating too many cookies. The burnt ones are the ones that Tom and Jerry share. They really like the crunchy ones best. A mother knows these things. I divided the rest of them.

"Chase and Nathan can have half, and the other half I will wrap up for Joel." I don't even know if he likes chocolate chip cookies! He will now. At least he'll say he does, if he knows what is good for him (not meaning my baking).

The cookies are all wrapped and ready to go. I was just wiping down the center island in the kitchen when the doorbell rang. I jumped, as usual. The boys went nuts and ran to the front door. I could see through the window it was Chase and Nathan. I opened the door.

"Ready for lunch, honey?" Nathan stood there with a big grin.

"Oh, yes of course." *I completely forgot.* "Come in for a minute. I just made you boys some cookies," as I handed Chase a paper plate covered in cellophane. "It probably has more cellophane than cookies." But it looked good.

"Why thanks hon," the look on Nathan's face wasn't too familiar. I know what they think about my cookies or cooking for that matter. But today, it isn't going to matter to me.

"Ready guys. Let's go!" I announced loudly to the world as I said goodbye to my babies and locked the front door. We walked down my flagstone pathway to the street where Nathan's car was waiting. We drove for a few minutes to our little downtown area and saw the new French Restaurant.

"It looks so quaint," I stated.

"Yes, it does," they both said in unison and smiled at one another.

"Amy, I'll let you and Chase out here to get a table, while I park around the back."

It was a cute little eatery, with great music, and the food looked delicious. I was so nervous about this afternoon. I probably didn't even taste how good the chicken salad sandwich was. I could hardly eat it. But I managed.

ക്ക

"I am so full. I will have the rest of my sandwich wrapped up. But it is really good." I just couldn't concentrate on eating the rest. My mind was wandering in different directions.

They both looked at me as if I was a nutcase right now. After lunch, Nathan thought we should window-shop, and that would help me take it easy. That actually felt relaxing and time flew by, a little too quickly. I glanced at my watch and saw that it was almost four in the afternoon. I panicked.

"Nathan, Chase, I need to get home. NOW!" I was shaking all over, looking for the car, grabbing the guys and running down the street.

"Is everything OK?" Chase asked while I practically choked him to death with his own shirt.

"I need to get ready for tonight. Joel is picking me up in forty."

We were home in a flash. I practically fell off the curb getting out of the car, said thanks for lunch, and sprinted inside. The message machine was flashing away. I pushed the button to listen to the messages and threw my sandwich into the fridge.

"Hey Amy. It's me, Carol. Just called to say HEY." She does that a lot.

"Big A, you didn't answer your cell phone. You need to make the ring louder, get a hearing aid, or both." That is obviously Michael. He is the only one of my four children who doesn't call me Mom, and has a masculine voice.

"Mom, I'm coming home for the weekend. Just me, myself and I." That was Mel because if it were the twins I would have heard two voices and it would have been twice as loud.

Last, but not least, another call from David. "Amy, I guess you didn't get my other messages, but I would like to know when we can have a picnic lunch on the beach."

"He just doesn't get it and he won't, figuratively and literally. It's time to move on David."

Four-thirty is here and I'm all ready, I hope. I'm wearing jeans, sneakers and a sweater. I have my purse with cell phone, loud enough to hear the ring. Just as I started pacing the kitchen island, the doorbell rang. I just about jumped out of my skin. Doorbells do that to me sometimes. I leisurely took my time getting to the door. Tom and Jerry beat me to it. They usually do. I didn't want to seem overly anxious, even though I was.

Joel was standing there with a single pink rose.

"For you M' lady." He handed me the rose as he kissed my hand. "Our chariot awaits," as he stepped aside, bowed down, and showed me a sparkling white BMW convertible.

I was blushing. I could feel it in my cheeks, "Where did you get this car? It's stunning."

"I know people." That was all he said.

I laughed, a nervous one I think. He helped me into the 'chariot' and closed the door behind me.

"May I ask what your plans are for this evening Sir?"

"It's a surprise."

"I love surprises!" (Most of the time I do. Usually, if they are good surprises).

We drove down to the Marina. There was a boat waiting for us. Not just a boat, but a BOAT. A blue and white, shiny, perfectly decorated boat, with white twinkling lights all around. A picnic basket sat on the edge of the boat. I could hear music in the background. It sounded like Frank Sinatra.

"Whose boat is this?"

"It isn't a boat, it's a yacht. I know people," he smiled at me and lifted his eyebrows. He raised his hand to help me aboard and signaled to the 'captain' to take off.

"Would you like a glass of red wine M' lady?"

"Of course, (*who wouldn't*).You know that red wine is good for heart," and he chimed in with me as I said it. We both laughed and said cheers. I can't believe this is for me. He really must like me, or something like that!

The sunset is early this time of year. We sat quietly with our glasses of wine, listened to the tide, birds dipping into the water, and watched the sunset from the yacht out at sea. It was so peaceful and serene. We had a picnic dinner and chocolate covered strawberries for dessert. It was perfect. What else could a woman want (*besides not having to make dinner and doing the dishes afterwards*)? I had all of his attention and he definitely had all of mine. We sat and talked about what we want from out lives from here on out.

"I want my children to be happy. That is the most important thing in the world to me. Also that they make something of themselves, give back to their communities and be healthy."

"What about you?" Joel stared at me as if something was missing from my life. "What do you want for you?"

"I already told you." I think I am confused a bit here. I tilted my head to one side.

"You said what you want for your children, but not what YOU want for yourself."

"My kids come first. I already had what I wanted; a husband, children, white picket fence; dogs, you know. What do you want?"

He stood up, walked towards the end of the yacht, and turned around, "You."

I'm sure my face turned as red as the strawberries we just finished off. I sure could feel the heat. Or is that another hot flash coming?

I gulped. Is he serious? Just as he said he wanted me, the lights on the yacht turned on. *How is that for timing?* I was living a dream. I had to pinch myself to make sure I wasn't dreaming. Joel walked over to me. He took the wine glasses and placed them down carefully on the table. He took me in his arms and kissed me ever so tenderly. Here I am back in paradise, (what a great place to be).

I didn't want this to end, ever. It felt so right. We took a heavenly ride around the harbor for a few hours. The weather was perfect, water was calm, and the lights were twinkling, (*and you know how I feel about twinkling lights).* I know I have never had a date like this before and probably won't ever again unless…

"All ashore that's going ashore," the captain announced when we reached land. Joel and I packed everything back into the basket and jumped back onto the pier where we first began our date in paradise. He helped me into the 'chariot'. It was a beautiful evening.

We drove to his hotel and we went up to his suite on the ninth floor (*I really am on cloud nine*). It has a balcony that overlooks the ocean. He had champagne sitting in ice on the coffee table with, what else, a dozen pink roses. There were some chocolates sitting there too. Everything I love in one place. What more could a girl ask for.

We both stood on the balcony looking at the full moon rising, and feeling the cool breeze. I could smell the ocean and hear the crashing waves. Here I am again in a dream and I don't want to wake up.

Joel broke the silence, "Amy, I love you and always have, and I want to be with you the rest of my life."

I stood there in shock, not that he loves me, but I think he just asked me to marry him. At least that is what I think I heard. I thought to myself, do I love him, can I love him, the rest of my life? I can't just forget about Cam, is this moving on? That is, if he keeps up the romance, roses, red wine, chocolates and such (who am I kidding?).

"What do I say? I, I, I'm speechless." I turned around so he couldn't see my face turning red as a beet now, not a strawberry as before. *I can tell the difference.*

"Let's get together, married," his hazel eyes had a luminous glow. He came closer to me and held me in his strong, safe, arms. The wind was blowing softly and sweetly as we could hear the waves crashing onto the sands below. He kissed me gently in the moonlight, backed away, and bent down on one knee.

"Will you marry me?" (This sounds like a Danielle Steel novel, doesn't it?).

"Marry you, now? I don't think the time is right. I feel it is too soon and we haven't even been together more than a day or two at a time. Don't you want to get to know me better?" I started to back up slowly, hoping he would pull me back.

He stood up and reached for my hand, "I've known you all my life. I've thought about you all my life. I have loved you all my life. I want to be with you for the rest of my life."

"You live on the East coast and I'm here. Don't you think that little tid-bit is important? We have never even lived with one another. You don't know what I'm like in the mornings or late evenings. I'm a clean freak. I don't cook much, or at all if I can help it. There are things you don't know about me. There are things I don't know about you. Doesn't any of that matter?" I threw my hands up in the air.

"The geographic difference can be changed anytime I please. I'm the boss and if I want to change offices from east to west, I'll do it." He paused for a moment, as he walked around in a circle on the balcony.

"Just like any other newlywed couple we'll learn about each other as we grow together."

"I don't want to grow anymore," I teased looking at my figure.

He laughed, "That is one of the reasons why I love you so much. You have a great sense of humor." He walked back into the suite and sat on the couch. I followed, sat down next to him, and turned towards him.

"I don't want to turn you down. I don't want you to walk away from me either," I started to say with a few tears forming.

"I'll never walk away or let you get away, ever again. If waiting is all you want, then I'll wait. I've waited thirty years, what's a little while longer going to matter?" Those twinkling hazel eyes were glazing upon me and I couldn't resist.

I reached over and gave him a gentle kiss on the lips. "What if I decide that I don't ever want to get married?"

"That is something I will have to deal with. I want to be with you. We don't have to be married to be together. I do want to make an honest woman out of you though," he smiled.

"Well, don't start tonight," I smiled and leaned over and kissed him again. This time I walked over to the light switch and turned it off. I walked slowly back to the couch, took his hands and wrapped them around me. He stood up and carried me back to my dream.

Chapter 24

Home Sweet Home

Weeks have floated by and the wondrous springtime arrived. The flowers are blooming and the birds are singing. This time of year means new life is growing from the earth. I love being able to open the French doors out back and sit in my comfy chair with a hot cup of coffee, Tom and Jerry sitting by my side, and the house is quiet.

Today is a great day for a walk to the park or a walk along the beach with my boys. I will let the boys decide, after I sit here and enjoy the peace and quiet of home, sweet home. Just when I was feeling so relaxed, the phone rang. I brought the mobile out with me.

"Good Morning."

"Well, good morning to you too M' lady. It looks like you are going to have a beautiful day in sunny southern California. What is on your agenda for today, if I may ask?" Joel was cheery and I could feel a smile upon his face.

"I thought about going for a long walk with my boys, why, are you interesting in joining us?" I teased as I smiled from ear to ear, and took a deep breath of fresh morning air.

"Well maybe I am interested. Are you drinking a hot fresh cup of coffee?"

"Why yes, I am drinking a hot fresh cup of coffee. Do you think you can make some time for me today?" I teased as I sat in my white wicker rocking chair.

"I'll see if I can get away." Joel clicked his cell phone with his left hand, leaning up against the French doors, with the coffee already in the other hand. He walked outside and kissed me on the top of my head. He sat down in the white wicker chair next to me and enjoyed the view, meaning me!

൭൫

We took Tom and Jerry for a nice walk to the park and wanted to sit, enjoy the weather, and people-watch. We sat on a hilly part of the park. It was a perfect day to be alive.

It was a Saturday afternoon in early spring, which means boys little league baseball games. My boys were soaking up the sun as they lay on the thick, green blades on the ground beneath them. They just love to roll around on their backs with their paws standing straight up in the air. Sometimes they even take a nap that way!

We were watching the boys play baseball when all of a sudden one of the boys, from the blue team, was hit by a pitch (*looks like it was intentional*), by the opposing pitcher in red.

"This looks like a little trouble in the making," Joel whispered to me. "Let's just watch."

Sure enough, a commotion was transpiring on the field. The kid was down for the count. A man came running onto the field, rather waddling out. He looked like he had a slight limp with his left foot and started to argue with the umpire.

"Oh, My, God. It's Joe Elliott down there," I was shocked.

"Who is Joe Elliott?" Joel had a puzzling look on his face as he continued to watch the argument and a little pushing going on down there.

"He's a long story, rather a few long stories that I'll tell you about another time dear." (*I called him dear!* I shocked myself but continued to watch the event in question on the field).

Sure enough, after a few minutes of yelling and screaming, Joe threw a punch. Another punch landed **him** on his ass, along with some pain in his somewhat healing leg.

We laughed and decided it was time to go home. We walked down the hill with Tom and Jerry on their leashes. We had to pass the boys' game to walk back to my house. I saw Joe and started to laugh. He saw me, turned around, and shook his head, as he must have been embarrassed. Joel and I were about thirty yards past the game now and Joe turned to me and yelled.

"I guess I'll never learn." I smiled back and shook my head in agreement, so he understood that I did hear him. I waved back and kept on walking.

When we reached the house, the message machine was blinking like crazy. I pushed the button and started to listen. The first message was from Joel's parents asking how we are and how he's settling in on the west coast. He bent over and caressed my neck with his soft lips. Rich called next and said he can't wait to be here Friday for the weekend with Carolyn. Michael called and said he was coming home with Liz next weekend. The twins called and said they wanted to bring some stuff home, which means half the closet, next weekend too. Melanie wanted to know when Uncle Rich would be here so she could come home and say Hi to her favorite (and only) Uncle, and mainly to meet his new girlfriend.

"Looks like I'll have a full house this weekend." I turned around into Joel's arms. "Care to help and barbeque some steaks on Saturday with me?"

"I would love to but I'll barbeque, not you. We all know what happens when you get near an oven or outdoor barbeque," We both laughed. *I hope he was joking.*

"And what happens when I get near a cooking appliance if I may ask?"

"You get all fired up!" He grinned and squeezed me hard. "You also get real hot, if you know what I mean." We both laughed, and I agreed to do the shopping and leave the cooking to anyone else.

The last message was from one of Cam's partners, Jeff. He wants me to stop by sometime during the week and pick up an envelope that he was holding for me. I know it's Saturday, late afternoon, but in that office, someone is always working, day and night. Will they ever learn?

∾

"I need to go to my office tomorrow for a few days and get some work done. What do you think Amy? Can you handle being here alone with Tom and Jerry?"

"I think just a few days would be fine. Then right back here for some 'R & R,' I announced. "I don't want you over-working this week and then telling me you won't be able to BBQ."

"Yes M' lady. I understand. Just a few more months of working hard and training others, then I can devote my time to more important issues right here," as he held me in his arms and kissed me.

"Are you sure that's something you want to do? I mean, work just part-time? Is it something feasible for you?" I had a serious look on my face.

"I'm the boss. I'm not giving it up, just letting some others work a little harder for their pensions."

"I just don't want you to let go of something so important to you, and feel guilty later on."

"The only thing I let go was **you** over thirty years ago. I won't let that happen again, ever," he held me, and I hope he never lets go.

Chapter 25

Cheesecake Anyone?

Monday morning is here and we have another gorgeous day in sunny southern California. I have a 'to do' list and want to get started early. I chose to go to the Law Firm first, and pick up the envelope in question. I parked down under the building, as always, and waited for the elevator.

While waiting, I decided to go the 'red ladies' floor and just say hi. I was a little nervous, but it's just something I need to do for myself. I got off the elevator, and approached the receptionist's desk.

"Hello."

Jeanine looked up and was amazed to see me. I think it was a happy surprise, even though I may never know.

"Well, good morning. It's nice to see you."

"How is the business doing?"

"It's growing like crazy, and we are having a hard time keeping up with all their clients. We just hired two men. Isn't that fabulous?" She was grinning and her eyes were as bright as a kid's on Christmas morning.

"Congratulations are in order, and I applaud you all. Say hello to the girls." I bowed my head and started to leave quietly. As I slowly walked to the elevator, I turned around and asked Jeanine, "By the way, why is it named 'Big Mac' Corporation?"

She laughed, "Because 'Mac' is Cam backwards. He gave us our start and we wanted to thank him in our own small way." I smiled and shook my head. He has been gone almost a year, and is still working away. Will he ever learn?

Traveling up in the elevator, I had to chuckle. The doors finally opened and I found myself standing in front of the tall beveled glass doors with my last name still on them. I haven't been in here for quite some time. I just stood there frozen in time, thinking maybe, just maybe, Cam is working at his office and has been all this time.

Jeff just happened to walk by at that moment, glanced at me, started to walk past me, then stopped in mid-step, and back-tracked. There he stood still, turned around, and reached over for a 'fake – have to do it' hug.

"It's so good to see you Amy. You look well. I hope everything is good with you and the kids," saying with a smile. It sounded phony to me, but what the heck.

"Everything is coming up roses," knowing he wouldn't acknowledge it, or ask me what I meant. After all, he is a lawyer and we all know they are into their work.

"Let me get the envelope for you. Come into my office and sit for moment." Jeff showed me into his office and I sat on the black leather couch. It was only a moment when he handed me the envelope.

"Cameron gave me this envelope over a year ago, and asked that I wait and give this to you this April. I didn't ask why, just said fine," as he handed it to me.

"Thanks Jeff. Is it a legal document or something that I would need you to interpret for me?"

"No, it isn't any type of legal document. Cameron said to take it home and you would know what to do," Jeff commented back. He actually sounded like he had no idea what it was, and didn't really care to find out. I sat for the longest time staring at the envelope with my name on it.

"Sit as long as you need to Amy. I will leave you alone." He left the room with a bunch of files that pretty much covered his suit from top to bottom.

I shook my head. I took a deep breath, and just stared at the envelope that I was holding now between my shaking hands. I felt numb. Is time standing still right now?

I don't know how much time went by before I made my way out of this mature, stale office building. I was on automatic pilot to my home. I don't remember how I got there or how long it took. I stared at the envelope again. This is all that is left of Cam.

I went into my bedroom, and sat down in my safe place, my rocking chair. Tom and Jerry hopped up on the bed. I just kept on staring at this envelope. I don't know why I am afraid to open it, but I am. This will be the last time I 'hear' from Cameron. What information lies in here that I couldn't or shouldn't have known until now? There's one way to find out. I carefully opened the envelope and took out the handwritten paper. It was in Cam's handwriting, which sometimes was not doable to read.

Dearest Amy,

You are my wife and my partner for life. There are times when a man must say, or write down, what is on his mind. This is my time. I love you and our four beautiful children we made together, though sometimes I have a hard time showing it. You know I am never one to show affection or be romantic. Maybe you didn't know that when we were younger and thought you could change my ways. After twenty-five years, I guess you have figured it out by now, and you are still here with me. That must mean something for the two of us.

I know I work many more hours than a normal person does. I want you and the kids to have everything I never had. I want you to be queen of the castle and enjoy watching our children grow up. You are their rock, not me. You have been there for them, good and bad, tough times and happy times. You will continue to be there for them after I am gone. That is why you have received this letter now. Obviously, I am gone. I knew I wouldn't live forever.

> *I knew I had a weak heart, and I didn't want you and the kids to worry about me, that is why I never told you. I didn't want you to suffer watching me. I told myself, 'when it's time, it's time and I will go quickly and quietly' (I hope I did).*
>
> *Amy, you are still young, adorable, full of spirit, and have a lot of love left in you, I know. You can find love again and I want you to love again. I know you are probably sitting in your rocking chair in our room, reading this and I hope you decide to get out into the world again and find another love. You are worth it, and anybody would be lucky to have you. I love you. I love our children.*
>
> *I wanted you to receive this letter in the April after I am gone. This is my last gift to you for your birthday. Happy Birthday Amy, and many more.*
>
> *Love, Cam*

I just sat, in my rocking chair, with full, salty tears streaming down onto the letter Cam wrote me. The gusher finally happened and I couldn't stop.

"Damn him."

It explains a lot, and yet, it explains so little. I really don't understand, and wish he told me everything when he knew. He didn't want to break my heart too. He did anyway, by leaving me so soon. Cam did say to move on and I think I have (*maybe sooner than he had hoped*). Maybe this is a sign that everything is going to be okay now. Maybe it is a sign that I can accept love and love again. I sat in my chair for hours on end. I just sat there, not rocking, just staring out into space with more tears streaming down my cheeks once again.

I don't know what time it is, but the doorbell rang. I jumped (*it scared me as usual when I am not expecting it to ring*). The dogs ran to the front door for their usual greeting. It was Carol. She knew about the letter because Larry saw me at the office, called her, and told her to check on me sometime this afternoon. I let her in and she just held me while I cried. No words. There didn't need to be.

We went into the kitchen and sat down. Carol made some coffee and poured us both a cup. "Are you okay hon? Is there something I can do for you right now?"

I just sat there for a moment, trying to gain my composure. I took a deep breath. It is time to move on.

"Actually Carol, you can help me plan a party." Carol looked shocked. Her eyes practically popped out of her head and her mouth dropped almost to the floor, which is a long way since she is six feet tall. She gave me the most puzzling look.

"Let me explain. Everyone seems to be coming home or visiting this weekend. All the kids, Rich is bringing his friend, Carolyn, and then of course Joel will be here. I want to make it a big celebration. We will celebrate being together. I haven't had my family all together in years, if ever. What do you think?"

"Whatever you want Amy. You know that hon," Carol was quiet now.

I made the plans while Carol listened and shook her head. We are going to barbeque some ribs and steaks. I called Rich and asked him to bring some New York Chocolate Cheesecake. I asked Carol to bring Larry and the kids around four in the afternoon and we can do appetizers. Carol volunteered to make them, knowing how I cook. I also called Nathan and Chase and invited them. They decided to make some of their famous cookies to nibble all afternoon, and fruit and veggie trays.

"It's late Carol. Your kids should be home now. I'll be okay. Go scoot now." I was trying to push her out the door. We hugged and then she gave Tom and Jerry kisses and left. I turned around and looked at Tom and Jerry.

"It's getting late. At least for today it is. Time to lock up the house as usual, boys."

I felt somewhat better. Maybe reassured too. I am moving on, as Cam wanted me too. I don't feel guilty about it, should I? I sat at my computer and emailed the kids telling them all that everyone will be here Saturday night for a big barbeque. I also emailed Joel, just saying that I am thinking about him and don't work so hard.

The next few days went by quickly. I had all the rooms ready for everyone to stay. I decided to give Rich and Carolyn, Michael's room while he sleeps on the sofa in the family room. It opens up to a bed. Liz can share the couch. I know nothing will happen while we are all watching. They'll be fine. Besides, I think I am a pretty hip Mom, if I must say so myself. They really are adults now. All my children are grown up, even though they will always be my babies, now and forever.

It's Thursday afternoon and all is quiet on the western front. I was running around the house wearing my sweats and socks, just checking each room. I lit candles earlier and made sure they were all out now. I don't want to start any unwanted fires. The garage door opened and Joel walked in with a dozen pink roses for me.

"They're gorgeous. Thank you dear." I kissed him as if we had been married for years.

"They aren't as pretty as you M'lady." I gave him the longest kiss of my life, (even though I looked like a homeless person right now). He couldn't believe it and wanted more. We both laughed and then went into hiding for the evening. It was a very nice evening indeed.

૭୦

Friday and all is well. Rich and Carolyn arrived early in the afternoon. It seemed like everyone was arriving one by one, right after one another. It is wonderful, a family reunion, a happy reunion. We ordered pizza for dinner. We all sat and talked for hours. We reminisced about Grandma and Grandpa, and about the old days when Rich, Joel and I were growing up in New York. I think the kids enjoyed hearing crazy stories about their Mom. I think Carolyn enjoyed it too.

I told my children they could figure out who was sleeping where and I wouldn't ask any questions. Unbelievably, I don't think I want to know.

Saturday afternoon and the rest of the Calvary is arriving. I turned the music on out back, and set out the tables and chairs for everyone. I put candles on the tables and lit them at sunset. I also turned on the twinkling lights out back. I knew they would come in handy someday out here. They do look fabulous and really brighten the yard.

The food is all ready for the barbeque.

"Who wants to barbeque the steaks and ribs?" I was holding the barbeque sauce.

Almost everyone, except for Carolyn and Carol's kids, all jumped up, "I will." Everyone laughed knowing they didn't want me near the barbeque.

"Fine with me. You can all fight over the honors. I am going to sit down and relax." I sat and talked with my neighbors while watching Joel and Michael stand watch over the barbeque. Everyone seemed happy. The girls were talking to their Uncle Rich, Carolyn, and Larry. Carol was busy yelling at her rug rats, in her apron and phone in pocket. Carol wouldn't be Carol without those two items.

We all sat down to eat and enjoyed the food (since I didn't cook it), red wine, conversation, and just being together. The girls cleaned up. I wonder what got into their food?

"I'll bring dessert out in just a minute Mom." Melanie was finishing up with the dirty plates. The girls all disappeared into the kitchen. Suddenly, all the lights went out.

"God damn it." The breakers went out. I started to get up.

Melanie, I think it was Melanie, was carrying a chocolate cheesecake with a million candles, at least it seemed like a million. The candles could be a warning for the fire department.

"Happy Birthday to you. Happy Birthday to you. Happy ...." Everyone sang to me. I completely forgot about my own birthday. A lot has happened this past year. I had a few tears in my eyes when the girls set the cheesecake in front of me.

"Make a wish." Everyone yelled.

Just as I was thinking of a wish, Joel came over to me, in front of everyone, and bent down on one knee.

"Amy, I want to make all your wishes come true from now on. Would you do me the honor and marry me?" He looked up to me smiling with those twinkling hazel eyes waiting for an answer (you know how I just love twinkling anything).

I looked around the table and saw that everyone was waiting for an answer as well. I thought I would be funny and said, "Well, I don't know. Where's the dazzling ring?"

"First things first. He cut a piece of the cake and placed it on a plate. He took a fork and dove into the middle. Nothing there. He cut another piece and mashed it up. Then he looked at Melanie. She looked puzzled and didn't say a thing.

"Third time is a charm," as he mashed another piece of delectable cheesecake.

"Take a bite please." I was somewhat confused and wasn't sure what to think.

I opened my mouth and let him feed me the first bite. Chocolate cheesecake is usually rich and creamy, except there was something hard in this one. I could feel something strange in my mouth. I opened my mouth and took out … a ring! Not just any ring, but a pink diamond ring. It was the most stunning teardrop-cut pink diamond I had ever laid my eyes on. Even more striking than the one Jack gave to Erica on All My Children years ago, when she was on her 11th husband?

I stared at it in shock. I was speechless, and still had some chocolate cheesecake melting in my mouth. Joel stood up, took the ring from my right hand and placed it on my ring finger of my left hand, and asked again…

"Amy Kayden, I love you and will love you the rest of my life. I promise I won't ever leave you. I will keep asking you, and follow you to the ends of the earth until I get the right answer. Will you marry me?"

How could I resist this man? He has loved me from afar. He would follow me around the world and to the ends of the earth, so he says, *I think*. He has given me the love I deserve and more. I was actually shaking (I probably needed more sugar), while he placed the stunning diamond on my finger.

It was a perfect fit. Some cheesecake on the side may have helped it slide on better too.

"How can I resist, when there's always chocolate," I laughed. Everyone else joined in and shouted congratulations. I was going to walk around the table and show everyone the ring.

"I think I should clean it off first so you all can see it better." I bent over by the pool just as Tom was running behind me and yes you guessed it. I fell in the pool. Once again, Joel jumped in to rescue me. So did Tom and Jerry. Everyone was in hysterics. The girls managed to get the dogs out of the pool, while Joel and I wrapped our arms around each other in the shallow end of the pool and kissed.

"You will always need rescuing Amy, and I am the man for the job," he whispered and kissed me again, and again, and again.

The party lasted until the wee hours of the morning. Would you believe that I forgot to turn the alarm on?

OH HOW I LOVE CHOCOLATE!